THE FURRY PRINCESS

"Princess Berzel was the light of Othion. And now..."
The herald buried his face in his hands, then wiped his
eyes.

"And now?" the wizard Kedrigern prompted.

"And now the beauteous Berzel, apple of her royal father's royal eye, flower of the kingdom, fairest of all
women, is accursed, blighted, blasted, and most foully
wronged, struck down by a baneful hand, her beauty desecrated, her young life tainted, her future devastated—"

"Could you be more precise?"

The king's messenger pulled himself together. "Riding
one night in the wood, Berzel stopped to pet a large dog.
The ungrateful beast nipped her fingers and fled. Then, on
the night of the next full moon, she turned into a wolf."

"I see," said Kedrigern. "It's a very tricky problem.
Maybe insoluble."

"Insoluble!"

"Bites just aren't in my field. I can't make promises,"
Kedrigern said, but at the sight of the man's dejected countenance, he pointed out cheerfully, "King Ithian always
was fond of animals."

"Yes, but not in his immediate family."

"A pleasant, leisurely...series of enchantments and adventures."

—*Publishers Weekly*

John Morressy
Kedrigern And The Charming Couple

ACE BOOKS, NEW YORK

This book is an Ace
original edition, and has
never been previously published.

KEDRIGERN AND THE CHARMING COUPLE

An Ace Book / published by arrangement with
the author

PRINTING HISTORY
Ace edition / January 1990

ISBN: 0-441-43265-4

Ace Books are published by The Berkley Publishing Group,
200 Madison Avenue, New York, New York 10016
The name "Ace" and the "A" logo are trademarks
belonging to Charter Communications, Inc.
PRINTED IN THE UNITED STATES OF AMERICA

10 9 8 7 6 5 4 3 2 1

For Susan Allison

. . . O who can tell
The hidden powre of herbes, and might of magick
spel?
—Spenser

⋯❦ One ❦⋯

a lodging for the night

DARKNESS FELL QUICKLY, impenetrably, bringing a dreary end to a filthy midwinter day. The full moon was obscured by thick clouds. Something was still falling, a nasty stuff too thick to be called rain and too wet to be called snow. The little horse, head lowered morosely, dragged its slow way through the clinging, sucking slop of the forest trail, slipping now and again but always recovering its footing in time to avoid a fall. Kedrigern shook the moist grayish clumps from his cloak, tugged his hood forward, and surrendered to gloomy thoughts. He was alone, on a weary horse, still days from his hearth and from Princess, with winter closing in; it was the stuff of bad dreams.

From a purely professional viewpoint, he had good reason to be satisfied. He had lifted an uncommonly intricate curse from a decent young king and been well paid for his work. But he would have been happier to practice his art nearer home, and preferably on a fine day in June. People in remote little kingdoms had a knack for getting themselves enchanted at the worst time of year . . . or so it seemed to Kedrigern. Summer and autumn, the times of dry roads and blue skies and pleasant breezes, passed without a word from anyone; but at the first trace of cold and gloom and snow, a dozen desperate victims of enchantment sent panting messengers to plead for his help at once, and always the kind of help that required the wizard's physical presence. And they all lived far from one another and from everyone and everything else, in inaccessible places to which they gave garbled directions.

But at least the worst was over now, and he was on his way back to the cottage on Silent Thunder Mountain. The homeward journey was the only excuse for traveling, in Kedrigern's view. And even that was a flimsy excuse, since any reasonable person did all in his power to avoid the outbound trip that made the homecoming possible. A man can't come back if he doesn't leave in the first place, and what man leaves home if he can help it? Not Kedrigern, certainly. Not unless it's a case of a friend in need; or a really serious enchantment that no one else can handle; or a whopping great fee. Or, as in this instance, all three.

A sudden gust blew cold drops in his face. As he wiped his cheeks, grimacing, a mournful howl came from the woods off to his left. An abandoned dog, perhaps, or a wolf; in either case, an outcast; a homeless creature like himself, he thought with an upwelling of self-pity, another wanderer doomed to pass the night in these cold wet woods, far from companionship and a warm fire.

He was pondering the wisdom of stopping right here and now and expending a bit of magic on a spell of light, warmth, and dryness, when he saw a gleam through the interlaced branches high ahead. He urged the horse on, and saw another light, and another, as of a village on a mountainside, and he was puzzled. There was no village on this road. He reviewed in his memory the landmarks King Comerance had described so precisely: the riven peak, the twin waterfalls, the row of aged oaks like gnarled sentinels along the roadside. And then he realized where he must be and what the source of the light was, and he sighed with relief. Tonight he would eat well and sleep soundly, in dry comfort, at the abbey on the mountain peak.

Kedrigern had never been given to attire that proclaimed

him member of a particular trade, calling, or profession. He had colleagues who sported silken beards to the waist and flowing white locks; who dressed in black robes bedight with glittering cabalistic symbols; whose eyes flashed under bristling brows and whose voices thundered like calls to judgment. But that was not for him; though a wizard, and a good one, he refused to dress the part and adopt the conventional mannerisms. He gave his chin, cheeks, and upper lip a thorough depilatory scraping every few days, wore plain clothing of homespun and comfortable old boots, and preferred to take the role of onlooker rather than be the object of interest. To a stranger, he appeared more like a successful practitioner of some sedentary trade—an apothecary, perhaps, or a goldsmith—than a wizard of formidable repute. And on this particular night, drenched and hungry and cold, far from home, he was glad of his choice, for however kind and generous the good monks might be, they did not offer their hospitality knowingly to a wizard.

Despite this prejudice of theirs against his own profession, Kedrigern had a high regard for monks in general. They were sensible. Not only did they retire from the world; once they found the place they wanted to be, they stayed put, doing good useful work and minding their own business. No gadding about for them. And as for not welcoming wizards under their roof, the practice was at least understandable. Kedrigern could think of quite a few colleagues whose presence placed a strain on his own good nature.

The monks of the mountain abbey were a mysterious lot, but that did not bother Kedrigern. Indeed, it reassured him. Men who had turned their backs on the world had a right—no, a duty—to be closemouthed about their work. It would ill suit a group of holy men to go from village to village and town to town proclaiming their holiness. Rumors might spring up, but idle people were always starting rumors, and the rumors were always malicious and silly. Kedrigern recalled some of the rumors he had heard concerning wizards and gave a sour little snort of ironic laughter. Nonsense, all nonsense. One simply could not pay heed to rumors.

The stories told about the abbey were so vague and conflicting that no sensible person would believe them in any case. No one knew for certain just what the monks' special mission was, or how and why they went about it, so everyone let his imagination run wild. There was one tale of a giant building containing a copy of every book in the world. Of course the monks would have a library, and probably a very good one—but all the books in the world? Now, there was patent nonsense for you. At least half the books in the world held things that no monk would want anywhere near him. And even if, for some strange reason, the monks had wished to gather all the world's books together, they certainly would not need a huge tower to house them. Kedrigern knew that he could house a copy of every book known to man right in his own cottage, and have shelf space left for mementos and knickknacks.

The thought of his cozy, distant cottage drew a sigh. That was where he belonged, not out here. But here he was, and the only shelter near was the abbey, so the sooner he reached it the sooner his immediate problem would be solved.

A student was always welcomed at the abbey on the mountainside, particularly a student of serious demeanor and mature years. And since Kedrigern was indeed a student (albeit an informal one, and often of matters frowned upon within monastery walls), he would present himself in that character. It was not, strictly speaking, deceitful; accounts of the library and the monks' work that had reached his ears had aroused his interest and provoked his curiosity, even after he discounted the exaggerations of the rumormongers, and he was grateful for this opportunity to study both at first hand, and gain at once shelter and knowledge. He rode on, pleased with his luck.

The howl came from the woods once again, closer this time. It sounded more lupine than canine. Kedrigern dug in his heels and gave the reins a sharp shake. Any creature alone and homeless on a night like this had his sympathy, but he thought it imprudent to offer it in person to a wolf. So, evidently, did his horse.

* * *

The doorkeeper, a great pale giant, welcomed Kedrigern with unfeigned heartiness. A groom led his horse to the stables while the doorkeeper took up his sopping blanket roll and personally conducted him to the kitchen, where the cellarer might see to his needs. The big monk stumped along at an uneven gait, apologizing all the way for the weather, as though he himself had brought the storm about by some clumsy oversight.

The cellarer, round and white-haired, brisk and bright-eyed, took the visitor's streaming cloak with exclamations of concern, and led him to a bench before the fire. By the time Kedrigern had tugged off his boots, another monk had placed a loaf of bread and a bowl of warm milk on a small table near at hand.

"I thank you for this hospitality," said Kedrigern, rubbing his hands together briskly and extending them to the heat.

Beaming, the monk said, "Does not the *Capitularia Regum Francorum* instruct us that every pilgrim is entitled to a room, a fire, wholesome water, and fresh bread?"

"This warm milk is more welcome to me now than the most wholesome water."

"Ah, yes," the cellarer said, and his smile vanished for a moment. "Our water is . . . it is not wholesome today. No. But the milk is, assuredly, and the bread is pure and nourishing. Our baker makes bread that a man could live on." He winced, as if he had said something unintentionally offensive, and Kedrigern spoke to reassure him.

"It will do very nicely. It smells delicious."

"You shall also have smoked meat and a salad," the cellarer announced, his cheer restored.

"Better and better. I thank you again. But I am no pilgrim, only a traveler."

"Are we not all pilgrims, in the true sense?"

"Well, yes. I suppose one might say that," Kedrigern conceded, eyeing the food before him.

"I will leave you to enjoy your collation in peace while I see to your sleeping quarters," said the cellarer, backing to the doorway.

The bread was fragrant and crisp, the milk rich as cream.

Kedrigern ate and drank, sighed with satisfaction, and held out hands and feet to the fire. The cellarer reappeared just long enough to whisk away the pitcher. He returned with a thick wedge of deep golden cheese and a pitcher refilled to brimming.

"A man must eat heartily on such a night as this," he said, and Kedrigern nodded and fell to. The cellarer looked on like an approving parent. "I had thought to bring you a bit of meat, but our smoked meats are . . . they have gone bad." He smiled weakly.

Kedrigern took a bite of the cheese and closed his eyes in rapturous gratitude. "I need no meat. The cheese is delicious."

"You are kind, traveler. Ordinarily, our water is the purest and our smoked meats are praised for their delicacy of flavor, but we . . . we have . . . the abbey has suffered misfortunes of late."

The monk's discomfort was almost tangible. To ease him, Kedrigern said, "The misfortunes, whatever they are, seem to have had no effect on the dairy or the bakery. My compliments to all, and especially to you, Brother Cellarer."

Displaying equal pleasure and embarrassment, the monk waved aside the compliment. He turned the talk to the visitor's affairs, asking Kedrigern where he had been and how long he had been traveling.

"I was visiting King Comerance of the White Wood. I left his kingdom eight days ago. It's good to be under a roof again."

"Are there no inns along the way?"

"Several."

"And you did not stop?"

"Does a man voluntarily give himself up to thieves and torturers?"

The monk laughed loudly, and seated himself on the bench at Kedrigern's side. "I have heard grim tales of the inns in this part of the world."

"If they were grim, then they were very likely true," Kedrigern said without elaborating.

The monk laughed again and nudged him in the ribs. "I have heard that at Zammaster's Inn the meat is putrid and the food glows in the dark. The beds are filthy and full of fleas the size of mice. The mice are the size of rats. And the rats—the rats are the size of—of . . ." He paused, groping for a suitable figure of comparison.

"Of innkeepers," said Kedrigern. "Sometimes the two are indistinguishable."

He and the cellarer fell to laughing like conspirators. In the midst of his mirth, Kedrigern had to cover a yawn, and the monk jumped to his feet, solicitous at once.

"How thoughtless of me to prattle away when you must be exhausted! Come, traveler, let me show you to the hospice."

The chamber was small and plain. It was located in an upper corner of a building near the outer wall, with a window that looked over the dark woods. Whatever rigors the monks might impose upon themselves, they afforded their guests every comfort. The bed was clean, the mattress soft, the blanket thick and warm. A weary traveler with a full belly could ask for nothing more.

Kedrigern had barely time to pull the blanket close around him before he was asleep. He was awakened once during the night by the howling of a wolf. It seemed to come from quite nearby, just beyond the wall, and in his sleep-befuddled state he conceived that the poor creature had followed him and was begging for shelter. But the wolf ceased to howl, and the wizard fell back into a deep sleep, awakening only at Lauds. He rose and dressed in the early light, and just as he finished pulling on his boots a tall, slender monk appeared in the doorway.

He stood nearly a head over Kedrigern, but he was a narrow man. His face was gaunt, his eyes hollow, his nose an abrupt, slender beak of nearly fleshless bone. His face had the high color of one who has spent a life in outdoor work, but the hand he raised in greeting was smooth and pale.

"I am Abbot Rectoverso. I bid you welcome," he said in a deep and solemn voice.

"My thanks, Abbot. I have been kindly treated."

"Duodecimo of Ardua, our cellarer, tells me that you have been at the court of Comerance. Our last visitor brought word

that Comerance had been placed under a spell by some filthy
sorcerer. Is that true?"

"When I left the court, the spell no longer afflicted the
good king," said Kedrigern with a noncommittal smile.

"Then you bear good news. It is welcome in these times.
Tell me, stranger, what is your name? Where is your home?"

"I am Siger of Trondhjem, a student and traveler," said
Kedrigern, giving a name he had employed now and then in
his wanderings.

"You have traveled far indeed. Men from many distant
places come here. Even among the monks there are men from
every corner of Europe."

"So I've noticed," Kedrigern said. "It's quite an interesting
mixture you have here. Your cellarer, for instance, is a Flem-
ing, educated in Paris. A kind man by nature. Though not
himself of high birth, he has passed his youth in a noble
household."

"You have learned much about Duodecimo in very little
time. I have never known him to reveal his past to a stranger,"
said the abbot, fixing his sharp eyes on Kedrigern.

With a shrug, Kedrigern said, "We did not discuss his past,
or mine. I observed his mannerisms and listened to the fram-
ing of his speech. They told me things he did not say."

"You are perceptive," said the abbot. "Tell me, what con-
clusions did you draw from your conversation with the doorkeeper?"

It seemed a harmless request, though the force of the
abbot's presence lent it weight; that taut, towering man could
charge the most casual utterance with significance. Kedrigern
reflected for a moment, then said amiably, "Aside from the
obvious facts that he spent his youth as a blacksmith's appren-
tice in Swabia before going to war in the Lowlands, and embraced the religious life while recovering from serious wounds
in the arm and leg, I could deduce nothing."

This was less a true deduction than a guess based partly on
Kedrigern's knowledge of recent events, partly on the doorkeeper's pronunciation of certain words, his imposing size, his
limp, and a long scar on his right hand and forearm. Its effect
on the abbot was dramatic. He stood for a moment as if frozen

to the spot, then stepped aside and gestured to the doorway.

"You must leave at once. Duodecimo will give you food for the day's journey," he said.

"I had hoped to visit the library. Would it be possible—"

"Go at once! Speak to no one, only leave us!" the abbot thundered.

Taken aback by this outburst, Kedrigern gaped at the lean figure standing like a signpost, one long arm pointing to the corridor. "As you wish," he said, with a curt nod of compliance, and left to see the cellarer.

The morning air was dry and clear, but a raw cold wind put a knife-edge of chill on the air. Kedrigern noticed, as he hurried to the kitchen, that the great dark tower of the library was covered with a web of scaffolding. Repairs, renovations . . . perhaps refurbishing with the generous assistance of a wealthy patron . . . or perhaps something else. It was too cold to stand and stare, and it made little difference to Kedrigern, anyway. The abbot's rudeness had soured him.

His spirits quickly revived under the kindly ministrations of Brother Duodecimo. Consoled by porridge, fortified by milk, heartened by bread and butter, gladdened by strawberry jam, he stood with his back to the fire as the cellarer bustled about his duties. When Duodecimo announced that one of his assistants was preparing a packet of food for the visitor's journey while another was brushing his cloak and rerolling his blankets, all nicely dried overnight, Kedrigern found himself feeling positively affable. No point in taking offense where none is intended, he told himself. The abbot was a busy man with much on his mind and no time to explain his actions to visitors. This brusque dismissal—however unsuited to the long monastic tradition of hospitality—was probably being done for a perfectly good reason. Be grateful for a warm bed, a dry room, and good food. Kedrigern settled himself beside Duodecimo, in the mood for a few minutes' amiable small talk.

"I noticed scaffolding on the library tower," he said.

"Oh, yes, yes. We are taking the stones from the present tower and using them to build a new library inside it."

"Something smaller and more convenient. Very sensible."

"Oh, no. The new library will be much bigger than the present one."

Kedrigern pondered that for a time, then frowned and turned to Duodecimo. "I don't understand that. How can you build one building inside another and make it bigger than the one it's inside?"

The cellarer laughed. "Others asked that very question when Abbot Rectoverso announced the plans. But it makes perfect sense. We will build a very deep structure, you see, going right down into the mountain. And on that foundation, we will erect an even higher tower."

"I see. An ambitious undertaking. And dangerous, too, I should think," Kedrigern observed.

"We won't see the end of it in our lifetimes, that's certain. But it must be done. Abbot Rectoverso says that the work requires it." Duodecimo gave a little sigh of resignation, as if to indicate that the abbot's word, and the requirements of the work—whatever that work might be—were beyond all question. Rather than sit silent, Kedrigern said, "Well, you'll certainly be busy here at the monastery."

"We're too busy as it is. All these things happening at once. Terrible," said the cellarer, shaking his head slowly. Duodecimo looked at Kedrigern, and seemed for an instant as though he wanted to speak further, but then he dropped his gaze and again shook his head. The two men remained silent for a time, Kedrigern expectantly and the monk despondently, until, without looking up, Duodecimo said, "Someone's been busy, that's for certain. Terrible things have been done. Terrible things. But it can't be. . . . I mustn't think of such things."

"If I can be of any help . . ." Kedrigern offered.

The cellarer looked up abruptly. "No, my friend, you can do nothing for us. Leave while you can. Go quickly, and leave us to our fate."

The monks certainly seemed anxious to see the last of him, Kedrigern thought, a bit chagrined. Before he could reply, a young monk entered the kitchen carrying a bundle wrapped in a clean white cloth. With a nod and a smile, he held it out to Kedrigern. "Bread and cheese to sustain you in this day's travel, pilgrim," he said.

"Thank you. May I fill my water bottle?" Kedrigern said, rising to take the bundle.

The young monk hesitated, glanced at the cellarer, and said lamely, "There is a spring... near the bend in the road. It is not far. A fine, clear spring it is, pilgrim."

"You should have had our pure water and a piece of good smoked meat, but you come in bad time... woeful time," said Duodecimo mournfully. He heaved a deep sigh, drew himself up like a man on his way to the gallows, and gazed into the fire. At a sudden thought, he turned to the young monk and asked sharply, "What's become of the wild man? Is he recovered? Has he been fed, and tended to?"

"He took some milk and went to sleep. He seems to be resting quietly," the young monk replied.

"Poor soul. He must have made his way here in hopes of finding peace and healing... and instead he has come to a place of... terrible things, terrible things," said Duodecimo in a despairing voice.

"What wild man are you talking about?" Kedrigern asked in perplexity.

"We found him this morning, huddled by the gate. A pitiful sight he was: his clothing in tatters, his body scraped and scratched, his feet bruised, mud covering him from head to foot. He raved of horrors... cried aloud of wolves and wizards."

"Wizards?"

"Yes. And wolves. Most strange. Oddly enough, he invoked the name of the blessed Briton, Kentigern," said the cellarer.

"Did he really?"

"No, not the good Kentigern," the young monk interjected. "It was a similar sounding name, but not that one. He seemed to be calling for a wizard."

"Fascinating," said Kedrigern, tucking the bundle under his arm and backing toward the doorway. "That's absolutely fascinating. Poor mad fellow. I do hope he recovers. I'll just be running along now, if it's all right with you. Thank you for your kindness."

"Your cloak, traveler! And your blankets!" the young monk reminded him.

"Ah, yes. Of course. Could you just bring them to the stable? I'd like to get an early start. It's a long way . . . and the weather . . . my horse . . . and you have so many things. . . . Goodbye!" blurted the wizard. He hurried from the kitchen, and in a quarter of an hour he was on the road home.

···⁌ *Two* ⁊···

wolf at the door

FIVE ARDUOUS DAYS of travel brought Kedrigern at last to Silent Thunder Mountain. The outlines of his modest cottage under the full light of afternoon were, to his eyes, more splendid than the grandest spires and tallest towers, and he urged the weary horse up the mountain with eager nudges of his heels and promises of equine dainties.

From far away he could see Spot's hideous little form bouncing up and down in paroxysms of delight, and soon the house-troll's joyous cries of "Yah! Yah!" crackled across the snowy meadow. Princess joined Spot in the sunny dooryard, fluttering up to the height of the rooftop, waving excitedly, and Kedrigern rose in his stirrups and returned the salutation with exuberance. He was home, and home he planned to stay.

After a long and leisurely dinner, accompanied by the finest wines from the vineyards of Vosconu the Openhanded, Princess and Kedrigern settled before the fireplace to exchange their news in full. Princess had made progress in her studies during his absence, but eager for word of courts and kings, she deferred her account until she had heard his.

Kedrigern made as much as he could of his stay with Comerance, but in spite of all his rhetorical embellishment, there was not a great deal to be said. Comerance was an austere and dignified young ruler, and the conversation at his table and among his courtiers was not the sort to amuse a wellborn lady. It was more likely to put her to sleep. Draining fenlands, scouring armor, and repairing bridges is useful and necessary work, but it is not the stuff of repartee. Princess showed all the outward signs of waning interest.

After her second politely smothered yawn, Kedrigern squeezed her hand and said, "It's probably best that you didn't come. You would have been bored to tears."

"You certainly make it sound as though I would. But at least I would have been bored somewhere new. I do like a change now and then."

"A change isn't necessarily an improvement. Comerance lives in a fortress. Great windy corridors, ice on the floors, fluttering tapestries . . . everyone sneezing and wheezing and coughing all through the night and snuffling and sniffling during the day. . . . It can be very depressing."

"I could have worn my heaviest cloak."

"It wouldn't have helped. Even with knitted wing-covers, you would have caught a chill, and the conversation wasn't worth it. The food wasn't very good, either."

"What about the fee?"

Kedrigern smiled broadly. He dug into the recesses of his tunic and drew out a large leather pouch that clinked sweetly as he hefted it and placed it in his wife's hand.

"In gold?"

"Of course. It was a very inconvenient curse, and Comerance is a busy man. We had no difficulty coming to terms."

"Comerance is a very generous man, too."

"I had the curse lifted before I shook the dust from my cloak. I don't waste time. Clients appreciate that kind of service."

Princess emptied the pouch into her lap. Coin fell upon coin with muffled metallic ring and glittered in the firelight, bright against the dark blue of her robe. "Comerance really is generous. There must be forty crowns here," she said.

"I like a man who isn't afraid to show his gratitude."

"You must have impressed him."

"Get there, lift the curse, collect the fee, start home," said the wizard, snapping his fingers in cadence with the rapid phrases. "That's the way I like to operate."

"Then why did it take you so long to get back?" Princess inquired, taking up a coin and examining it.

"I couldn't just jump on my horse and ride off, could I? It wouldn't have been polite, and you're always telling me to be more polite to kings. And I had to stay for a few days to make sure there were no adverse aftereffects. The follow-up is every bit as important as the quick cure, you know."

"You were gone for over four weeks. That's a lot of follow-up."

"I spent most of that time traveling. I really did hurry back —even took a shortcut that Comerance suggested."

"Did it save time?"

Kedrigern shook his head. "Comerance has no sense of direction. His shortcut took me three days longer than the route I had originally taken to his kingdom. The roads were about the worst I've seen, and the inns were absolutely awful. I looked in at two of them, and decided I'd be more comfortable in the woods. The only night I spent under a roof was when I stopped at the abbey on the mountain."

Princess's eyebrows rose. "Did you really stay there? I didn't think monks took kindly to wizards."

"I don't suppose they do, but they're considerate towards travelers. Very good people, actually. They seemed a bit . . . well, sort of on edge. Anxious. They were very kind, but they did their best to get me on my way first thing the next morning."

"Maybe they realized that you're a wizard."

"No, I don't think it was that. Something was bothering them. Duodecimo—the cellarer—kept hinting at awful things happening, and the abbot became quite touchy when I mentioned a few details I had observed. It was all very odd."

"Not so odd, when you think of it. Men living apart from the world like that must lead very quiet lives. The slightest incident could be upsetting."

"Their lives didn't look to be all that quiet, and I didn't get the impression that I had arrived on a particularly busy day. The very morning I left, they found a wild man raving at the gate."

With an impatient flutter of her hand, Princess said, "You're liable to find a wild man anywhere these days."

"I think this one was raving my name."

"Why would a wild man rave *your* name?"

"I can't imagine, and I didn't think it prudent to wait around and find out. But, my dear, I've been going on far too long about what was essentially a rather dull business trip, and I'm anxious to hear the news from home. What did you do while I was gone? Any visitors? Any clients? Any excitement?"

"There was no excitement. One messenger came, with a long letter from Vosconu. It wasn't confidential, so I read it over and told him to come back in the summer for a reply. Nothing pressing. Vosconu is thinking of clearing some forest land and he wants you to check it for enchantments and curses before his men get to work."

"Very sensible of him. His castle is in dryad country. You don't want to go cutting down trees at random in places like that. Anything else?"

"Nothing. Absolutely nothing," said Princess with a sigh. "I spent the rest of the time working on wand use and advanced spelling, and watching Spot clear away the snow."

"How's your wand work coming along?"

"Slowly. They're tricky little things, wands are," Princess said, the set of her jaw hinting at episodes of frustration that she preferred not to mention.

"Yes, but useful—provided one doesn't become dependent on them. I recall a witch I once knew . . . long ago it was, too, but I'll never forget . . . Dalaban was her name, poor old thing," said the wizard softly and wistfully, gazing into the fire and slowly shaking his head. He raised his goblet, found it empty, and reached for the decanter. "I think I'll have one more wee sip before turning in. A few drops for you, my dear?"

"What happened to Dalaban?" Princess demanded.

"Yes, of course, Dalaban. Poor old Dalaban," said Kedrigern, settling himself once again. "She was a very popular witch. I don't believe she had a single real enemy, and you know how rare that is, especially among witches. Well, for her three-hundredth birthday, all her friends chipped in and bought her a wand. I was studying with Fraigus then. We both contributed something. Dalaban was presented with a really lovely first-class wand. She had had no wand training at all, but she set to work at once, and soon she was quite proficient. She came to rely more and more on the wand for her day-to-day work, and in time she forgot all the other magic she knew. Then she lost the wand."

"Oh, the poor creature! How awful for her!" Princess cried, looking genuinely concerned.

"There was some unpleasantness with a demon, I believe. I never did learn the details. But poor old Dalaban found herself pushing four hundred and all her magic lost or forgotten. All she had left was a minor charm to keep her up and about, but she was unsteady on her feet for a long time."

"Whatever became of her?"

"Last I heard, she was cook at some inn up north. That was a while ago."

"But couldn't her friends do anything?"

"No one knew about it until long after the fact, and they all assumed that it would be rather an embarrassment to Dalaban to bring it up. Actually, she didn't mind the job. She liked to cook, and she was accustomed to spending hours on end over a hot cauldron. And she enjoyed the company. Witching's a lonely business. There's usually no one around to talk to but a cat. At an inn, though, you've always got someone on hand for a nice chat."

After a lengthy pause, Princess said, "That isn't such a tragic story."

Kedrigern thought for a time, then said, "No, I suppose it's not. But I didn't say it was, did I?"

"Then why did you bring it up? What's the point?"

"I thought the point was very clear: Don't become dependent on your wand; you may not be as lucky as Dalaban."

"I'll never become dependent on this wand. I don't think I'll ever get the hang of it."

"You underestimate yourself, my dear. You have a natural talent for magic. It's just a matter of application. Practice, and more practice."

And practice she did. After the first relaxed and cozy days of homecoming, Princess and Kedrigern settled down to their work, she on wands, he on the subtleties of counter-counter-counterspells.

The worst of winter was soon behind them. Each day was longer than the day before. The sun rode a bit higher in the sky and worked its way farther north at each sunrise. The snow mantle shrank and melted, and dwindled to dirty patches in shady dells and north-facing slopes. Spring was not yet arrived, but it was near at hand and coming nearer every day.

On a pleasant, bright, almost-spring morning after the last full moon of the winter, Kedrigern came to the breakfast table late. His eyes were puffy, his expression benumbed. He slumped into his chair and planted his elbows on the table. With a sigh, he rested his chin on the heels of his hands and gazed vacantly across the table at his wife. Princess paused in the act of buttering a muffin. She looked disapprovingly at his elbows, but did not speak.

"Sorry, my dear," Kedrigern said, removing his elbows from the table top and sinking lower into his chair. "I didn't get much sleep last night. All that howling."

"There did seem to be a lot more howling than usual. It woke me up around midnight, but I went right back to sleep," she said.

"One expects a certain amount of howling when the moon is full, but last night . . ." He broke off to yawn once again. "Excuse me, my dear. I suppose I should have worked a little spell for silence."

"Why not just plug your ears? You're always telling me not to squander magic."

"I wouldn't call that squandering magic. What's the good of being a wizard if you can't get a decent night's sleep?"

"You should take a bowl of warm milk before you go to bed."

Kedrigern gave a noncommittal grunt, thought for a moment, and said, "No, that doesn't work, either. That night I stayed at the abbey I had some lovely warm milk just before I turned in, and I was awakened by howling in the night. I was bone-tired, too. I'm afraid there's nothing for it but a spell."

"If that's what you prefer," said Princess, reaching for the jam pot.

"A very simple spell: Start at bedtime, end about an hour before dawn. Nothing fancy, and I'd only need it once in four weeks. All things considered, it's the—"

Kedrigern stopped in mid-sentence as a loud knock sounded on the front door, followed by two more, equally loud. He and Princess exchanged a quick glance, of annoyance on his part, interest on hers.

"Someone's at the door," she said.

"Spot can get it."

"Spot tends to frighten people off."

"Good. I'm not expecting anyone. If some stranger wants to intrude at a ridiculous hour of the morning, he deserves to be frightened off."

The knocking came again. Kedrigern did not stir. Princess gave him a hard look and put down her muffin.

"It may be a client. Someone may need help," she said.

"What about me? I need sleep. I need fewer interruptions. I need peace and quiet if I'm going to do my work properly."

"Yah! Yah!" came the cry of their house-troll, and the slapping of its huge feet as it hurried to the door.

"Has it occurred to you that someone might be asking for *me*? If that's the case, I do not want Spot opening the door. What if it's a fair damsel in distress? Will you please attend to it, or do you prefer that I do?" said Princess impatiently.

Kedrigern rose hurriedly. "I'll go, my dear. No telling what's liable to be banging on the door at this hour."

"I'm perfectly capable of protecting myself."

"Of course you are, but why take chances?" Kedrigern turned and cried, "I'll answer the door, Spot."

Muttering irritably to himself, he hurried to his front hall. He paused for a moment to work a short-term spell against physical violence, then drew the latch and opened the door.

The intruder was a young man, and the word that occurred to Kedrigern at sight of him was *disreputable*. His clothes were ripped and stained, stuck with bits of leaf, twigs, crushed berries, and clots of muck. The knees of his trousers were worn through. His hands were wrapped in dirty rags, and much dirtier rags were wound around his feet. He looked like a sturdy but very unsuccessful beggar.

He blinked, focused red-rimmed eyes on the wizard, and in a hoarse, strained voice said, "Master Kedrigern . . . are you Master Kedrigern, the great worker of counterspells?"

Untidy the fellow might be, thought Kedrigern, but he was a man of discernment. "I am he," he replied.

"You must help me. I'm so weary. I've been seeking you . . . since autumn," the visitor said weakly, swaying and reaching out one bandaged hand to steady himself against the doorjamb.

Kedrigern saw blood seeping through the rags, and his irritation vanished. This poor fellow was hurt and needed help. *His* help. He had no choice but to offer it.

"Come in, come in, young man. We'll get you cleaned up, and give you some breakfast, and then we'll see what we can do. Understand, I'm not a physician."

"I'm not an invalid. I need a counterspell."

"Ah. In that case, I may be able to help. Well, come in." As the visitor staggered over the threshold, Kedrigern called out, "Spot, fill the tub with hot water and fetch some clean cloths. Quickly, now." Taking the young man's arm, he said, "Don't be put off by Spot's appearance. A troll is a great help around the house."

"Thank you . . . Master Kedrigern. You're very kind," said his guest feebly.

"Just don't let Spot scrub your back. It means to be helpful, but it's a lot stronger than it realizes."

"I'll remember that."

"Good. Go right into the kitchen," said the wizard, pushing open the door. His guest stopped short and stiffened at his first glimpse of the knee-high house-troll. Spot was mostly head, and its head was mostly nose, and its nose was mostly warts. Large ears stuck out like open shutters bordering a window; the rest of Spot was chiefly huge hands and feet.

"Yah! Yah!" Spot greeted them, amid clouds of steam.

"This is a client, Spot. He's going to take a bath, and while he does, you're to wash his clothes and mend all the rips and tears."

"Yah!"

"Bring him my gray robe to wear while his things dry."

"Yah!"

"And when he's ready, show him into the breakfast room."

"Yah!"

"And bring him eggs and rashers and oatmeal and a pitcher of milk."

"May I have plain bread and butter? My stomach is a bit . . . delicate," the visitor interrupted.

"Of course. Make that bread and butter, Spot."

"Yah!"

Kedrigern left his guest in Spot's care and returned to Princess, who was consumed with curiosity which he could not allay. The young man's appearance suggested great hardship and long struggle. He was clearly on the brink of exhaustion. Could he be a fugitive? If so, was he fleeing from justice, or from injustice? His appearance was unprepossessing, but he was well-mannered and clearly intelligent. And he had spoken of his need for a counterspell, but he showed no manifestations of enchantment. It was a puzzle.

They speculated, made suggestions, theorized, and debated one possibility after another without result. When the visitor finally entered, accompanied by a gust of warm, moist air from the kitchen, they welcomed him with enthusiasm. Kedrigern undertook the introductions.

"Princess, this is a new client . . . whose name I don't know. Young man, would you mind . . . ?"

"Zorsch. My name is Zorsch."

"Oh. Zorsch, my dear. And this is my wife and collaborator in the subtle arts, Princess."

Zorsch bowed low. Such evident good breeding only deepened the mystery of his predicament. Princess took the direct approach to a solution.

"So pleasant to meet you, Zorsch. Do tell us what brings you here and how we can help you," she said sweetly, gesturing to a place at the table.

"Thank you, my lady. You are very kind. You have both been very kind," said Zorsch, seating himself gingerly, like a man resting after long and strenuous labors.

"Your problem, Zorsch . . . ?" Kedrigern urged.

"I'm a werewolf. I need a counterspell to release me."

"Werewolf?" said Princess, raising an eyebrow.

"I'm afraid so, my lady."

"Was that you howling last night?" Kedrigern asked.

"Very likely it was, Master Kedrigern. If I disturbed your rest, I'm sorry. I couldn't help it."

"Don't give it another thought, Zorsch. Your mind was on other things, I'm sure."

"I suppose it was. I never really know."

"Have you no memories at all?"

"Absolutely none. I have no idea where I've been or what I've done while I was transformed."

"How terribly awkward for you," said Princess, moved to empathy by her own memories—or, more accurately, the absence of them.

"It's most unsettling, my lady. I wake up on the morning after a full moon in some strange place, full of fleas, with a stiff back and my hands and feet all scraped and raw, and I have no idea of what I did or how I got wherever it is I am. My bones ache for a week, and my throat is sore, and my stomach is in a terrible state."

"Dreadful," the wizard murmured.

"But the worst part is the uncertainty. It's like being two entirely different persons."

"One person and one wolf," Kedrigern corrected him.

"Possibly. I assume that when I'm a wolf I'm all wolf, because when I'm a human I'm all human, but since I have no memories, I can't be sure."

"You poor thing," said Princess, patting his hand in a soothing gesture.

"As a matter of fact, I'd be willing to remain a wolf permanently if that's the only solution. At least I'd be able to make plans. This way, it's very difficult to hold a job, and impossible to form any kind of lasting relationship. All the girls I've met want to go out walking under the full moon, and of course that's out of the question."

"Oh, absolutely," said Princess.

"So I have to keep making excuses, and they think I'm sneaking off to see someone else, and that's the end of it."

Kedrigern nodded profoundly to express his sympathy and understanding. "A difficult predicament, Zorsch, no doubt about it, but I'll do whatever I can. First I must know exactly how you became a werewolf. Be accurate. It's very important."

"There's not much to tell. I was bitten by a dog—I *thought* it was a dog—on the night of a full moon, and when the next full moon came, I felt something happening to me. I was on my way through the woods, to meet a girl. . . ." Zorsch fell silent, then sighed and said, "Meerla was her name. The miller's daughter. Lovely girl . . . but as I was saying, I felt something happening to me, as if my body were suddenly being pulled all out of shape. I could see coarse hair sprouting on my hands and arms . . . my nails growing thick . . . and then everything went black. The next thing I knew, I was waking up in the woods next morning, my clothing in rags, every muscle strained, my voice hoarse. And every full moon since then, it's been the same."

Kedrigern grunted. "Bitten, eh? Not a curse, or a spell, or enchantment of some kind?"

"Bitten, Master Kedrigern."

"I was afraid of that. I do counterspells, Zorsch. I don't have anything for bites."

"But you're a great wizard!"

"That's true, but even a great wizard . . ."

"Keddie, you can try. You must. The poor boy needs you," Princess said.

"I do, I do, Master Kedrigern!" Zorsch cried, throwing himself at the wizard's feet. "I've been following you since the harvest moon. I arrived in the kingdom of Comerance two days after your departure. I nearly caught up to you on the road, but then the full moon . . ." He buried his face in his hands.

With a start, Kedrigern said, "It was you howling outside

my window at the abbey—you were the wild man at the gate!"

"I was. By the time the good monks had nursed me back to health, you were far away. It's taken me all these months to find you."

"You traveled ... in this weather ... all that distance. ... Oh, do get up off the floor, Zorsch. Sit down. Eat your bread and butter." Kedrigern raised the youth to his feet and helped him into the chair. Returning to his own seat, he said thoughtfully, "All that way ... in the cold and snow ... "

"I'll be grateful for anything, Master Kedrigern, anything at all, if it will only stop the changing back and forth. That's the part I can't bear. Make me a full-time human being if you can; but if you can't, then make me a bat, a cat, a toad—"

"Not a toad!' Princess broke in sharply. "Be a wolf if you must, but never be a toad!"

"All right, a wolf. Please, Master Kedrigern. Help me, and I'll serve you faithfully."

"Serve me? I take it that means you can't pay me."

Zorsch shrugged. "As I said, it's difficult to hold on to a job."

"What about your family?"

Zorsch shook his head. "Everything they have is tied up in real estate. My father is a great landowner, but he's always short of cash."

"Keddie, don't be mercenary," Princess said sternly.

"I'm thinking of Spot. I don't know how Spot would take to having a wolf around the house."

"It would only be for one night a month," Zorsch said.

"And this wouldn't be your ordinary wolf," Princess pointed out.

"I'd be useful, Master Kedrigern. I could keep away intruders, and save you a lot of protective magic. I can learn to fetch. We could have wonderful romps in the fresh air."

"Oh, all right," said the wizard with a sigh. "Finish your bread and butter, Zorsch, and then come to my workroom. I'll see what I can do."

⋯⋰ *Three* ⋱⋯

a summons to othion

TEN DAYS LATER, the Zorsch problem was still unsolved. The young man did his best to be cooperative, and cheerfully helped out around the house. So eager was he that Kedrigern had almost forcibly to restrain him from fetching his slippers after dinner.

But as the moon waned, and the prospect of the next full moon began to oppress him, Zorsch's cheerful manner became difficult to maintain. Kedrigern, too, showed signs of strain as his frustration grew. Finding relief for Zorsch was proving to be a slow process. When, on the eleventh day of Zorsch's stay, Princess suggested that Kedrigern call in a consultant, the wizard bridled.

"A consultant? Me, call in a *consultant*?" he retorted, charging the word with revulsion.

"Why not? You said yourself that this kind of work is outside your field. A consultant might be helpful."

"My dear, have you never heard the saying 'Those who can, do magic; those who can't do magic settle for alchemy; those who fail at alchemy become consultants'?"

"No, I haven't. You just made it up."

"It's a wise saying, all the same. Consultants are utterly useless. The very suggestion is insulting. Here I am, doing everything I can, working around the clock with no hope of payment, and you want me to call in a consultant. Have you no faith in me?"

"It's two weeks to the full moon, and Zorsch is getting nervous."

"Well, so am I. I don't want a werewolf around the house, even if it's a client. Do you?"

Princess looked thoughtful. "Can I do anything to help?"

"You can stop talking about consultants."

"It was only a suggestion. I want to help. Isn't there anything practical I can do?"

"You might start going through these books and see if you can find a formula for adapting counterspells to treat bites," said the wizard, indicating by manual gesture four waist-high stacks. "While you're looking through those, I'll be going through these." He indicated, by similar means, four additional stacks on the other side of the room.

"Are you sure it's in one of these?"

Gloomily, Kedrigern said, "No. I'm not even sure such a formula exists. I'll probably have to improvise, but I want to avoid that if I can. One can never predict the side effects."

At that moment, before either of them had had time to open a cover, an uproar burst upon them. First came a blare of brass, then Spot's excited "Yah! Yah!" drowned out by a second flourish, followed by more cries from Spot, a final tucket, and then Zorsch's shouts of "Master Kedrigern, my lady Princess, a herald comes! A herald in rich livery! With trumpeters, and men-at-arms!"

"Company! Oh, how delightful!" cried Princess, clapping her hands and flying from the room to greet them.

Kedrigern flung up his arms with a groan. "Always interruptions! How am I supposed to get anything done? I might as well try to research spells in the middle of a fair!" He looked to Princess for sympathy; not seeing her, he heaved a martyred sigh and trudged from the room, carefully closing the door behind him.

By the time he rejoined her, Princess had already thrown a

cloak over her shoulders and admitted the herald and two burly men-at-arms. They all stood, rather crowded together, in the entry hall. The herald was attired, as Zorsch had declared, richly, and in excellent taste. He removed his plumed hat, tossed back his black cloak, and made a low, sweeping bow. The men-at-arms took up position behind him, arms folded, eyes alert. Kedrigern studied their colors and the herald's livery, and as the herald straightened, said warmly, "A servant of King Ithian is always welcome in the home of Kedrigern and Princess."

"You reassure me doubly, Master Kedrigern," said the herald, bowing once again to him, then to Princess, with an accompanying, "My lady."

"And how are things in Othion?"

"All things in Othion go well, save one. And it is to seek his old friend's help with that single difficulty that the king has sent me, his faithful servant Uldindal."

"If I can help Ithian of Othion in any way, I'll be delighted to do so," said Kedrigern.

"His Majesty will be most pleased. He still recalls with gratitude the timely assistance you offered him in the days of his youth."

"Ah, yes. That business with the ogre . . ." Kedrigern nodded slowly and smiled a faint, nostalgic smile. At a sharp jab from Princess's elbow he snapped to alertness, saying quickly, "But you must come inside. We can speak more comfortably within."

"I thank you, Master Kedrigern," said Uldindal. He dismissed the men-at-arms with a nod, and followed his host and hostess.

"Your men must be hungry and thirsty after all that riding. I'll have Spot bring refreshments out to them," Princess said.

Uldindal bowed once again. "My lady is too kind."

"I think I'd better go out with him. The sight of Spot can be off-putting if one is not prepared."

"As my lady wishes," said Uldindal, with one final bow and flourish. When Princess was gone, and he had settled into the chair offered by Kedrigern, he said, "Perhaps, Master Kedrigern, you might like to know the problem that brings me here."

"I would indeed," said the wizard. He seated himself facing the herald, hitched the chair a hand's-breadth closer, inclined forward in a posture of eager attentiveness, and with a gesture, said, "Please proceed. I am all attention."

"You will recall that King Ithian married the radiant Kanvanira of the Dales shortly after his victory—with your generous aid, Master Kedrigern, for which he and his people are still grateful and ever will be—over the ogre that threatened both his kingdom and that of Kanvanira's parents. Their happy union produced one daughter, the beauteous Berzel. When a fever carried off Queen Kanvanira, the king was, for a time, inconsolable; but he soon redirected all his affection to Berzel. She became everything to him, and to his people. She was the light and the joy of Othion. And now. . ." Uldindal choked up. He buried his face in his hands for a moment, then looked up and wiped his eyes.

"And now?" Kedrigern prompted.

"And now the beauteous Berzel, apple of her royal father's royal eye, flower of the kingdom, fairest of all women, is accursed, blighted, blasted, and most foully wronged, struck down by a baneful hand in one of those instinctive acts of kindliness and love that were so much her nature; her beauty desecrated, her young life tainted, her future devastated."

"Could you be more precise?"

Composing himself, Uldindal said, "Riding one night in the wood, on her way to bring toys and sweets to the children of an ailing forester, Berzel stopped to pet a large dog and to offer it a scrap of food from her own hand. The ungrateful beast nipped her fingers and fled. The wound scarcely broke the skin, and Berzel gave it no thought until the night of the next full moon—when she turned into a wolf."

"I see. A fascinating coincidence," said the wizard thoughtfully. Noting Uldindal's perplexity, he began to recount Zorsch's story and his own efforts on the young man's behalf. As Kedrigern proceeded, the herald's mood changed from gloom to hope to exuberance, and the wizard had scarcely completed his account before Uldindal leapt up, seized his hands in a firm clasp, and burbled, "O providential accident! O felicitous misfortune! Now you need only apply those efforts already afoot to two afflicted souls instead of one!"

"I'm afraid it isn't that simple. In fact, it's a very tricky problem. Maybe insoluble."

"Insoluble? For a master of the subtle arts?" said Uldindal, recoiling in dismay.

"Well, lycanthropy isn't brought on by a curse, or spell, or enchantment, and those are the things I'm trained to handle. I don't know much about bites. They just aren't in my field."

"But surely you can adapt an existing spell. You can improvise."

"In my profession, improvisation is the last resort. It may come to that, but I'll try everything else first. It's going to take time."

"King Ithian was hoping that something might be done before the next full moon."

"I can't make promises." At sight of Uldindal's dejected countenance, Kedrigern pointed out cheerfully, "King Ithian was always fond of animals."

"Yes, but not in his immediate family."

Kedrigern raised a hand to concede the point; it was a complication that could affect one's judgment. But quickly brightening, he said, "Berzel can stay in the royal game preserve on nights when there's a full moon. That way, she couldn't hurt anyone, and there'd be less danger to her, too."

"A sound suggestion, Master Kedrigern. But still, only a stopgap. We must solve the problem, not adjust to it."

"And solve it we shall. But we don't want Berzel running all over the countryside biting people while I'm looking for the cure, nor do we want people pursuing Berzel with silver arrows and garlic and things like that."

At this point Princess returned, to announce that generous portions of bread and cheese, cold meats, and pitchers of ale, had been taken to Uldindal's men. Kedrigern apprised her of the herald's mission, and she was deeply moved.

"Oh, the poor, dear thing! I know exactly how she feels. Transformation is a terrible sensation, even if it's only for one night at a time. Keddie, you must do something," she said, wringing her hands.

"I shall, my dear. Uldindal," said the wizard, "you may tell Ithian that I am at work on his daughter's problem. He will hear from me the moment I find the remedy."

Uldindal did not appear reassured. There was a note of apprehensiveness in his voice as he said, "His Majesty had hoped to confer with you in person. I am to invite you to be honored guests in Othion."

"Honored guests?" Princess repeated in joyful surprise.

"I'm afraid that won't be possible," said the wizard, edging toward the door.

Princess seized his arm. "I want to be an honored guest in Othion. I want to enjoy the company of a king and a princess and noble lords and ladies, and to hear court gossip, and see court ceremony, and eat at the royal board. I want that very much."

"Othion is only a hundred leagues distant," said Uldindal.

Kedrigern scowled at him. "A journey of a hundred leagues begins with a single argument, followed by days of packing, maddening confusion, wasted time, crippling expense, and a murderous headache."

"That's not the way the saying goes," said Princess.

"It is when I say it. I hate travel."

"This is no time to be selfish. Berzel needs your help. Ithian needs your support. I need a vacation."

"My dear, how can I help Berzel without my books?"

Eagerly, Uldindal broke in, "Every book in Othion is yours to command, cherished master."

"That's no help. My work requires a very specialized library."

"But the king's own wizard, the renowned Master Traffeo, has placed the entire contents of his private library at your disposal, Master Kedrigern. King Ithian insisted upon it."

Princess beamed. "Well, there you are. Zorsch can do the packing. Spot can watch over the house. What are we waiting for?"

"It's a hundred leagues away! The roads are muddy, and there are thieves and robbers everywhere—I'll have to use up piles of magic just getting us there safely, and then use up more getting us back!" Kedrigern cried in growing exasperation. He sensed a losing battle.

With gestures of reassurance, Uldindal scuttled to the wizard's side. "You need have no fear for your safety, Master Kedrigern. I have come with eight men-at-arms selected by King Ithian himself to escort you to Othion. When Princess Berzel is her royal self once again, they will escort you home. Your reward will be two hundred golden crowns."

Kedrigern's eyebrows rose at mention of the sum, but he did not speak. Princess stepped forward and said, "Leave us, Uldindal. We have matters to discuss."

"Yes, my lady. At once, my lady," said the herald, bowing and backing from the room. When he was gone, Princess confronted Kedrigern, her arms folded, her visage stern. He avoided her eyes.

"You're being impossible," she said sharply.

"Well, I don't want to go to Othion," he muttered.

"Why on earth not? You won't have to use any magic to protect us, we'll enjoy the royal hospitality, and the fee is enormous. Besides, Berzel needs an understanding friend at a time like this. We princesses must stick together. We simply have to go, Keddie. What possible objection can you have?"

"I don't want to use someone else's books. I want to use my own, and work in my own study. Working in Othion could take me twice as long."

"You'd have another wizard to help you. It might take only *half* as long."

Kedrigern shook his head. "Not with Traffeo helping me. He's said to have an impressive library, but from what I've heard, he's not much of a wizard."

"All the more reason for him to want you finished and on your way as quickly as possible."

Kedrigern grunted sourly. "All the more reason for him to make a mess of things and try to blame it on me."

"All right, then: We'll send Traffeo off somewhere and I'll help you. So there's no problem."

"Not with the magic, maybe," Kedrigern said grudgingly, after a long pause, "but Ithian probably won't give us an escort back. He'll make all kinds of deductions from the fee, too. I've had dealings with kings. Promise anything, and then when you have what you want, renege. That's royalty for you."

"*I'm* royalty," said Princess in an icy voice.

"Yes, but you're different. We both know that."

"One of us sometimes forgets."

The room was very still. Kedrigern looked at Princess and smiled. She did not return the smile. He sighed. For a long time, there was no other sound in the room.

"Well, if you help me, it shouldn't take too long. And Traffeo might have a few books I've been looking for. It's possible. And if Ithian tries to renege, I'll just have to take stern measures," said the wizard resignedly. "So I suppose . . ."

Princess's expression softened. "To Othion?"

Kedrigern threw up his hands. "To Othion."

Princess found the journey pleasant and diverting. Uldindal was a repository of court gossip and noble small talk, a source of diversion unavailable on Silent Thunder Mountain and one which, on principle, she sorely missed. Her memory of youthful days at the court of her parents was still almost completely lost to her, but Princess was aware of what was done and not done in such circles and happy to be able to exercise her birthright.

Uldindal, for his part, was relieved to be heading home with his mission accomplished, and exerted every effort to be obliging. Zorsch, once his initial disappointment at the intrusion into the wizard's single-minded attention had passed, drew encouragement from the thought of this added incentive to the search for a counter-lycanthropy spell, or some equally effective substitute. Two weeks remained before the next full moon; they would be in Othion before that time; with any luck at all, he might not have to undergo another transformation. His spirits revived at this happy prospect, and he spent much time diverting his fellow travelers with droll tales, merry song, and skillful whistling.

Kedrigern, who hated travel with unwavering intensity,

consoled himself as best he could with the promise of an enormous fee. When that began to pall, he turned his thoughts to Traffeo's library and facilities. They were certain to be absolutely first-class. Othion was a wealthy kingdom, and Ithian was known as a generous patron of learning in all forms, especially those that might come in handy in times of trouble. He was one of the few kings of Kedrigern's acquaintance who could, and did, read. His royal wizard's library would want for nothing, and the wizard would have the very best equipment.

Traffeo himself, though, might prove a problem. It would be unprofessional simply to ignore him, and naive to accept him as a trusted assistant. That Kedrigern might require assistance was likely, and that it would all be provided by Princess was his hope. Princess could be relied on, and her natural talent for magic was considerable; but she was still learning, and it took long experience to work variations on a spell without unforeseen consequences. Even for an experienced wizard, nothing was certain. Of course, with magic, nothing was ever certain anyway; one took great care, followed instructions to the letter, and hoped for the best.

And the best—when working with, and perhaps depending on, a wizard of doubtful abilities and injured feelings, acting under enforced hospitality—was likely to be indistinguishable from the worst. Kedrigern pondered this for a time, then went back to thinking about his fee.

For the journey to Othion, Princess and Kedrigern rode horses from their own stable; they seemed appropriate to the occasion. Hers was transparent. Except for the rich caparison of white, trimmed with gold, that covered its body, it was a vague shape of shimmering iridescence. Princess seemed to be riding on a beam of sunlight, and was a lovely, graceful sight.

Kedrigern's mount was a giant, black as polished onyx, red-eyed, with silver hooves and a silver horn as long as a man's arm jutting from its forehead. Between the wizard's gloomy silence, and the awesome presence of his horse, the men-at-arms were inclined to keep their distance. It was not until the very last day of their journey that one of them worked

up his courage and came close enough for Kedrigern to acknowledge his company with a smile and a nod of greeting.

"And a good day to you, master wizard," said the guard in
a voice like a kettledrum reverberating at the bottom of a deep
well. "That is a fine horse you be riding."

"He's a wonderful horse," said Kedrigern, patting the creature's neck with affection and respect.

"Has he a name?"

"Not that I know of. I think it would be presumptuous of
me to give such a horse a name of my own devising."

The guard's heavy brow furrowed and drew down to
shadow his battered nose and scarred cheeks. He pondered the
wizard's words for a time, then said solemnly, "That is good
thinking."

"Speaking of names, what's yours?"

"I am Kolma, master wizard."

"That's not a local name, is it?"

"No, master wizard. I was born in the east, beyond the
mountains, on the high plain."

"You've seen something of the world in your lifetime,
haven't you, Kolma?"

"Oh, I have. I have indeed," said the guard with a faint,
reminiscent smile. "Sea and land, great kingdoms and empty
deserts, high places and low. I've been shipwrecked, served as
a galley slave, been a king's champion. . . . I fought in the
siege of Meodahad, and in the battle of the four fleets at Sam-
midar. I shared in the plunder of the Ivory Palace. And
once—" Here he stopped, looked around cautiously, then
leaned closer and in a lowered voice said, "Once I crossed the
Desolation of the Loser Kings."

"A hard journey that was, I'm sure," said the wizard sym-
pathetically.

"Horrible, master wizard. Thirty of us started out from the
Inn on the Outer Edge. I reached the mountains alone, two
months later, crawling on my hands and knees, and was out of
my true wits for a year after that. And glad I am, too, to be
quit of the memories of that crossing. Sometimes they come
back in a dream, and I wake up. . . . A bad place, master wizard, a bad place that is."

"Not any more, Kolma. Now grass grows there, and flowers. Trees are beginning to bloom, and the streams and brooks are flowing again with clear, sweet water. It's become rather a pretty place."

"The Desolation? A pretty place?" said the guard, his heavy features transfigured by wonderment. "How could such a thing happen? Who would have the power to work such a mighty magic?"

Kedrigern glanced down, smiled shyly, and with a little dismissive gesture of his hand said, "Well . . . one does what one can."

"You, master wizard?"

Kedrigern nodded. Kolma simply gaped. They rode on for a full minute, with no sound save the dull beat of the horses' hooves on hard-packed earth. Then the wizard said, "That's where my wife and I got our horses, as a matter of fact. There was an eruption of pent-up magic going off in every direction. All sorts of things happened—translations, transmutations, transformations, enchantments, disenchantments—a very busy time. It was interesting, certainly, from a professional point of view, but I don't think I'd care to go through it again."

From above them came a faint sweet voice, crying in joyous tones, "There it is! Othion! Oh, it's lovely!"

Kedrigern looked up. Princess was overhead, just above treetop height, one hand shading her eyes as she gazed upon their destination. Kedrigern waved, and she swooped smoothly down and hovered at his side, her little wings fluttering with a soft hum.

"You never said how lovely Othion is, Keddie—It's a beautiful city! Oh, we're going to have a wonderful visit, I know we are!" she exclaimed, clapping her hands excitedly.

"Ithian must have made some improvements since I was here last. It's been—oh, my—well over twenty years. Closer to twenty-five. Time for plenty of change."

"There's a fine high wall of white stone, with watchtowers, and pennants everywhere, and a really magnificent palace."

"Yes, it was a nice palace, as I recall. A bit drafty, but lots of room."

"And gardens. Nothing much is blooming yet, but they're beautifully laid out. They'll be lovely in summer."

Kedrigern nodded. "Ithian's father was known as Gurnian of the Green Thumbs. He didn't actually have green thumbs, you understand—he was called that because of a certain knack he had with plants."

"We'll be there before midday, at this pace. I must have another look," said Princess, soaring upward and onward.

Kolma had not spoken a word since hearing Princess's delighted cries from above. Now he wet his lips, looked about furtively, and in a small voice said, "The lady has wings."

"Yes. Very handy things to have."

"She flies," Kolma said in a voice even smaller.

"She certainly does. In weather like this, I can't keep her down," said Kedrigern with a good-natured chuckle.

"Is the lady a fairy? A . . . witch?"

"Oh, dear me, no. Nothing of the sort. She's a perfectly normal princess who happens to have wings. Got them at the Desolation, as a matter of fact, where we got these horses. On the very same day."

Kolma edged his horse to a safer distance. He looked at Kedrigern with wary respect for a time, and then, wetting his lips once more, and clearing his throat, he asked, "And you, master wizard—what did *you* get on that day at the Desolation?"

Kedrigern thought for a time, then turned to the guard and with a sphinxlike smile said, "Experience, Kolma . . . and a few new tricks."

···⚜ *Four* ⚜···

with ithian in othion

WHEN THEIR LITTLE party reached the edge of the forest and the walls of Othion came into view, Uldindal signaled for a halt. At his direction, the trumpeters proceeded at stately pace to the crest of a knoll. There they dismounted, and with showy gestures readied their instruments.

"We must announce our return in a fitting manner," Uldindal informed Princess and Kedrigern.

He flung up a hand dramatically. The trumpeters turned to face the city walls, raised their instruments, and blew an elaborate fanfare which Kedrigern, out of curiosity, timed by counting his pulsebeats: forty-two. Scarcely had their last notes faded before a flourish came from the ramparts of Othion. It lasted for a count of sixty-seven.

Uldindal beamed upon his company. "Our arrival is noted. Now we must identify ourselves," he said, flinging up his other hand.

This time Kedrigern's count went to eighty-nine before the trumpeters were done. They were quite red in the face. As they lowered their instruments, the sound of their breathing was audible to all. The response from the wall went on for a hundred-and-sixteen count.

"This is the best part. We're going to let everyone know that the mission was a success," said Uldindal with a nod to the trumpeters.

Success was proclaimed in a shorter, but much more energetic, fanfare. When it was over, both trumpeters were a bit unsteady on their feet. One had to lean against his horse for a time. The response from the walls was equally brief, but more subdued.

Uldindal rubbed his hands together with evident delight. "His majesty is pleased. We may request permission to enter Othion," he said.

Princess and Kedrigern exchanged a glance of alarm and looked toward the knoll. Uldindal showed no sign of concern, and indeed, the trumpeters' florid coloration had faded slightly, so they did not voice their misgivings. Uldindal raised both hands. The request for permission to enter the city went on for a ninety-one count, during which Uldindal winced several times at cracked notes. When it ended, the trumpeters' faces were as red and shiny as polished apples. The response from Othion came quickly.

When he saw the trumpeters readying themselves for another blast, Kedrigern could contain himself no longer. "Will this go on past dinner time? Those men look as though they're about to explode."

"Just a brief acknowledgment of permission, Master Kedrigern, and we'll be on our way. Must observe protocol, you know."

The acknowledgment was indeed brief and simple: a rising three-note motif taken in turns by each trumpeter. At its conclusion, Uldindal formed up the party and they rode for the gates, which opened wide to admit them.

The streets of Othion were smoothly paved and surprisingly clean. The people, too, were clean beyond ordinary expectations. Doorways were swept, front steps scrubbed, and several of the shops and houses appeared newly painted. The paint was of a drab muddy hue, as were most of the colors of Othion's buildings and the garments of her residents, but all was very clean. As the procession rode to the palace, bells began to ring. Princess waved to a group of children, and they waved back wildly, squealing and shouting welcome. Two women began to toss flowers, and others joined them.

"They seem happy to see us," Princess said.

"Oh, yes, my lady," Uldindal assured her. "The people of Othion love King Ithian and his daughter, and their love extends to all who befriend and aid them."

"That's very nice of them. They're lovely subjects, really. Do you think I ought to fly a little? They might like that."

Kedrigern frowned with concern and shook his head. "It could be dangerous, my dear. There are a lot of sharp edges on the gables, and low-hanging shop signs. You might give yourself a nasty knock on the head."

Princess looked up. In places, the jutting gables of facing houses were within arm's length of one another. Ridgepoles and downspouts projected beyond the rooflines, and they and the rafters were, on many houses, elaborately carved and decorated with pointy embellishments. Heavy carven shop signs swayed within easy reach above a rider's head, depending from sagging spear-like poles. The airspace was undeniably hazardous.

"My lady can safely fly from the walls," Uldindal suggested. "Or around the tiltyard."

"I'll wait and do that," said Princess, waving and smiling to a group of apprentices, who cheered loudly.

They rode up the gently sloping street toward the gates of the palace, which stood at the highest point of Othion. The gates opened smoothly and silently to admit them, and closed noiselessly behind them, shutting out the populace. On the steps of the palace stood King Ithian, surrounded by a crowd of courtiers, members of the royal household, soldiers, and the upper echelon of servants.

Ithian was a handsome, well-formed man in the prime of life. He was dressed in black, with a gray cloak over his shoulders. Beside him stood a slender, delicate-looking girl in a hooded brown cloak trimmed with rather uninteresting fur.

"Is that Berzel?" Kedrigern asked.

"That is our unfortunate princess," Uldindal informed him.

"She's a pretty child," Princess observed, withholding comment on her attire.

"Princess Berzel is the light of Othion. Her grace and beauty and the unfailing sweetness of her disposition—it is said by some that she is gentle even while a werewolf—make her predicament all the sadder."

"Cheer up. My husband will put her straight."

"We have every confidence in him."

"And I'll be assisting."

"Our confidence is redoubled, my lady. And now, if you will permit . . ."

Uldindal signaled a halt some ten paces from the steps. While the escort formed up on either side of Princess and Kedrigern, he rode forward, dismounted, and climbed the steps at stately pace to kneel at Ithian's feet and present the honored guests.

"Kedrigern! We knew you would come!" cried Ithian. His voice was deep and strong, but his handsome features were marked by grief.

Kedrigern dismounted and started forward and up the steps. Ithian descended to the first landing, a plateau broad enough for a carriage to turn in, and said, "Again you come to our aid. Thank you for such touching loyalty."

"I'll do my best for you, Ithian," said the wizard, embracing him.

Ithian returned the embrace, and held the wizard by the shoulders. "We can ask no more of any man. We have no false hopes. Berzel's condition is grave."

"It is indeed. Pity she's not suffering under a spell, or a curse. I know how to handle such things. But a werewolf's bite . . ." Kedrigern shook his head slowly, indicating his perplexity at the situation.

"If our Berzel can be helped, you will help her," said Ithian, clapping the wizard firmly on the shoulders. "If not, then there is no hope for her."

The crowd cheered and applauded loudly at this display of amity between the two men. Ithian waved, and they cheered louder.

"Don't say that, Ithian," said Kedrigern, waving and smiling at the onlookers. "There's always hope."

"Not in this case. We wanted Berzel to marry some day, when we deem her ready, and continue our royal line."

"She can still marry."

Ithian glowered. "We hope for grandchildren, not cubs."

"That is something to consider," Kedrigern conceded.

"Besides, who would wish to marry a woman—even a sweet, gentle, beautiful creature like our beloved daughter— who turns into a wolf every time the moon is full? Think of the dowry we would have to give. There is not enough wealth in Othion and the neighboring kingdoms."

Kedrigern nodded. "Another consideration. I seem to have my work cut out for me."

"The royal wizard's library is at your disposal, and Traffeo will assist you in any way you wish. Have you brought servants?"

"Just one young man who came to me recently with the same problem as your daughter. I hope you don't object."

"Not at all. Berzel would be pleased to think that by helping her, you help others as well. She is a very generous person."

"And, of course, I brought—"

"Merciful heavens!" Ithian exclaimed, recoiling in astonishment.

Princess had tossed aside her cloak and unfurled her wings. She was now approaching them, gliding smoothly through the air about a yard above the steps, smiling her sweetest smile. The sun glinted on her coronet and wand, and struck highlights from the transparent horse that stood patiently where she had left it.

At sight of her, the onlookers gasped, then began to shout encouragement. She waved to them, and they cheered wildly.

"Ithian, I'd like you to meet—" Kedrigern began to say.

"Your fairy godmother!" Ithian blurted.

". . . my wife, Princess," the wizard concluded. "Princess, this is Ithian of Othion."

"Delighted to meet you," said Princess, alighting and

dropping a graceful curtsey. "It's so good to see a genuine king again."

"Wife?" Ithian said softly, looking from Princess to Kedrigern and back to Princess. "Are you sure you're not someone's fairy godmother?"

"Quite sure, Your Majesty."

"But you have those little gossamer wings . . . and that wand. . . ."

"I do, don't I?" said Princess with an airy shrug of her shoulders. "But I assure Your Majesty that I am a perfectly normal princess in all other respects."

"Yes. We see," said Ithian. His tone and facial expression made it clear that he did not see, and did not expect to; but he was a ruler and their host, and he acted as his roles required. He took Princess's hand, raised it to his lips, and kissed it, then favored Princess with a warm smile. She returned it radiantly. Everyone cheered some more.

"May we speak to Berzel? The sooner we meet her, the sooner we can get to work," said Kedrigern.

"Of course. Yes. Certainly," said Ithian with a start. He turned and extended his hand, and the beauteous Berzel stepped forward to join the threesome, her head bowed, her eyes lowered demurely. "Berzel, our dear child, come, meet the man who will free you from your affliction . . . and his lovely wife," he said to the maid.

Berzel curtseyed. In a sweet childlike voice she said, "It is kind of you both to come so far for my poor sake."

"My dear young lady, it's a pleasure and a privilege," said the wizard in his most ceremonious manner. "I will set to work this very day, and I will not rest until your problem is solved."

Princess went to Berzel at once, and took the girl's hands in hers. Her voice was at its most maternal and consoling as she said, "Oh, you poor, dear, unfortunate child. I know exactly how you feel. But be of good cheer. We will leave no spell unwoven in your cause."

"My lady is kind, and I am grateful for her sympathy. But alas, no one can know truly how I feel," said Berzel wearily.

Giving Berzel's hands a reassuring squeeze, Princess released them and said, "I can. I had a similar problem myself, and this is the very wizard who helped me."

Berzel started, and gazed at her with eyes rounded in wonder. "Was my lady, too, a wolf?"

"Not a wolf, dear. I was a toad. I was a toad all day, every day, for ever so many years. I had just about given up hope when Kedrigern of Silent Thunder Mountain came along."

"*All day*? Was there no respite?"

"Not for an instant. I was a toad in a bog, and that was that. It was not a very pleasant bog, either," said Princess.

Berzel looked at her with tear-filled eyes. "Oh, my poor Princess! I am a wolf for but one short night each month, and I shudder at the mere thought. But to be a toad . . . and to *remain* a toad . . . Oh!" and she threw herself, weeping, into Princess's arms. The crowd cheered louder than ever, and dozens of hats were flung into the air.

As Princess and Berzel wept on one another's shoulder and poored one another in throbbing voices, Ithian drew Kedrigern aside and said softly, "That's Berzel for you. All sympathy. She's four days away from turning into a wolf, and look at her, weeping for the past sorrows of a woman she's just met."

"A sweet child, Ithian. You have raised her well. She looks a bit like her mother, as I recall."

Ithian's grip on the wizard's arm tightened convulsively. He covered his face with his other hand as he whispered, "Her mother! Yes, she is the image of our Kanvanira. Alas for our poor lost love!"

"Steady, Ithian," the wizard urged.

"Yes, of course. Forgive us, Kedrigern." Ithian released his grip and straightened, sweeping the crowd with a cool and regal eye, raising a few subdued cries of "Hurray for King Ithian!" which he acknowledged with a nod and a wave of the hand. To Kedrigern, he said, "We have never gotten over our loss. Actually, it has been worse for our poor little girl, growing up without a mother . . . no one to turn to . . . especially now, in this time of trial."

"Princess will help all she can. My wife is a very understanding woman. Absolutely insisted on coming with me. She feels that beautiful princesses ought to stick together."

"A lovely woman, Kedrigern. You are a lucky wizard."

"I am." Kedrigern paused for a moment, then said, "Tell me, Ithian, have you never . . . I know how deeply you loved Kanvanira, but hasn't anyone . . . I mean, in all those years, haven't you once considered . . . ?"

"Remarrying?"

"Yes."

"We have been urged to do so for Othion's sake and Berzel's, and for our own," Ithian quickly assured him. "But we have found no one even remotely suitable. Beautiful princesses are rare these days."

"I don't wonder," said Kedrigern. "The last few I've met have all had problems like Berzel's. One was a fly. Another was a sword, when she wasn't a shillelagh, and her sister was a crown. Then there was a cousin who was a wand."

"You have interesting acquaintances."

"We do indeed. The trouble is, most of them have serious problems with enchantment."

"It is shocking," said Ithian, shaking his head.

"Princess, too. She was a toad when we met, you know."

"She has made a remarkable recovery," Ithian said, regarding Princess appreciatively as she comforted his daughter, to the accompaniment of sympathetic murmurs and scattered applause from the onlookers.

"Yes, she certainly did. They all did, as a matter of fact, except for Lalloree, and even she seems to have adjusted well. She's happily married, at any rate. But that sort of thing does reduce the number of beautiful princesses in circulation."

"Would that we had found someone suitable. If we had another child, there would still be hope for the succession, even if Berzel cannot be cured."

"Then I must see to it that Berzel is cured. Have faith, Ithian. Remember that ogre."

"We do, Kedrigern. And we trust you, and welcome you and Princess to Othion. Come, honored wizard—all Othion is at your service," said Ithian, taking Kedrigern by one arm and Princess by the other and conducting them at a dignified pace up the steps, with Berzel still clinging to Princess and the crowd cheering itself hoarse.

After an elaborate, delectable, but rather somber dinner, Princess and Berzel withdrew and Kedrigern was shown to the royal library. It was a lovely place for a browser, heaven for a bibliophile, but almost entirely worthless to a wizard: On those long shelves of exquisitely bound volumes, standing as trim and orderly as various divisions of the king's own household, were exactly eight works dealing with the subtle arts, and all eight were at the beginner's level. There was a wealth of genealogy at Kedrigern's disposal; ages of history, actual, fanciful, and mixed; marvelous big books of maps and charts of every corner of the world, known and unknown, real and imagined, explored and unexplored; volume upon volume of poetry—epical, heroic, narrative, lyrical, meditative, devotional, satirical, and various blends of these types—in volumes ranging from ornate and massive incunabula to tiny 64mos that scarcely covered the palm of his hand; books on economy, cookery, herbals, architecture, warfare, gardening, woodworking, monument-building, falconry, horsemanship, swordsmanship, musicianship, shipbuilding, navigation, hunting, philosophy, engraving, theology, animal husbandry, heraldry, and court etiquette. And eight skinny books of magic whose contents, combined, would scarcely enable one to make a flea disappear. The priorities of the Librarian Royal were deplorable.

As he slid the eighth book back into place with a frown, a sigh, and a muttered phrase expressing his disappointment and chagrin, Kedrigern heard a soft cough behind him, as of a visitor announcing his unnoticed arrival. He turned and saw a refined-looking man of perhaps two hundred or so, dressed in resplendent wizardly regalia, regarding him with mixed curiosity and uneasiness.

"Master Kedrigern, I presume?" the newcomer said.

"I am he. And you must be Master Traffeo."

"I am Traffeo. Yes, that is my name. Traffeo, Wizard Royal of Othion, by appointment of King Ithian," the other

announced with a sweeping bow and a flourish of his voluminous robes. The cabalistic symbols on his garments flashed
and glittered in the candlelight.

"I'm pleased to meet you, Traffeo. I hope we'll be able to
work together to solve Princess Berzel's problem."

Traffeo straightened, and at once moved back into the
shadows. "You are kind, Master Kedrigern, but I fear I have
little to offer to one of your skill and accomplishment. My
library and I are at your service, but I think you will find my
books more useful than I can ever be."

"You are too humble, Master Traffeo. One is not appointed
Wizard Royal of Othion unless one has a great deal to offer in
the way of wizardry."

"What can be learned from books and done by rote, I can
do. But I lack the stuff of a great wizard," said Traffeo dispas-
sionately, raising a hand to forestall Kedrigern's objection. "I
am aware of my limitations, Master Kedrigern, and aware that
while my small accomplishments might astonish others, they
will neither deceive nor impress one of your stature. I offer
my assistance, such as it is, but I cannot persuade myself that
I will be of use to you. I have already drunk deep from the cup
of failure."

Traffeo's manner, as much as his words, bespoke a bitter
disappointment. Hoping to console him, Kedrigern said,
"Berzel's case is a difficult one. It's not really in our line at
all."

Traffeo sighed deeply and shook his head. "I was ac-
quainted with failure long before the good princess's misfortune. I am a worthless travesty of a wizard, and I have learned
to live with my disgrace. But enough of this—come, let me
show you my books. I have searched them through, and found
nothing to suit the current situation, but such a wizard as
yourself will no doubt make better use of them."

"We'll find the answer together, Traffeo," said Kedrigern
confidently, falling into step at his side.

They left the royal library and made their way along a hall,
through a door, along a shorter hall, through another, smaller
door with heavy triple locks, up a flight of narrow winding
stairs, through still another locked door, and finally into a

spacious tower room. As Traffeo ignited torches, a room much like Kedrigern's own workroom, only much cleaner and tidier, came into view. The walls were lined with books, and Kedrigern's eyes lit up at the sight of them. Most of them were familiar friends, trusted tools, faithful servants. He turned to Traffeo with a grin of anticipation, rubbing his hands together briskly, eager to get to work.

"This is more like it. You've got a wonderful collection, Traffeo. May I?" he asked, gesturing toward the shelves.

"Please do. My books, my instruments, and I are at your service," said Traffeo.

He looked mournfully at Kedrigern, his features illuminated by the light of a candle on the table before him and the torches on the walls all around. Kedrigern had his first clear sight of the Wizard Royal, and it perplexed him.

"Traffeo, have we met before? It seems to me—"

"No, we have not," said the other flatly, turning aside and averting his face. "You have never seen me before, I am certain of it."

"If you say so. Just for a moment, you reminded me of someone I once knew."

"A trick of light and shadow, nothing more. I will leave you to your investigations, if you have no objection. Please treat this room as your own. Stay as long as you please, use whatever of my instruments you like, take what books are of interest," said Traffeo, laying a ring of keys on the table. "I ask only that you lock the doors whenever you leave."

"I'm surprised that such a precaution is necessary."

"It was not, until recent years. But since I possess some volumes that might, in the wrong hands, lead to mischief . . ."

"I understand. I'll be sure to lock up."

"Then I will take my leave of you," said Traffeo with a low bow. He backed from the room, keeping his face in shadow, and closed the door behind him.

Kedrigern stood for a time bemused, looking down on the keys. Then he turned to gaze at the door. Traffeo was a puzzle. The man could not have been more gracious, or more cooperative, and his manner seemed genuine. But he seemed, too, to be one of the saddest men that Kedrigern had met in recent memory.

Memory . . . that was a puzzle, too. Something about Traffeo's face . . . the shape of the eyes . . . the way he held his head at a certain angle . . . It was annoyingly familiar, but Kedrigern could not recapture the image that had flickered across his mind and then vanished back into the murky mental labyrinth of half-forgotten things. He had a good memory for faces, but a poor one for places and circumstances in which the remembered faces had been encountered. At times, the combination proved a source of embarrassment, and he had learned to wait until the full picture was clear before speaking out.

In any event, his primary concern was not with Traffeo but with Berzel. Unless a cure could be found within a very few days, she would turn into a wolf. Kedrigern cleared a place on the long worktable, took up the candle, and started his search of the Wizard Royal's library.

···❧ *Five* ❧···

the furry princess

"You had quite a late night," said Princess when Kedrigern cautiously opened his eyes to a bright and sunny mid-morning. "Were you carousing with the Wizard Royal?"

"Certainly not, my dear," said Kedrigern righteously. He yawned and closed his eyes. "I can assure you that the Wizard Royal is not a carousing man. And even if he were the prince of merrymakers, I have far too much to do, and very little time to do it. There will be no carousing for me until Berzel can look at a full moon without dropping to all fours and howling."

"If you're that pressed for time, you'd better be up and doing. The morning's half gone. Open those eyes. Come along, up we go," said Princess, snatching the pillow from under his head and tugging the bedclothes free.

"You're chipper this morning," Kedrigern observed morosely.

"I had a lovely long chat with Berzel last night. She's not at all as shy and retiring as she first appears to be. She's very chatty. Loves to talk. It's such a treat to talk shop with another princess."

49

"Shop? Princesses don't talk shop."

"Well, not exactly shop. She told me all the court gossip, and I told her about Louise, and Lalloree, and all the other princesses I've met. I described what it was like being a toad, and she told me what she could recall about being a wolf. The poor girl doesn't remember much. It's just the way Zorsch described it."

"You don't remember much yourself," Kedrigern pointed out.

Princess shook her head. "I remember my life as a toad in excruciating detail. It's the time before that I can't recall."

"It will come back, my dear. You must be patient."

"You've been saying that for years."

"We don't know how long you were in the bog. That's a factor. And when you consider the amount of magic you've been subject to . . ."

"Fortunately, that's all behind me."

"Yes, and this is a perfect opportunity to make use of your experience and your talent," said Kedrigern, covering a great yawn. He swung his legs over the side of the bed and rubbed his eyes in a childlike gesture. "You can help me go through Traffeo's library. He's got some fine books. You'll learn a lot."

"What's Traffeo like? You said he's not a carouser, but what *is* he?"

"A joyless fellow, I'm afraid. Very cooperative, full of praise, willing to help, but gloomy. He seems to have lost all his self-confidence."

Princess gave him a curious look. "A Wizard Royal without self-confidence? That's unusual."

"It's practically unheard of. Traffeo is an unusual man. He talks as though he has some great failure in his past. His face bothers me, too."

"Is he ugly?"

"Oh, no. Quite decent-looking. What bothers me is that I think I've met him before, but I can't recall where, or when, or under what circumstances."

Princess smiled sweetly and patted him on the head. "It

will come back, Keddie. You must be patient. Now, get moving."

Traffeo's tower workroom was a calm and restful sanctuary far from the routine noises of the castle workday. No thumps or clanks or hoofbeats or rumbles or shouts or whinnies reached the ear, only the murmuring of doves and the occasional whoosh of wings, and the breeze whuffling around the high window openings and in the chimney. Shaded but not gloomy, cool without chill, cozy yet unconfining, it seemed to Kedrigern an ideal base for his efforts. Princess inspected it closely and carefully, peering and peeking, checking for dust and other less identifiable substances that experience had taught her to expect in a wizard's workroom. Having completed her tour, she seated herself at the table and delivered her verdict.

"It's very tidy."

"Traffeo hasn't been busy lately, I imagine. It's hard to be tidy when one is busy," said Kedrigern. Princess gave him a look that bespoke a difference of opinion, but pursed her lips and said nothing. He went on, "I told Zorsch to bring up a good lunch. He can help carry the books to the table. Some of these are too heavy to lift."

"Traffeo has a very nice library," Princess observed.

"Yes. Quite . . . adequate," said Kedrigern indifferently.

"He has more books than you do."

"He does, but they're mostly on curses. Nasty things, curses," Kedrigern said, half to himself, as he stood before a shelf crowded with oversized volumes bound in various shades of black.

"You've got books on curses," Princess reminded him.

"Of course. Every wizard does. But just the basic ones. I have to know a certain amount about curses if I'm to deal with them, but Traffeo seems positively obsessed by them."

"What's so terrible about curses?"

"A curse is intrinsically malevolent. You can put a nice helpful spell or enchantment on someone, but who ever heard of a friendly curse? Curses are usually hissed out *in extremis*, just as the axe is about to fall, or the faggots to be ignited.

Curses are angry and mean by their very nature. I'll take spells any time."

"Spells can be mean, too. It was a spell that caused my problem each time, if you recall."

Kedrigern raised his hands defensively. "I don't deny that a spell can be pretty wicked, too. But a curse can't be anything *but* wicked. I don't like to work with things like that. Besides, they're so subjective that half the time they're useless, anyway."

"Don't belittle things just because you don't like them," Princess said impatiently.

"It's true, my dear. One must think very carefully before working any magic, but with a curse one must think twice as carefully. And as I pointed out, the circumstances of your typical curse are not conducive to dispassionate reflection and cool objectivity. Quite the reverse. And when one works a bit of magic in the heat of passion . . . well . . ." Kedrigern came to the table and perched on the edge. He folded his arms and looked solemnly down on Princess. "Did I ever tell you about Bleggendrettle, the gourmet witch? A perfect illustration of the dangers of impulsive cursing."

"I don't recall the name."

"It happened quite a while ago. Fraigus mentioned it one evening. Fraigus has a wide acquaintance among witches, so he heard the whole story. Bleggendrettle was unusual among witches in that she was a marvelous cook. None of your 'eye of newt and toe of frog' for Bleggendrettle, thank you. It was all choice cuts and fresh ingredients. She could do a dinner that would have people talking for years. Her sauces were like silk. And her desserts . . ." Kedrigern paused, closed his eyes, and sighed at the thought of culinary delights.

"What does this have to do with cursing?"

"Ah, yes, cursing. Well, it seems that a local farmhand, a fellow named Grumf, stole a pig that Bleggendrettle was planning to use as a main course at a very important dinner. In a fit of fury, she cursed Grumf with what, to her, was a terrible affliction: She destroyed his sense of smell."

Princess winced. "What a cruel thing to do!"

"To a gourmet, yes. To a swineherd, no. And a swineherd

is what Grumf became once he found that he had no more sense of smell. He did nicely for himself. In a short time, he married a very clever, very pretty, farmer's daughter who saw possibilities in him. She cleaned him up and taught him how to dress decently and behave among civilized people, and at her urging, he opened a moat-cleaning business. Within five years, he was a wealthy man, employing over two hundred people. He built a lovely home, acquired a lot of land, and changed his name to De Grumffe. By all accounts, he was as happy as he was successful. Two of his children married into noble families, and his wife was a confidante of princesses. He himself often went hunting with the local lord, and was consulted on all matters of architecture, land defense, and drainage."

"It's a relief to know that everything worked out well," said Princess, brightening.

Shaking his head, Kedrigern raised an admonitory hand. "For Grumf, yes. For Bleggendrettle, no. She had a terrible temper, even for a witch. When she learned what had become of the man she intended to punish, Bleggendrettle was livid. She flew into an uncontrollable rage, screaming, throwing things, dashing about madly. The upshot was that she had a stroke and died on the spot. She was terribly overweight, you see, and all the excitement . . . well, that's what comes of thoughtless cursing. Bleggendrettle never stopped to think that what would have been a terrible blow to her might be a boon to someone else. She was all wrapped up in her own mean-spirited desire for revenge, and it turned out quite differently from what she had intended."

"A kind of rough justice," Princess observed thoughtfully.

"In Bleggendrettle's case, I suppose it was. But then there's the curious case of Purn the Peacemaker, which was an exercise in irony all around. Purn was a warlord, always out laying waste to something or other, and finally an angry wizard cursed him with confusion of directions. Now, that would seem to be the perfect punishment for someone who likes to lay waste to things. You can't very well lay waste to something if you can't find it. Purn kept getting lost, and missing battles, and everything became peaceful. He wound up getting all the credit for it. The truth didn't come out until years later, and by that time—Ah, who's this, now?" Kedrigern said, as the sound of footsteps on the staircase reached their ears.

He went to the door, opened it, and beheld Zorsch, bearing a tray containing a cold joint of lamb, a loaf of bread, a golden round of cheese, and a bowl of fruit, as well as a pitcher of ale and two tankards. Kedrigern indicated by a simple digital gesture that the tray was to be placed on the table. Zorsch entered the chamber with great caution, looking about warily, and made his way with reluctant steps to the indicated place, where he set the tray within Princess's easy reach.

"Thank you, Zorsch," she said.

"Happy to serve you, my lady, I'm sure," Zorsch replied, ducking his head. "May I go now?"

"I think my husband has some work for you."

Zorsch's face fell. He looked around with quick, nervous glances and shuffled his feet.

"I need your strength, my boy," Kedrigern said, smiling to put Zorsch at his ease. "Nothing too strenuous. There are some books we'll want moved onto the table. I may be wanting some equipment moved, as well, but I'm not sure about that yet."

"And we may want to rearrange the furniture," Princess added.

"May I leave when it's all done?"

"What's wrong, Zorsch? Don't you like Traffeo's workroom?" Kedrigern asked.

"It makes me nervous," Zorsch confessed uncomfortably.

"Why on earth are you nervous? You've been in my workroom, and you didn't act nervous there."

"I *wasn't* nervous, Master Kedrigern. There's something about this room. All those books on shelves, all tidy and neat . . ." Zorsch's voice trailed off. He gazed at the shelves and shuddered. "It's like being back in that awful library."

"What library do you mean, Zorsch?" Princess asked.

"At the abbey, my lady. I spent the winter there."

"Whatever did you do when—when the moon was full?"

"I slipped out into the woods, my lady."

"Oh, you poor boy," said Princess. "It must have been awful."

"Well, I dressed warm when I left, and I don't suppose I minded the cold so much when I was a wolf, having a nice thick coat of fur as I did. But coming round in the early morning all scraped and tattered and exhausted . . . that was unpleasant. Very uncomfortable."

"We're doing all we can to help you, Zorsch. The solution may be in one of these books. Why do they make you so uneasy?' Kedrigern asked.

"After I got to feeling better, I offered to help out around the abbey. They were getting ready to do some work on the library, so they set me to moving books for them."

"Nothing so unnerving about that, surely."

"Oh, no, Master Kedrigern. It was good light exercise, and pleasant, for the most part. Very nice people, those monks. But one day a monk I hadn't seen before asked me to help him move some books from a different part of the library. He led me down flights of steps to a room inside a room inside a room—a very deep structure, it was—where the light was so dim I could barely see at all, but even so, he covered all the books with a piece of cloth before he'd let me touch them, so's I couldn't read their names. He said it was best for me to know nothing about these books, not even what they looked like, because they were thoroughly wicked. And they *felt* wicked, I swear they did! The wickedness was like something that oozed out of them, through the cloth and all. Ever since then, I haven't liked being around books. Yours aren't so bad, but these make me feel all queer and queasy."

"Keddie, why would the monks keep wicked books?" Princess asked.

"For the same reason wizards do, I suppose: They have to know what they're up against."

"Master Kedrigern, will I have to touch any wicked books?" Zorsch asked piteously, wringing his hands, shifting his weight from one foot to the other.

"I can't really say. Probably not, though. In any case, you'll only have to carry them a few steps. It won't be all that bad, Zorsch. And remember, the time is running out. In just three days, you and Berzel . . ." Kedrigern spread his hands and looked at Zorsch expectantly.

Zorsch gave a mournful sigh. He nodded. With a reluctant step forward, he said, "Show me the books you want moved, Master Kedrigern."

Though he did his best to keep up a confident front, Kedrigern had little expectation of finding a remedy for Berzel and Zorsch in the time remaining before the next full moon. Traffeo's library was simply too extensive to master in such a short time without Traffeo's help, and the Wizard Royal— whether out of deference, or diffidence, or petulance—did not come forward. Kedrigern was too busy, and too proud, to seek him out, and the frequent, increasingly emotional visits by Ithian made concentration impossible until the king and his lugubrious entourage had left. Zorsch controlled his fears and shuttled huge volumes back and forth between bookshelf and worktable, his keenness growing with each passing hour. Princess, when she was not occupied giving comfort and reassurance to Berzel, dedicated herself to the search, and Kedrigern drove himself to exhaustion, dining on sporadic snacks and abandoning sleep entirely. But it was all to no avail. The days passed, the night of the full moon was upon them, and no remedy had been found.

As Kedrigern yawned and blinked red-rimmed eyes, Princess patted him on the shoulder. He reached up to take her hand. Zorsch sat across the table from them, his chin in his hands, gazing vacantly at the book that lay open before the wizard.

"I'll have it by the next full moon, Zorsch. I promise you. If the answer is anywhere in these pages, I'll find it and cure you and Berzel," Kedrigern said, his voice raspy from fatigue.

"Maybe there is no answer. No cure. I'll be a werewolf forever," Zorsch said without raising his eyes.

"Impossible. 'For every spell there is an equal and opposite counterspell.' That's a fundamental law."

Zorsch looked up, his eyes dull and hopeless. "But I'm not under a spell, Master Kedrigern. Or a curse. Or an enchantment."

"You're a victim of magic. The law pertains to you. Don't give up hope."

"And don't worry about tonight," Princess said. "I'll see that whatever is being done for Berzel is done for you. We'll make everything as safe and comfortable as we can."

"I'll be all right, my lady," said Zorsch with a deep sigh. "I've been through it all before. Just lock me away somewhere with a dish of water and a chunk of raw meat. I'd appreciate it if you could get me something with a nice big bone in it. That will keep me occupied."

"Of course we will. Would you like a blanket, too?"

"No, thank you, my lady. It promises to be a warm night, and I'll have my fur."

"How about a ball? Berzel takes a leather ball with her. She says it always looks well-used in the morning."

"Anything you say, my lady."

"Just leave it to us, Zorsch," said Princess, reaching over to give him a friendly scratch behind the ears. "Keddie, don't you think we ought to see Berzel and Ithian before . . . ?"

"Yes, certainly," said the wizard, starting out of a light doze. "How long do we have?"

"Two hours and forty-one minutes," Zorsch said.

"We'll be back to take care of you," Kedrigern assured him. "Meanwhile, you might look over the chamber at the foot of the stairs. It's clean, and there's room to lope. The windows are high, and securely barred, and the door is solid. You'll be safe in there, and everyone else will be safe once you're inside."

"I'll sweep it out," said Zorsch, rising. "May I borrow the bucket, for my drinking water?"

"Of course."

"And do you think Master Traffeo would mind if I used his board and chessmen while I'm waiting? I can keep my mind on chess problems. It makes the waiting a bit easier."

"I'm sure he wouldn't object. And we'll be sure to bring you back a nice piece of meat. With a bone in it."

"Are you sure you don't want a blanket?" Princess asked.

"Quite sure, my lady. A wolf doesn't need much."

The three of them left the chamber together, locking it behind them. Kedrigern and Princess left Zorsch at the foot of the stairs, then continued on to the royal apartments. Though both were deeply concerned and grieved by their failure to find a remedy, the wizard and his wife were too exhausted to speak all the way there.

Upon being admitted, they found Ithian slumped in a chair by the fire, a silver goblet in his hand. He was oblivious to the bustle of courtiers and ladies all around him. Berzel, dressed in a plain, rather drab robe, greeted them cheerfully.

"You're a brave girl," said Kedrigern, raising her hand to his lips.

"It isn't so terrible, Master Kedrigern. Really, it isn't. Except for the soreness and stiffness afterwards, it's no trouble at all," Berzel said with a plucky smile.

"Is everything prepared?" Princess asked.

"Oh, yes. Daddy had a nice roomy corner of the game preserve walled off. My ladies will be in constant attendance just outside the gate."

"I'll go in with you, if you like," Princess offered, hugging Berzel.

"Oh, I couldn't ask you to do that. There's always the chance that I might do you some harm while I'm . . . not myself," Berzel said, returning the hug.

"Everyone says you're a very well-behaved wolf."

"I do hope I am, but I'd hate to risk hurting you."

"No fear of that. I'll just fly over the wall at the first sign of wolf behavior," said Princess with a flutter of her wings that took her a hand's-breadth off the floor.

"I couldn't dream of imposing. You have that poor servant to look after. He doesn't have a powerful, generous father to protect him in his time of need. It would be cruel and selfish of me to take you from him."

"Listen! Will you listen to the girl!" cried Ithian, bursting from the chair, staggering a bit, spilling wine down his shirt-front. "She's an angel! A living saint! In two hours she'll be a wolf, but is she worrying about herself? No! Oh, the cruel injustice!"

"Now, Daddy, you mustn't get upset," said Berzel, hurrying to his side. She took the goblet, handed it to a servant, and urged Ithian back into his chair.

"Our angel. Our baby. Our sweet child!" he blubbered.

"I'll be fine in the morning, Daddy. Just a bit scuffed up, that's all. You promised me you wouldn't get upset."

"The Wizard Royal can't help. Kedrigern can't help. Our little girl is going to be a wolf for the rest of her sweet, innocent life," Ithian wailed, slurring several of the words.

"It's only once every twenty-nine days, Daddy," Berzel said sweetly, kissing his cheek. "Don't you worry."

Ithian gave an anguished cry. He turned bleary eyes on Kedrigern and said, "Look at her! Listen to her! How can you let this go on, wizard?"

Kedrigern, who had been dozing off, blinked, stepped forward, and with a dramatic sweep of his arm, said, "If a cure for your daughter is to be found, Ithian, it will be found. You have a wizard's word."

Ithian looked at him stupidly for a time, then a glint came into his eyes. "When?" he demanded.

"Soon. Very soon," Kedrigern said solemnly.

"What does that mean, wizard? It might be years! Decades!"

"It won't be decades. It will be soon."

"That's easily said. *How* soon? If you're such a great and powerful wizard, tell me that: how soon?"

"Before the next full moon has set," Kedrigern declaimed in a voice that filled the room.

"You heard him. Everybody heard him," said Ithian to Berzel and the crowd of servants and attendants. "Before the next full moon has set. You promised, wizard. You gave your word."

"I said *if* a cure is to be found."

"Well, of course a cure is to be found. That's your business, isn't it? Aren't you always telling people that any spell can be unspelled and any enchantment can be disenchanted? Aren't you?"

"I may have said something like that."

"All right, then. Find the magic before the next full moon

sets. If you can't find a cure for our poor sweet little baby, you don't deserve to call yourself a wizard."

Before Kedrigern could reply, Princess took his arm and whispered, "Don't say another word. Ithian's drunk and you're too tired to think clearly. Let's go and see about Zorsch."

Kedrigern glowered at Ithian, but said nothing. He turned to Princess and gave a single curt nod, then swept from the chamber. Princess gave Berzel a farewell hug, waved to Ithian, and left the room to find Kedrigern angrily pacing the hall.

"Miserable ingrate!" he cried. "He as much as called me a fraud in front of his daughter and half the people in this castle! And if it hadn't been for me, Ithian would be one more notch in an ogre's club."

"He's under a strain," Princess soothed.

"Is that what you call it? So full of wine he sloshes when he tries to move is what *I* call it. And not very good wine, either. Of all the tenth-rate, bumptious, two-for-a-penny nonentities I've ever had to deal with, Ithian is—"

"Now, Keddie, relax. Just relax. Don't upset yourself. I'm sure Ithian didn't mean a word he said."

"He said it, didn't he?"

"It was the wine talking," said Princess, tugging him away.

"Well, the wine talked good and loud, and everyone in the room heard every word it said!" Kedrigern stopped in his tracks and waved a fist in the air. "I deserve it, though. I should know better than to expect gratitude from a jumped-up knight-errant who can't even take on an ogre without help from a wizard. I should have turned him down cold, but I came running to his castle, ready to help, ready to give selflessly, ready to . . . to help. . . ." He fell silent, fuming. Princess got him moving again.

"You'll help. You'll find the remedy," she said.

"If there's a remedy."

"Certainly there's a remedy. And you'll find it before the next full moon, too. You've already promised Zorsch that you would."

"Zorsch was decent about it. Grateful. *He* didn't call me a

fraud in front of a crowd of courtiers and servants and attendants and who knows what else."

"Zorsch isn't paying you two hundred crowns, either,"
Princess pointed out.

Kedrigern grunted unhappily. They went down the hall for
a way in silence, and at last he said, "The worst part of it is,
we won't get an hour's sleep with all the howling."

Princess squeezed his arm and smiled. "If it's any consolation, neither will Ithian."

⋯⋰ Six ⋱⋯

should old acquaintance be forgot?

AFTER THE STRAIN of anticipation and the shock of fulfillment, the setting of the full moon ushered in sensations of anticlimax. Berzel and Zorsch came through their metamorphosis unharmed but exhausted. Ithian remained apart, sulky and slightly hung over.

Princess devoted the entire next day to Berzel. She remained by the girl's bedside, pressing cool moist cloths to her forehead and reading cheerful stories aloud to her. Kedrigern applied himself to the search. He had given Zorsch the day off to rest and recover, and so was alone. After a morning of solitary and unbroken work, he descended to the kitchen for a snack. Upon his return, he found Traffeo in the workroom.

The Wizard Royal was standing before the bookshelves, looking proprietary and very comfortable. His hands were clasped behind his back, and he was rocking gently back and forth, up on the balls of his feet, down on the heels, in slow rhythm, whistling softly to himself. Like Traffeo's face, the tune nudged Kedrigern's memory with annoying vagueness. He seemed to recall it, but could not fix it in a time and place.

"Hello, Traffeo. Haven't seen you here for a few days. Been away?" he said by way of greeting.

Traffeo did not turn or interrupt his rocking. "Away? No, not at all. What makes you think I'd want to go away?" he asked.

"No reason. I just haven't seen you around."

"Oh, I've been around. No one's noticed me, perhaps, but I've been here, moping around the castle, useless and unwanted."

"Really, now, Traffeo, there's no need to feel that way. I'd be happy to have your assistance."

"I'll bet you would. Oh, I'll just *bet* you would," Traffeo said, turning to face him, smiling a thin and humorless smile.

Kedrigern paused for a moment before asking, very calmly, "What's bothering you, Traffeo?"

"Me? Bothering *me*?"

"You. Bothering *you*."

"Nothing's bothering *me*, my dear colleague. I should think *you'd* be the one to be bothered. Berzel changed into a wolf last night, didn't she?—despite your efforts. And your servant changed, too, I believe. Another failure. How very trying. And I've heard of an unpleasant scene between Ithian and his overpaid, overpraised, visiting wizard from Silent Thunder Mountain. I can see where *you* might be bothered, dear master, but I'm feeling more cheerful than I have for years." Traffeo folded his arms, smiled broadly, and began to rock back and forth once again, whistling. The tune was maddeningly familiar, but Kedrigern had no time to spend on such matters.

"Traffeo, I didn't ask to come here. Ithian sent for me," he pointed out.

"By now, he may be wondering why he bothered."

Drawing a deep breath to calm himself, Kedrigern said, "He bothered because he knows what I can do. He is aware that without my assistance he would not be alive today, ruling in Othion. He would never have won the hand of Kanvanira, and he would have no daughter."

"So he owes it all to you, does he? I'm sure he'll be

pleased to hear that you go around his own palace boasting of it."

"Traffeo, if you're looking for trouble, you can—"

Raising his hands, palms forward in a peaceful gesture, and assuming a benign expression, the Wizard Royal said, "I will not repeat your words, I assure you. There's really no need for me to do so. In fact, I need do nothing but wait."

"For what?"

"For about twenty-nine days. I heard of your boast to Ithian. When his darling Berzel turns into a wolf at the next full moon, you will be sent packing, empty-handed, and I will be treated decently once again," Traffeo said with evident pleasure.

"What makes you think I won't find a remedy?"

"Several things," said Traffeo. He held up his hand and enumerated, finger by finger. "First, this kind of magic is not your specialty. Secondly, whether or not a remedy for lycanthropy exists is a matter of lively speculation. Thirdly, if a remedy does exist, it may not be written down. Fourthly, if it has been transcribed by someone, at some time, it may not be in one of the books in this chamber—if, indeed, the book in which it is contained still exists. And fifthly, if it is in one of these books, it is highly unlikely that you will locate it before the next full moon. It took me eight years and five months to familiarize myself with the contents of the books in this room —not to master the contents, mind you, or even to grasp their full import, merely to achieve a degree of familiarity—and while I have a high regard for your abilities, I do not believe that they will enable you to achieve in twenty-nine days—actually, twenty-eight-and-a-half days—what I could not do in eight years and five months."

Kedrigern's face clouded. "Probably not," he said thoughtfully.

"So I will be patient. One more full moon should do the trick. Two, at the very most. Even three would not be an intolerable wait." Traffeo rubbed his palms together and favored Kedrigern with a smug smile.

"You could help me," Kedrigern said.

"I could. But I will not."

Kedrigern nodded. He scratched his jaw and looked gloomily at the rows of books. "I didn't think you would."

"In truth, my dear master, even with my wholehearted cooperation, your task would be formidable. I could help you avoid a lot of wasted effort and dead ends, but I assure you, I have seen nothing in any of these volumes that could be of the slightest use to Berzel."

"Maybe you just didn't recognize it."

Raising an eyebrow, Traffeo said coolly, "It is a tribute to your integrity that even when desperate, you do not flatter. Quite the contrary, you add insult to injury, and do so gratuitously. It will give me great pleasure to see you driven from Othion in disgrace."

"I wasn't trying to insult you. It's very easy to miss the subtler ramifications of an obscure spell—particularly when it's not pertinent at the moment. Before Berzel's problem, you never went through this library looking specifically for an anti-lycanthropy spell, did you?"

"Of course not."

"So you might easily have skimmed over one while looking for a different spell."

Traffeo pondered the suggestion for a moment, then dismissed it with an impatient wave of the hand. "Impossible. An experienced wizard like myself could never have been so slovenly where spells are concerned."

"You've certainly regained a lot of confidence since I first talked to you."

Traffeo chuckled. "I thought, when you arrived, that you might overshadow me with your superior magical skills. Now I see that my fears were groundless."

"What about the failure you kept moaning over on the day I arrived? What about the disgrace?"

Drawing himself up, Traffeo said huffily, "I was distraught at being displaced from my position. I spoke impulsively."

"Are you telling me now that you're *not* a travesty of a wizard? You've never drunk deep from the cup of failure? That you don't lack the stuff of a great weaver of spells?" Kedrigern said, stepping closer.

Traffeo stood fast. "Nobody wins them all, not even a great

wizard. Surely you know that, my clever and experienced master. And if you do not know it yet, you will soon learn."

Kedrigern glared at him, but said nothing. Traffeo put his hands behind his back, smiled blandly, and resumed his rocking. Kedrigern wanted very much to tweak the man's nose, tug his long white beard, or pull his steeple-crowned hat down over his eyes. He did none of these things. Traffeo began to whistle that irritating tune. Kedrigern fumed; and then, in an instant, things came together in his memory like broken shards of pottery fusing magically into a beautifully intact urn: the habit of rocking back and forth; the familiar face; the song from his youthful days, "Mopsie, the Maid of the Mill." He remembered. He remembered the whole story, and he smiled.

He took a few steps back, keeping his eyes fixed on Traffeo, and seated himself at the table. He leaned forward, over an open book. Traffeo ceased his whistling, but not his rocking.

"Back to work, eh, Master Kedrigern? Good thinking. Time is precious," said the Wizard Royal.

"So it is. But far more precious, Master Traffeo, is fraternal spirit. Cooperation. A helping hand. Wizards working side by side, all rivalry forgotten."

"Precious to you, no doubt. Not to me."

"You won't help me?"

"I will not lift a finger," said Traffeo with a pleased grin.

"I offer you one last chance."

Traffeo made a vulgar noise. Ostentatiously, he covered a languid yawn, and then commenced to whistle.

Kedrigern sighed loudly. He gazed up into the gloomy recesses overhead and said, "How unfortunate. When one thinks of the spells we might discover if we worked together in this splendid library . . . spells to bring relief to all sorts of unfortunates."

"Tough on them," said Traffeo.

With a wise and tolerant smile, Kedrigern waved the utterance aside, saying, "No, Traffeo, you may pretend to be heartless and unfeeling, but I know you have your soft spot."

"Try and find it," Traffeo jeered.

"I know it well. I know that you've been seeking one particular counterspell these past ninety years. You dream of it at night; you muse upon it by day. You brood over it when unhappy, anticipate it when cheerful, hunger for it at all times and everywhere."

Traffeo stopped rocking. "Nonsense. That's all nonsense. I do nothing of the kind."

"Of course you do," said Kedrigern in the gentlest of voices, like a kindly uncle hearing a child's tale of woe. He rose and approached Traffeo. "Ever since that unfortunate incident during the War of the Six Princes, when—"

"What do you know about the War of the Six Princes?" Traffeo cried in alarm, starting back wildly.

"A dreadful time," Kedrigern said, shaking his head solemnly. "No one was safe, nothing was sacrosanct. Every young maid feared for her virtue and her life. Only fat ugly old men had a chance of escaping the eye of the marauding bands that harrowed the countryside, looting, burning, raping, killing, and putting all to the torch when they had had their will. And so parents sought the aid of magic to save their daughters. They learned of a wizard named Imberwick, who had the power—"

"He's dead! Imberwick is dead! Vanished without a trace!" Traffeo cried in panic. Kedrigern listened politely, then went on.

"—to turn beautiful young ladies into fat ugly old men, and they flocked to him, weeping and wailing, pleading and beseeching him to turn their lovely daughters into men so old, ugly, and fat that no marauder could look upon them with anything but revulsion. And Imberwick did so, and much more. In a very short time, the land was teeming with ugly fat old men, and not a woman under eighty was to be found in five days' riding."

"Obviously, Imberwick—the deceased Imberwick—was a brilliant wizard," said Traffeo. He was pale, but his voice was steady.

"Obviously. And perhaps because of his brilliance, the War of the Six Princes soon came to an end. The rival armies disbanded and returned to their homelands, peace was restored, and men began to think once more of normal life—a home, and marriage. And so the parents returned to Imberwick, pleading and beseeching him to turn the ugly fat old men back into nubile maidens. Unfortunately, Imberwick had never made clear to his clients that no counterspell was known, and that all the fair young maidens were doomed to—"

"Stop! Stop! Not another word, Kedrigern, I beg you!" Traffeo said in a cracked voice. He staggered to the worktable, dropped into a seat, and buried his face in his hands. Kedrigern came around the table and stood beside the Wizard Royal, patting his shoulder gently, murmuring, "There, there. It's all right."

"How did you know? What magic did you use to unearth my secret?" Traffeo asked, his voice muffled.

"There was something familiar about your face. We met once, at Fraigus o' the Murk's place."

"I had no beard then."

"The beard confused me, but I recognized the eyes. And your habit of rocking back and forth when you're contented. And the tune you whistled. Not many people know 'Mopsie, the Maid of the Mill' these days."

"I thought I was safe, after all those years."

"You made a mighty clean getaway. How did you manage it?"

"An invisibility spell."

"Really? They're tricky things."

Traffeo shrugged. "It was my only chance. One does not attempt to explain the complications of magic to a mob of enraged peasants and heavily armed nobles. I made myself invisible and slipped away. I worked my way south, and finally settled just outside of Otranto."

"That's pretty far south."

"I thought it prudent to establish distance between myself and my . . . clients. I stayed in Otranto, in a very pleasant small castle, until about twenty years ago, when I learned that Ithian was looking for a wizard. I thought it would be safe to return. After all, seventy years had passed since . . . I never expected . . . Kedrigern, you won't expose me, will you?"

Kedrigern favored him with an expression of consummate

benevolence. "My dear . . . Master Traffeo. How could I do such a thing to a man who has volunteered to work at my side, day and night, until we find a remedy for Berzel?"

Traffeo nodded. "Of course. Foolish of me to ask. Well," he said, rising and rolling back his sleeves, "let's get to work."

With Traffeo to guide his research, and Zorsch to do the heavy lifting, Kedrigern made steady progress. Nevertheless, when eight days had passed, and all but a few score thick volumes had been eliminated from consideration, he still had a formidable task ahead. Traffeo was cooperative; Zorsch was indefatigable; Princess was on hand to assist at every moment she could spare from Berzel. But despite their generous aid, Kedrigern found himself at an impasse.

Two more days passed. On the tenth night after the full moon, Kedrigern, Princess, and Traffeo sat half-asleep at the worktable while Zorsch snored softly in a corner of the room. Before each wizard was an open book, and each looked down with bleary eyes on tiny black letters that seemed to wiggle and slide about on the page. Midnight had passed. Birds and insects slept; the bats were off on the hunt; there was no wind. The silence was absolute, except for the periodic crackle of a turned page, an occasional yawn, and the irregular muted burr of Zorsch's snores. Princess's weary voice broke the stillness.

"Can either of you tell me what a *snille* is?" she asked.

"*Snille*?" Kedrigern repeated. Traffeo merely shook his head and shrugged.

"I think that's the word. Come and have a look."

Kedrigern rose, groaning as he did so. He stretched, yawned, and made his way to Princess's side. She pointed to a word. He blinked, rubbed his eyes, and focused on the tiny, cramped script.

"The word isn't *snille*, my dear. There's no such word," he said.

"What is it, then?"

"It looks like *simils*, to me."

"Is there such a word?"

"Not that I know of."

"Well, it isn't gibberish, Keddie. It's a very clear reference to a book: *The Book of Five Blue Snille*, or *Simils*. See for yourself," Princess insisted.

"Wait a minute, now. Wait just a minute," said Traffeo, digging among the volumes heaped by him on the table top. "I came across a reference to *The Book of Five Blue* something-or-other just after lunch."

"What did the reference say?"

Traffeo pulled out a book, leafed through it, pushed it aside, took another, turned pages quickly, then more slowly, then ran his finger down one page, then down a column, and at last cried, "Here it is! I knew I had seen it."

"What does it say?" Princess asked eagerly.

"It's a very skimpy allusion to other books of spells. Doesn't look very helpful, though."

"Read it to us," Kedrigern said.

" 'Strong spells there be, not herein writ,
    That call for greater skill and wit.
If ye dare seek them, go and look
    In Glaggid's handy spelling book,
Or in the closely written columns
    Of Isbashoori's final volumes.
For spells that work when all else fails,
    Seek out *The Book of Five Blue . . . Snails*'?"

They gazed at one another in bewilderment. Princess and Kedrigern came to Traffeo's place at the table to see the lines for themselves. They read and reread, and were no less bewildered after the seventh reading.

"It looks like *snille* to me. It might just possibly be *simils*, but I don't think it's *snails*," said Princess.

"It's *simils*," Kedrigern said confidently.

Traffeo shook his head. "It's *snails*. There can't be any question. Doesn't it rhyme with *fails*?"

"That doesn't mean anything. Someone who would rhyme *columns* with *volumes* would be perfectly capable of trying to rhyme *snille* with *fails*," said Princess. "And maybe it's in dialect."

"My dear, why don't you read out the passage you came across?" Kedrigern suggested.

"All right. Good idea. Fortunately, it's not rhymed." She cleared her throat and began to recite: "'But if, for all thy will and skill, these spells serve thee not in thy time of most need, then blame not him who writes them, for he sets down all he knows. Go then, and seek the book of never-failing spells, but be of stout heart and rare power in spelling, else the words of *The Book of Five Blue Snille* be thy undoing.'"

"*Snails*," Traffeo said under his breath.

"Whatever it is, I think we'd better try to find that book. Do you have it here?" Kedrigern asked.

"I never heard of it before."

"I thought you knew everything in these books."

"I don't know it word for word. Look at the size of this library! Can I be expected to remember every reference to every book?"

"It might help," said Kedrigern impatiently.

"And did you hear what she read? It was a warning! It said *The Book of Five Blue Snails* would be your undoing!"

"*Snille*," Princess murmured.

"Only for those who lack power in spelling, and surely that doesn't apply to us. This is the first good lead we've had, Traffeo."

"Well, the book isn't here. I'm sure of that."

"How can you be sure it's not here if you don't even know what it looks like?" Princess demanded.

Zorsch stirred in his corner and stretched himself. He yawned loudly. Kedrigern took advantage of the slight interruption to take Princess and Traffeo each by an arm and say in his most placating voice, "Let's all take a break before we get ourselves excited. We'll send Zorsch to the kitchen to fetch us a snack, and then we'll think of a way to search out this book."

They agreed. Zorsch, yawning and scratching himself, shuffled to the table. He glanced idly down on the open book at Princess's place, then looked up expectantly. Kedrigern had an idea.

"Zorsch, you can read, can't you?"

"Oh, yes, Master Kedrigern."

"And you have good sharp eyes, too, I'll bet. Here, read this passage out loud for us," he said, indicating the desired lines with a finger.

Zorsch started back and looked at him with wide, fearful eyes. "Not a spell, is it, Master?"

"A pair of straightforward expository sentences, and no more. Go ahead, read it."

Zorsch leaned forward, wet his lips, and in an uninspired monotone recited the words Princess had read out minutes earlier.

"You said *snails*," Princess said. "The word is *snille*."

"Begging your pardon, my lady, it's *The Book of Five Blue Snails*. That's because of the five blue snails on the cover. Lovely inlaid enamel, they are."

"Have you . . . seen . . . this book . . . Zorsch?" Kedrigern spoke as if he expected the young man to vanish in a puff of smoke.

"Oh, yes, Master Kedrigern. It was in the room with those evil books I told you about, only it didn't feel evil at all. I had to carry it to another place, and while I was carrying it, the cloth slipped off and I saw the cover with the five blue snails."

"It's at the abbey, then?"

"It is."

"Then we leave for the abbey in the morning," said Kedrigern decisively. "Will you come with us, Traffeo? Your help would be invaluable." The Wizard Royal assented with a graceful gesture, and Kedrigern turned to Princess. "It's going to be difficult to get you into the abbey, my dear, but I wouldn't think of having you miss out on the final moments."

"I can't come with you. Berzel needs me here. She puts up a plucky front, but this is all very difficult for her."

"Whatever you think best, my dear. I know you've become fond of the poor child."

"I have. And besides, you'll be able to travel faster without me, and time is of the essence."

"Master, may I stay here with my lady? She should not be left unprotected," Zorsch said.

"That's sweet of you, Zorsch, but I'll be all right," Princess said.

"It's a sensible suggestion. You should have at least one servant of your own, my dear. And it might lead to complications if Zorsch and I showed up at the abbey together."

"What complications?"

"Well, the last time I was at the monastery—when the abbot sent me packing so abruptly—Zorsch turned up the very morning of my departure, raving about a wizard named Kedrigern. I wouldn't want the monks to see anything that might stimulate their memories and get them asking questions."

"I didn't tell them who you are, Master," Zorsch assured the wizard. "Once I was myself again, I told them I was subject to strange fits, when I said and did all manner of things I couldn't remember afterwards. They didn't ask me anything more."

"You displayed admirable foresight. But under the circumstances, I think it's best you remain here with Princess. Do you agree, my dear?"

"Yes. You must stay with me, Zorsch."

The news delighted the young man, and gave him new energy. He thanked his master and mistress effusively, packed the two wizards' gear swiftly and expertly, and bade them farewell in the morning with a grin that lit up his weary face.

⋯⋅⁂ *Seven* ⁂⋅⋯

royal favor

THE WIZARDS LEFT Othion at dawn on sturdy horses from Traffeo's stable. A few hours sleep had refreshed their weary bodies, and the prospect of an end to the search had lifted their spirits. They rode off like small boys going on an outing.

Princess flew a short way with them, then kissed Kedrigern goodbye, waved to Traffeo, and soared to the battlements of the castle, where she watched until the two figures vanished into the mist. Tired though she was, she resisted the temptation to go back to bed and remain there until mid-afternoon. There was no point in giving oneself up to sloth. Besides, Berzel would be awake and asking for her in a short time, ready to talk. The girl did talk. Princess covered a yawn and flew languidly back to her chambers.

At breakfast with Berzel, she attempted the customary chat, but her manner and the color in her cheeks revealed her excitement. Berzel pressed her. She was evasive, feeling it only proper to break the news first to Ithian, but under Berzel's repeated appeals to their friendship, she gave in.

"They've found the answer! I'll be cured!" Berzel cried,

bouncing up and skipping about the room, clapping her hands and laughing.

"Dear girl, you mustn't get your hopes up," Princess chided. "They're not positive that *The Book of Five Blue Snails* contains the necessary spell, and even if it does, they may have some difficulty obtaining access to it. And even if they get it—"

"They can just say that Daddy sent them," Berzel broke in.

"That may not help. Apparently the library at the abbey is in disarray. The book may be hard to find."

"They'll find it. They're wizards, aren't they? And they'll copy out the spell, and hurry back here, and I'll be cured by the next full moon, thanks to your wonderful Kedrigern," said Berzel, pirouetting gracefully several times.

"Traffeo helped, too." Princess was silent for a moment, then she said thoughtfully, "He's been very cooperative since the night of the full moon. He can't seem to do enough for us. I'm glad he overcame his shyness."

Berzel looked at her curiously. "Traffeo isn't shy."

"Well, then, his uneasiness. His diffidence. He may have been afraid that Keddie would take his job away."

"Oh, wouldn't that be wonderful?" Berzel said, with a little skip of joy. "Wouldn't you just *love* it? I'll tell Daddy he must make your Kedrigern Wizard Royal, and then you can both stay here forever."

"I don't think Keddie would like that. He prefers to be self-employed."

"Daddy would give you lovely quarters."

"We have a nice place now. Very snug. It gets a bit cramped at times, but it's ever so cozy with a nice fire going and the smell of Spot's cooking in the air."

"Daddy would give you a whole tower all to yourselves," said Berzel, dropping down at Princess's side and taking her hand. "He'd arrange alterations to suit. You could have all the servants you want. Lots of clean linen, and lovely furniture. Daddy's been so much more cheerful since you and Kedrigern arrived in Othion. Everyone has noticed."

"He wasn't cheerful the night of the full moon," Princess reminded her.

"He was worried. I think he worries more about my changing than I do. But he's been nice since that night, hasn't he?"

"Yes, he has," Princess admitted.

"Then say you'll stay. Daddy will make Kedrigern his Wizard Royal or anything else you want, and you'll both live here forever and ever. You can teach me all the things a princess should know."

"I'll think about it. Keddie and I would have to discuss it fully before we commit ourselves."

"Make him agree, Princess dear. You can do anything you want, and you know everything, and I want you to be near me always," Berzel said, resting her head in Princess's lap.

"Not always. One of these days you'll meet a handsome prince, or a bold knight . . . perhaps even a nice wizard."

"Like Traffeo? Ugh."

"I was thinking of someone younger. In any event, you're bound to meet *someone*. I'm surprised you haven't already done so, a pretty little thing like you."

"Handsome princes and bold knights don't come to Othion," said Berzel with a sigh.

"We can fix that easily enough. Your father can proclaim a festival to celebrate your recovery, and hold a great tournament. That always draws young men."

Berzel bounded up, giving Princess a bit of a start. "Oh, let's do that! Let's have a tournament, and jousting, and a great feast, and peasants dancing and singing, and lots of handsome young men in gleaming armor bashing away at each other, and the bravest and handsomest gets to marry me! Let's do that, dear Princess, oh, let's! You must tell Daddy at once!"

"Would you really like that? It will mean a lot of work, but it's sure to be fun. And you'll meet dozens of nice young men from good families."

"Yes! Yes! Oh, that's a wonderful idea, Princess! You're the best friend I ever had! Do run and tell Daddy now, right away!" Berzel cried, in a paroxysm of skipping, dancing, and hand-clapping.

"I will," said Princess, rising. "I really should have seen him first thing this morning, to let him know that Keddie and

Traffeo have left for the monastery. He'll be relieved to know they've narrowed the search to one book."

"It must be the most magnificent festival ever held anywhere, with all the finest and bravest young men—be sure to tell him that."

"I will, Berzel dear."

"What shall we give for prizes? Are saddles in good taste? Do you think they'd prefer swords? What about horses?"

"We can discuss the details later," Princess said, moving to the door.

"And what will we *wear*?"

"Later, dear," said Princess, slipping from the chamber.

She hurried down the hall to the stairs, and at the first alcove she sat on a chest to catch her breath. Berzel was a dear child, she reflected, but exhausting to be with. The absence of a mother's nurturing hand was all too evident. Princess had only to show a perfectly normal sympathy and understanding for her concerns, and Berzel seized upon her as a sister-best friend-auntie-mother-confidante and vowed never to be away from her side.

What the girl needed, even now, was a mother. Especially if she were to find a proper husband. It was all very well for Ithian to be inconsolable—that was all to the good in a man —but Berzel's needs should have been considered. Even if eligible princesses were in short supply, Ithian could have tried. He was not an unattractive man. He was vain, pompous, self-centered, inconsiderate, rude, unfeeling, and utterly devoid of a sense of humor, but one expected that of rulers. At least he looked, and dressed, like a king. Not a great king, to be sure, but a king all the same, with a decent little domain and a tolerable stronghold. Othion was bearable for a short visit, though Princess shuddered at the thought of taking up permanent residence amid such drabness. A woman's presence over all these years might have made it rather a nice little kingdom; at present, it was more like a remote outpost of some decaying empire where all attempts at civilized behavior had been abandoned. Poor Berzel had never been taught the things that every princess ought to know. She had no idea how to dress. That would have to be seen to, and quickly. Her hair needed attention, too. All in all, there was much to be done before she was ready to preside over a tournament.

At the thought of the tournament, Princess sprang up with a little cry of annoyance. In her weariness, she had been wool-gathering. She had much to say to Ithian, and the morning was nearly gone.

She hurried to the state chamber, and was admitted at once. The ministers and attendants rose at her entrance, and Ithian acknowledged her with a nod.

"I have news about the remedy for Berzel," she said.

"Then by all means, speak!" Ithian said, his look severe.

"Kedrigern has learned of a book that may hold the spell to cure her. He and Traffeo left at dawn to seek it."

"They left!" Ithian cried. "They did not ask our permission! They left Othion without permission!"

"It was Your Majesty's sleeping time. It would have been rude to wake you."

"They should have waited for us to wake up."

"Every minute is precious."

Ithian weighed her words for a moment, then gave a grudging nod of assent. "We will overlook their transgression, since it was done in the best interests of our beloved Berzel." He leaned forward, looked searchingly at Princess, and said, "They left you behind."

"I chose to stay behind. I feel that I am needed in Othion." When Ithian did not respond, Princess decided to say what was on her mind. "Berzel has been without a mother's guiding hand for too long. She is a young lady, and soon she will be considering marriage."

"Marriage! To whom? We were not consulted! If any man dares—!" Ithian reddened and waved his scepter about like a club.

"She has no one in mind. I mean only that she is of marriageable age, and once she's over this unfortunate werewolf problem, she—"

"Our Berzel is a child. A tot. How can you speak of marriage when she is barely out of the nursery?"

"Your Berzel is a very pretty young lady. She needs someone to do her hair properly, and to tell her that she does not look her best in baggy mud-colored gowns, but she has the makings of a beautiful princess, there's no question about it."

Ithian shook his head and gestured with his free hand, as if trying to wipe out Princess's words. "It cannot be. Why, it was only yesterday—practically yesterday—that Berzel was a babe in arms."

"Obviously, Your Majesty has been so immersed in affairs of state that the years have slipped by unnoticed."

"Nonsense. Nothing slips by us unnoticed," Ithian said haughtily.

Princess smiled. "Ask your council."

The councilors, who had been looking on with mild amusement, glared at Princess and exchanged nervous glances among themselves. Ithian pondered, tugged at his ear, scratched his chin, and said, "We will do so. Erandron, speak—Tell us truly, is our Berzel a fair young lady?"

The unfortunate councilor looked wildly around. His companions all averted their eyes and moved away from him. Erandron cleared his throat, smiled in a ghastly, terrified grimace, and said, "Could the child of Your Majesty and the resplendent Kanvanira of the Dales be anything but fair? And not merely fair, but dazzling in her beauty. Incomparable!"

"Berzel has always been a comely child! We ask whether she has passed beyond that state, and into womanhood," Ithian said, with a dangerous edge in his voice.

"She is . . . she is seventeen, Your Majesty," said Erandron.

Ithian was thunderstruck. "The very age of Kanvanira when we met! Why did no one tell us?"

"We were . . . we thought Your Majesty had noticed," Erandron said weakly, trying to shrink back into the crowd, which shrank from him in turn, in a slow and stately movement, like a solemn dance.

"Noticed? *Noticed*!" Ithian cried. "We have noticed the royal treasury dwindling like sand down a rat hole while the number of tax collectors increases and the treasurer grows fatter every day. We have noticed trade with neighboring kingdoms expanding while import duties shrivel up like worms under a hot sun. We have noticed leaks in the north tower, loose paving stones in the courtyard, rust on the guardsmen's mail shirts, mice in the grain, water in the wine, and incompetence everywhere! Are we to notice our daughter's age, as well? Must we do everything in Othion?"

The councilors milled about like cats at feeding time, making low, soothing noises and calming gestures. Ithian rose and stood with his feet wide apart, hands on his hips, head thrust forward, glowering at the lot of them, and roared, "And stop oozing about! Stand still when we are having a tantrum!"

"If Your Majesty please . . ." Princess said softly.

"Yes? Speak."

"This is the very point I was attempting to make. Because the cares of state have weighed so heavily upon Your Majesty's shoulders, Berzel has reached the brink of womanhood untutored in those little things that every girl should know. She is attractive. She is of marriageable age. The prospect of bold and wellborn men vying for her hand does not displease her. She needs a mother's guidance."

Ithian fixed his eyes on her thoughtfully, then turned to his councilors. They nodded eagerly, exclaiming, "Yes, Your Majesty! The very thing! Our opinion, exactly!"

Seeing her advantage, Princess said, "I would like to discuss these matters further with Young Majesty, since we are both concerned for Berzel's happiness."

"It likes us well," said Ithian weightily. "We will summon you. Meanwhile, attend Berzel."

The man's manner was insufferable, Princess thought as she left the chamber. "We will summon you" indeed! He treats a princess as one would hesitate to treat a servant. And "Attend Berzel" if you please! Easy to see that he needs direction as badly as his daughter. Spoiled rotten, that's what he is. No doubt about it, Ithian was long overdue for remarriage.

As she made her way back to her chambers, Princess went over the names of likely candidates. For the woman's own sake, she would have to be someone of royal blood, she decided. A man like Ithian would make a woman's life miserable if she lacked noble birth. He would speak of "stooping" a dozen times a day until the woman felt lower than a serf. Louise of the Singing Forest would provide just the sort of firm, no-nonsense supervision that Ithian required . . . but

Louise might be too overbearing for Berzel. That was the first consideration: finding a good stepmother for Berzel.

Louise's cousin Wanda would be ideal as a stepmother. She was gentle and delicate . . . but she was just the sort of woman Ithian would browbeat into transparency. No, not Wanda. The sister, Alice, might fall somewhere between these two extremes: firm with Ithian, gentle with Berzel, accustomed to ruling. But Alice had been a crown for quite a long time. One never knew what effect that might have on a person. And Louise had been a sword, and Wanda a wand. It was difficult to think of a princess who had not been something else at one time or another.

There had to be someone. Princess thought and thought, but all the best candidates were either married or still enchanted. That seemed to be the usual fate of princesses these days, she thought, frowning.

Perhaps the next wife of Ithian did not have to be a princess if she had some other claim to distinction. That would widen the field considerably. But what, in all honesty, was equal in distinction to royal blood? Princess could not imagine. She thought and thought . . . and at last a possibility occurred to her: magic.

Being a wizard, witch, or sorceress was not quite the same as being born a princess, of course, since it was the sort of thing one could acquire. But in this case it might be just the thing. Even Ithian would tread softly in his dealings with a woman who, when sufficiently provoked, might turn him into a hedgehog.

But that list was even shorter than the roster of available princesses. Bess the Wood-witch was decidedly not the marrying kind . . . and who else was there? Princess thought, for just a moment, of Memanesha, the sorceress, and smiled. Now, there was a woman who would put Ithian in his place soon enough, and keep him there. But she was off in some unknown corner of existence with her afreet, and unlikely ever to return to this world. And sorceresses did have a terrible reputation as stepmothers.

No, it would have to be a princess, that was clear. Princess sat by her window, looking out at the sky, trying without success to think of someone suitable.

The sky was clear, except for high fat woolly clouds. It was ideal flying weather, and a few turns around Othion would, she believed, clear her head and help her think. She rose and tossed her cloak aside, and just as she was ready to launch herself, she heard a familiar merry voice.

"Oh, Princess, Princess, dearest Princess, what did Daddy say? When will we hold the tournament? What kind of invitations shall we send? Oh, I do hope we have lovely weather! What if it rains! It would be dreadful having mud splattered all over everything, and all that shining armor getting rusty. Say it won't rain. Promise me it won't rain, Princess dear! Your Kedrigern can do a little thing like stopping rain, can't he? I'm sure he can. And then we can put on lovely dresses and distribute prizes to all the handsome princes and valiant knights..." And so on, and on, and on, went Berzel, skipping and capering and twirling and clapping her hands.

Princess sighed, took up her cloak and threw it over her shoulders, and turned to welcome Berzel. A charming girl, a sweet girl, a lovely girl—but exhausting.

Ithian's summons did not come until well after dark. Princess found him alone in the council chamber, wearing a long robe trimmed in gray fur. He rose to greet her, bowed low, and kissed her hand. Rather an elaborate greeting for someone coming to discuss a family problem, she thought, but a distinct improvement in manners. Much better than curt commands and displays of temper.

Ithian waved her to a chair beside his own. She seated herself, and before she could speak, he took up a delicate silver goblet, mate to the one near his own hand. "Wine for our honored guest?" he asked.

This was more than mere improvement, it was regeneration. The man was actually being polite and considerate. Princess wondered what had brought about the change. Awakening of paternal feeling, perhaps? Surely that must be the reason. Underneath all those repellent vain mannerisms beat the heart of a loving father. Smiling sweetly, she said, "I would be delighted, Your Majesty."

With a wave of his hand, Ithian said, "You need not be formal, dear lady. Call us Ithian." He poured a goblet of dark red wine and gave it to her, then raised his own, saying, "We drink to Othion's loveliest visitor."

"Ithian is too kind," she murmured.

"This morning you broached matters of some significance touching ourselves and our daughter. It is our hope that you will elaborate upon them."

"As I said, Berzel needs a mother. She is at a vulnerable age, and a mother's guidance is essential."

"Our councilors agree. We, too, concur," said Ithian.

"Very good. And as soon as Berzel is cured of her unfortunate condition—and Kedrigern will cure her, you may be certain—I think you should proclaim a festival, with a great tournament."

Ithian's eyebrows went up. "A tournament in Othion... There has been no tournament here since we celebrated the birth of Berzel. Ah, that was a tournament to be remembered, my dear Princess. Thirty days of jousting, thirty nights of revelry. We challenged all comers, and unhorsed every one. We were bruised from head to foot, and scarcely able to move for months afterward, but we were magnificent." Ithian sighed and turned to gaze into the fire. Something of the bold young warrior was still visible in the pallid, slightly puffy features. He laid a hand on his waist and said, "Of course, it would not be fitting and proper for us to participate at this time. We must leave the field to the suitors for our Berzel's hand."

"Of course," said Princess.

"There is much to be done. Banners must be repaired. Armor must be scoured and polished. There must be clowns and jugglers, exotic animals in splendid cages... a lion. We must have a lion. And the tiltyard will require extensive work."

"Mere details, Ithian. A tournament is the perfect way to have Berzel meet a lot of suitable and eligible young men in the shortest time. That's important at her age. We want the world to see her. She'll need a completely new wardrobe. Work on that should begin at once. Her clothing is a disaster."

"It would please us greatly if you took this responsibility on your capable and most attractive shoulders. More wine?"

"No, thank you. No wine, I mean—I'll see to the wardrobe. And something must be done about jewelry. Berzel doesn't even have a ring on her finger."

Ithian, looking uncomfortable, said, "We have a few caskets of magnificent jewelry in our treasury. We had intended to present them to our Berzel when she is grown."

"She's grown. Let her have them."

"We shall do so. We give you leave to do whatever must be done for our daughter's happiness. Be as ourselves in Othion. Now, touching on the other matter . . ."

"The other matter?"

"Berzel's need for a mother. Our remarriage. It would please us to hear your suggestions." Ithian hitched his chair closer and looked into Princess's face expectantly.

"Well, I think you'd be happiest with someone of royal blood. I'd say a princess, at the very least. It would be awkward for Berzel to outrank her own stepmother."

"Very sensible. And should it not be a woman for whom our Berzel feels an instinctive affection?"

"Yes, but that should be no problem. Berzel gets along with everyone. We've been close since the instant we met."

"That has not escaped our notice." Ithian drained his goblet and took up the decanter. "Is our exquisite friend sure that she wishes no more wine?"

"Quite sure."

Ithian refilled his goblet to the brim. He drank deeply, looking closely at Princess in the light of the candelabra that burned at either side of the table, then said abruptly, "Can you suggest a likely candidate for the next queen of Othion?"

"I've been trying to draw up a list, but without any luck. Beautiful princesses are hard to find."

"They are indeed. Even passable ones are uncommon, it would seem. Kedrigern was a fortunate wizard to win the heart of such a beautiful princess as yourself."

She smiled to acknowledge the compliment, and said, "I hope Kedrigern is all right. I do miss him when he goes off on these expeditions. It's dangerous out there, even for a wizard."

"We are content to let wizards come and go, dear lady. As long as you remain in Othion, it matters not who departs," said Ithian, raising his goblet and drinking. He set it down, wiped his lips, refilled the goblet, and said, "So, you believe that we should seek a beautiful princess who has the love and respect of Berzel."

"I think that would be the best thing for all parties."

"We agree wholeheartedly. Your hair gleams most prettily in the light of the candles."

"So kind of you to say so, Ithian, but let's stick to the subject."

"We speak plainly. Your eyes are wondrous blue. Your shoulders are like a swan's breast. Such beauty has not been seen in Othion since the passing of our beloved Kanvanira."

"Well, that's very nice of you, Ithian, and I do appreciate the compliments," said Princess, rising, "but I really think—" She sprang back with a cry as Ithian drained his goblet, flung it aside, and fell to his knees before her, blurting, "Princess, be ours! Sit at our side in Othion!"

"Ithian!"

"Othion loves you. Berzel needs you! We approve of you!"

"Ithian, I am a married woman!"

"Arrangements can be made! You are the one, dear Princess, lovely Princess! By your very own criteria, you are the perfect match for us!"

"Not only am I married, Ithian, I happen to love my husband," Princess said, retreating.

Ithian pursued her on his knees, arms outstretched, crying, "Your husband is a wizard. We are a man and a king!"

"You'd do well to remember that," she pointed out.

"And you do foolishly to ignore it. Kedrigern will live for centuries, and scarcely change at all. In fifty years he will still look like a man in the prime of life—as we ourselves do now—while you will be an old woman. A crone. What kind of life is that for a beautiful princess to look forward to? Leave him, and be Queen of Othion! If he truly loves you, he will release you."

"He's more likely to turn you into a toad."

"We defy toadhood!" Ithian cried, climbing to his feet and shaking a fist. "We have made our choice, and you must obey."

"I don't want to hear any more. You've had a few goblets too many, Ithian, and you're going to—"

Ithian made a lunge for her, and Princess instinctively took to the air. He crashed into her chair, and he and the chair toppled to the floor. Ithian's shouts of anger, the falling chair, and the clatter of Princess's goblet made for considerable uproar. Ithian scrambled to his feet, breathing loudly. Princess rose out of reach.

"Come down at once. This is no way to treat a king," said Ithian with unexpected calm, and even a touch of injured dignity.

"Well, it's no way for a king to treat a lady, either. I'm staying up," Princess said, fluttering higher.

With surprising agility—considering his bruises and the amount he had drunk—Ithian dashed to the door and shot the bolt home. Only a small window remained to provide egress, and Princess beat him to it by a hair. In his wild grope he caught her shoe, and she flew off, leaving it in his hand.

Her chambers were in the opposite wing. She judged that she would have just enough time to roll a spare outfit in a blanket, hunt up a comfortable pair of shoes, and be on her way, before Ithian came bursting in. She was tired and cross, and the thought of having to sleep in the forest annoyed her very much. For just a moment, she weighed the possibility of a spell on Ithian—he would make a perfect toad, she thought —but realized that this would only complicate things, and probably upset poor Berzel. For the child's sake, then, it had to be the forest.

She decided to take two blankets and a pillow. She was just slipping her foot into the second of her most comfortable pair of shoes when she heard loud shouts and clamor in the hall. She tucked her wand into her belt and went out the window, headed for the forest.

⋯⋊ Eight ⋉⋯

refresher course

SOME THREE HOURS after leaving Othion, the two wizards paused for rest and refreshment in a glade by a lively brook. They plunged their hands into the cold fresh water, splashed their faces, and reclined in the shade of a beech tree to nibble on slabs of fresh dark bread, thickly buttered. Traffeo stretched out his legs, interlaced his fingers behind his head, and looking up into the sun-spattered leaves, took a deep breath and exhaled with a sigh of pure contentment. Kedrigern yawned audibly.

"This is the life. Thanks for getting me out of Othion," Traffeo said, closing his eyes and smiling. "I'd forgotten how good it is to be on the road. It's years since I've done any traveling."

"Lucky you. I'm always being dragged off somewhere."

"Then I can only envy you, Kedrigern. Just smell this good air. And listen to that brook. Was there ever anything as clean and refreshing as cold water from a woodland brook?"

"Yes. A soft bed with clean linen. Chilled wine. A big chair before a fire on a snowy night. A nap in one's own dooryard. The smell of Spot's home cooking," Kedrigern enumerated lovingly.

With a tolerant chuckle, Traffeo said, "Good things, all of them, I'm sure, but I'll take the open road."

"You can have it."

"I mean it, Kedrigern. Othion was stifling. It changed me for the worse. I behaved very badly toward you, and I'm ashamed of myself."

"Don't give it a thought."

"I can't help thinking about it. All those years cooped up in Othion had me thinking like a courtier, all full of envy and suspicion. I was even dressing like a typical courtier, all useless fancy frippery. These plain traveling clothes are much more sensible. More comfortable, too," Traffeo said. He wore a dark blue tunic and trousers and low boots, with a cloak of brown wool over his shoulders. He looked like a moderately prosperous merchant from a good family.

"I've always preferred ordinary clothing, myself. It attracts less attention. And, of course, going to the abbey. . ."

"Oh, yes. Certainly. It's the only way to dress. But one's attire affects one's attitude, I'm finding. I'm free of the jealousy and uncertainty that torment courtiers. I was actually terribly insecure in Othion. I should have welcomed you with open arms and been grateful for your help, but instead I suspected you and feared for my place."

"Not all that unreasonable, really. Totally unfounded, of course—I have no ambition to be a Wizard Royal, for Ithian or anyone else—but it's still understandable. After all, when you're Wizard Royal and the king calls in outside help—"

"But you're a specialist," Traffeo broke in. "Berzel's case is most unusual. I should have understood and cooperated to the full. If I'd been thinking clearly, I'd have realized that such a course was in my best interests. Instead, I was peevish and obstructive."

"Don't be hard on yourself. No harm was done."

"Time was wasted. Why, if I had helped from the very start, we might be on our way back with the cure this very day." Traffeo sat up, looking troubled by this speculation.

"You're being helpful now. Forget what happened before.

With any luck we'll find the book, the cure will be in it, and we'll have Berzel set to rights before the next full moon."

"I hope so. You're being very good about all this."

Kedrigern brushed aside the compliment. Traffeo hauled himself up, stretched, and walked to the stream. He drank deeply, rose, and scanned the bank for useful herbs. Kedrigern remained supine beneath the tree. Traffeo, finding nothing, returned and sat beside him.

"Better and better. Wonderful. It's grand to travel," he said.

"Don't judge all travel by this. We've only been on the road a few hours," Kedrigern replied without moving or opening his eyes.

"That's long enough to convince me. This outdoor life clears the cobwebs from a man's mind. Warm sun, cool shade, lots of bracing air, delicious water . . . why, even an ordinary bit of buttered bread tastes like a feast out here. Think of the freedom, Kedrigern. Think of the peace, and the solitude, the sheer joy of utter unpredictability! How wonderful it is not to know exactly what's going to happen from minute to minute, day after day!"

"Think of rain. Think of mud, and flies, and wolves—real ones—and ogres, and giants, and bandits, and cursed woods. Think of inns with terrible food, and fleas, and ale that would curdle a moat. That's travel for you, Traffeo."

"You have to look at the good side."

"The only good side of travel is staying home."

"But then you're not traveling."

"Exactly," said Kedrigern with a small, comfortable smile.

"You're getting crotchety. You're losing your love of adventure."

"Not at all. Adventure can be very diverting, under the right circumstances. What I've lost is my willingness to tolerate unnecessary peril, acute physical discomfort, spiritual misery, exploitation by thieves, surprise enchantments of the vilest sort, and an upset stomach."

"It's a wonder you ever get out of your house, if you feel that way."

"It's not a wonder, it's an unfortunate side effect of the

profession. A wizard has to go where the work is." Kedrigern
sat up. He scratched his head, yawned loudly, and said, "I
also do some traveling for Princess's sake. She seems to enjoy
it."

"Women like to meet people and see new faces."

"I can't imagine anyone's wanting to see some of the faces
we've encountered on our travels," Kedrigern said with dis-
taste. He hauled himself to his feet, groaning, and brushed his
back and seat. "This is a comfortable spot, but we'd better be
moving on. It's at least five days' ride to the abbey—unless
we run into an enchantment, in which case it could take centuries."

"Think positive," Traffeo said as he shook out his cloak.
"We're two accomplished wizards. We're unlikely to come up
against anything we can't cope with between us."

"You're certainly sounding confident."

"I owe it to you, Kedrigern. You forced me to confront the
truth, and I realized that I've been trying to live down something that wasn't my fault." Kedrigern raised his brows in a
show of interest, and as they made their way to their horses,
Traffeo went on, "Well, all those farmers and millers and tan-
ners came to me, just like the merchants and nobles; I didn't
seek them out. And I never said anything about the spell's
being a one-way transformation, because they never asked.
They hardly gave me chance to open my mouth. It was,
'Please, great wizard, make my little girl an ugly fat old man'
and 'O mighty Imberwick, save my daughter—turn her into
something that looks like the Lord Chamberlain' everywhere I
turned, and all of them offering huge fees that went up with
every rumor of an approaching enemy. I always asked them if
they were sure they really wanted to go through with it, and
they always reassured me that they were. No one ever hesitated or asked questions. Even the young ladies themselves
couldn't wait to be transformed. It became a sort of social
thing, you see. Parents felt that if they weren't interested in
having their daughter changed into an ugly fat old man, perhaps they didn't love her, or considered her unattractive. So
everyone came to me. And busy as I was, I still took every
precaution."

"Why did you run, then? That made you look bad, you know."

"I'm sure it did, but it was that or try to reason with a mob of outraged parents, all of them armed. I suppose I could have turned them into crickets until they came to their senses, but I had been concentrating on that one spell for so long that I was rusty. So I ran. And when one is a fugitive, it isn't long before one begins to *feel* and *think* like a fugitive: furtive, and guilty, and ashamed. It's true, my friend, all too true. Every once in a while—even in Otranto—the name of Imberwick would come up, and the story made me feel worse with each retelling. For a time, when I made a new start in Othion, I thought I was over it; but then I'd see an ugly fat old man, and it would all come back to me, worse than ever. When Berzel was bitten, and I couldn't help her, I lost all faith in myself."

Kedrigern shrugged. "I can't help her, either, without the right spell. Maybe no one can help her. You can't let the tough cases get you down."

"I realize that now. And I owe it all to you. But we will help Berzel. I'm sure of it. *The Book of Five Blue Snails* has spells that work where all others have failed."

"I hope so."

Kedrigern mounted and led the way back to the road. About an hour farther on, they came to a fork. It was unmarked, and Kedrigern halted to study the terrain.

"I don't remember this," he said uneasily.

Traffeo raised his open palms in a gesture of helplessness. "I know nothing of these roads. I've never been out here before," he said.

"Well, I have, and I don't remember this fork. Are there any enchanters in these parts? Any cursed or enchanted spots? Any magical goings-on?"

"Oh, all sorts of things. There's The Grove of Shadows up to the north. A dreadful place, from all accounts. But that's at least a day's ride from here, I believe. The Black Jester works a lot of wicked magic in these woods, but he's never been known to tamper with roads. He works out of his own manor house. The fairies keep off the roads entirely, so this is none of their doing. Then there's The Mad Miller, The Witches of the Burning Well, The Beckoning Hand, The Ghoul of Grongon's Fen . . . elves and gnomes, of course, but they keep to themselves."

"It's a busy place, for such a small wood," Kedrigern said thoughtfully. "Ithian's messenger never mentioned any of them."

"Well, this is a very dense, dark wood in places, and there are deep caves and windswept fells, and terrible crevasses—just the sort of country to attract wizards and witches and sorcerers. We've had scores of them over the past few centuries. Some of them were careless spellers, and they didn't always dispose of their unsuccessful enchantments properly."

"If there's anything I can't stand, it's sloppy workmanship. If we're going to lose a lot of time over a failed spell that some idiot has left lying around . . ." With an angry grumble, Kedrigern reached in his tunic and drew out a silver medallion. He raised it to his eye and examined the branching road.

Seen through the Aperture of True Vision at the center of the medallion, the road ran straight on without branching. Off to one side, where the second road appeared to the unaided eye, was poised a hideous creature, wide of maw, sharp of fang, long of talon. It bestrode the illusory track, hunched and waiting, its jaws dripping. Ghastly parasites, rat-like things with glowing pincers, crawled over it, snapping at one another blindly.

Kedrigern lowered the medallion and rubbed his eye. When he looked unaided at the way before them, he saw two roads. "We keep to the left, Traffeo," he announced. "The other road is an illusion. There's a fiend lying in wait."

"What sort of fiend?"

"Very ugly. Covered with little eyeless parasites."

"A big fiend?"

"Quite big."

"That's a new one. I never heard of anything like it before."

Kedrigern looked over his shoulder. "Just one of the pleasures of travel. The glorious unpredictability," he said sourly.

They proceeded along the left-hand branch, the true road, and when they had gone about forty paces, a chilling cry arose behind them. The trees to the right of the road trembled, and the ground shook.

"Sore loser," Traffeo said.

"I wouldn't want to be the one who . . .," Kedrigern started to say, then fell silent and reined in his horse. "Traffeo, we have to do something. Sooner or later some unsuspecting wayfarer is going to take the right-hand fork and fall into that thing's clutches. We can't permit that."

"I couldn't agree more. What do you suggest?"

"A banishment, I should think."

Traffeo patted his restive horse to calm it. He weighed Kedrigern's idea, smoothing his beard with rhythmic strokes as an aid to reflection. At last he nodded slowly and turned a businesslike gaze on his companion. "May I ask your indulgence? I'd like to cast this spell myself. The sooner I start acting like a real wizard again, the better."

"An excellent suggestion. I leave the matter entirely in your hands," said Kedrigern, with a sweeping gesture of largesse.

Traffeo dismounted and handed the reins to Kedrigern. He took a moment to collect his thoughts, ticking off points on his fingers, his lips moving as he rehearsed words long unspoken. He drew six deep breaths, then turned toward the invisible fiend. Rolling back his sleeves with slow, deliberate movements, he extended his hands.

There was a flurry of activity in the wood, but Traffeo ignored it. He stood motionless for a time, absolutely silent, then he threw his head back and began to speak. The language was harsh; the words growled and grated and sometimes snarled. Kedrigern watched with professional interest as the activity in the wood increased to a frenzy: Small trees were uprooted and flung into the air, accompanied by sizeable rocks and great amounts of dirt. Traffeo spoke on, unperturbed, and suddenly all was still.

Traffeo stood in the silence for a full minute, then slowly and dramatically lowered his hands. He turned to Kedrigern and bowed with great dignity, and Kedrigern applauded and said, "Well done, Traffeo. Well spelt, indeed."

"Thank you," said Traffeo. He took a long drink from his

water bottle, wiped his lips, and leaned against his saddle for a moment before remounting. Once they were on their way, he said, "It takes something out of you, casting a spell does. I'd forgotten."

"It can be very taxing," Kedrigern said.

They rode without much talk for the rest of the morning. At midday they paused once again, and this time Traffeo fell asleep directly after eating. Kedrigern let him rest for well over an hour, then roused him and took to the road again.

When they stopped for the night, Traffeo was still subdued. He was sound asleep by sundown, snoring loudly. Kedrigern turned in early, and they were up at the first hint of light and on the road before sunrise. Traffeo was a bit livelier this day, but still showed the effect of his unaccustomed exertions.

A second night's undisturbed rest restored Traffeo's spirits and strength. When they stopped at mid-morning on this third day of travel, he was talkative once again, as ebullient on the subject of their profession and its glories as he had been two days previously on the joys of travel. Kedrigern chewed his slice of bread, munched on a piece of cheese, sipped his water, and let his companion rattle on with ever-increasing enthusiasm. When Traffeo began to rhapsodize about the glowing future of wizardry, however, he felt obliged to bring him back to reality.

"I can't agree with you there, I'm afraid," he said. "I love the wizard's profession as much as anyone in it, but when I look to the future, I become very depressed. We may be the last generation to practice wizardry as we know it."

"How can you say that? Scarcely a year passes that I don't receive an inquiry from some talented youngster."

"Ah, but are the talented youngsters willing to put in the years of apprenticeship? Will they study, and practice, and master the basics? Not a chance. They inquire, but they don't follow up. All they want to do is pick up a few impressive-sounding terms so they can learn spell-management and become consultants." Kedrigern shook his head ruefully. "The worst part is, they can't even spell correctly, and they refuse to learn. They think that they'll rake in big fees, and hire some poor old retired wizard to check their spelling for them."

Confidently, Traffeo said, "They'll change once they get some experience. You'll see."

"I doubt it. And even if they do, there's the alchemists. Absolute frauds, every one of them, and totally shameless, but clients flock to them, and the bright young people are all bedazzled by their jargon and the fancy titles they confer on one another."

"We don't have any alchemists in Othion."

"You're the better for it. A dull and dreary lot they are. If they have their way, all our knowledge will be replaced by pills, or powders, or something you mix in your wine. No more spells, no more magic, everything all dry and formulated, cash and carry, no personal contact."

"That's dreadful to contemplate," Traffeo said, his voice pained.

"The only consolation is that if they succeed, they'll put themselves out of business as well as us."

"That's not much consolation."

"None at all, really."

They sighed, and both were silent, gazing gloomily into the surrounding wood. After a time, they rose and slowly readied themselves for travel. Traffeo mounted, and Kedrigern was raising his foot to the stirrup when a terrible noise burst from among the trees, very close at hand. It was a part-human, part-animal, but mostly demoniacal combination of screech, snarl, growl, howl, roar, bellow, and shriek, with a strong undertone of grinding metal, and it was accompanied by a sudden, violent agitation of the flora.

Kedrigern's horse jerked away. Traffeo's mount reared. Both animals whinnied in terror. As Kedrigern started after his horse, the trees beside the road parted, and there stood the banished fiend, fully visible. It looked much bigger than it had when viewed through the Aperture of True Vision, and even more hideous. Its eyes, all five of them, were fixed on Kedrigern. It drooled a thin ribbon of ugly slime and flexed its long bladelike talons. The eyeless parasites clustered about its waist, snapping their jaws excitedly.

"I thought you banished this thing," Kedrigern said, backing away.

"I did!"

"Where to?"

"Nowhere special. I just banished it," Traffeo said as he struggled to control his plunging horse.

"Traffeo, when you banish a fiend, you have to banish it *to* someplace, or else it can return unexpectedly—like this one," Kedrigern said in a tight, angry voice, keeping his eyes on the fiend.

"Oh . . . Yes, now I remember. Sorry, Kedrigern. It's been a long time since I did anything like this."

The fiend turned its eyes on Traffeo. It made a few hissing noises and bent forward until its elbows rested on the ground. Its legs tensed for a spring.

While the thing's attention was fixed on his companion, Kedrigern slowly raised his hands, preparatory to casting a quick displacement spell. Before he could utter the first syllable, the fiend launched itself, with a twisting sidewise motion, not at Traffeo but at Kedrigern, catching him unprepared. He threw himself to one side, rolling out of the range of the fiend's sweeping talons, and just as he scrambled to his feet, the thing vanished. It was gone, utterly and completely and instantaneously, so swiftly that the air gave a little pop as it rushed into the vacated space.

"I got him that time," Traffeo said. He was pale, and looked a bit shaken, but his voice was confident.

"Nicely done. A banishment?"

"Yes. This time I did it right. Sent the thing back to the one who originally summoned it up," said Traffeo with a broad smile.

"Good thinking. Whoever called that fiend to earth deserves to have it drop in for a visit. How do you feel?"

"Quite drained. But good. I feel as though I've had a healthy workout."

Though both wizards were shaken by their experience, they were ready to move on at once. Rest could wait; distance was more desirable at the moment. Kedrigern brushed himself off, recovered his horse, and mounted, and they hit the trail at a good pace, not stopping until late in the day.

They had no further encounters with magic in the woods

around Othion, and met no travelers on their way. There was one day of rain, steady but mild, at times scarcely more than a heavy mist. By sundown they had passed through the rain, and found a dry campsite for the night. The next day was sunny.

Just at sundown on their fifth day of travel, as the wizards rounded a hillside, Kedrigern called out to Traffeo and pointed across the valley, to the peak of the mountain opposite them. There, on the mountaintop, silhouetted by the descending sun, stood the abbey.

···✦ *Nine* ✦···

an unexpected pleasure

A TREETOP WAS a quiet place to sleep, very private, and safe —provided one could fly, and the night was dry and the winds gentle. Princess enjoyed an untroubled repose and awoke to a cool, bright morning.

All was still around her save for the hushed rustle of leaves and distant birdsong. She lay snug in her blankets, dozing and dreaming, and at last roused herself. Spreading her blankets over the uppermost branches to air, she flew above the treetops to get her bearings. The towers of Othion rose dimly through the mist in one direction; in the opposite direction were the mountains, Kedrigern's destination, and now hers. She planned to catch up to him, inform him of Ithian's perfidy, and work out a suitable punishment.

That Ithian would be punished was beyond question. Though it might be difficult explaining the circumstances to poor Berzel, the man's behavior could not be countenanced. To act in such a manner to a guest, a princess, the wife of an old friend, the companion of a daughter . . . it was not to be borne. Much as she longed to get right to it, Princess felt that

Kedrigern should have the opportunity to participate; after all, he, too, had been insulted.

She thought for a moment of Zorsch, and hoped he would not do anything rash when he learned of her flight. It was unlikely that he would hear the true circumstances, but he might try to follow, out of loyalty. If he came alone, he would be in danger, and if he came accompanied by Ithian's men, he would bring the danger with him. Unless he stayed put, Zorsch could be a problem.

But at least Zorsch might bring a horse for her. That would save a lot of flying. And an extra cloak, for cool weather, would be welcome.

There would be time enough to think of these things later, when she found Kedrigern. Right now, the pressing need was for sustenance. She had left Othion in a hurry, bringing no water and only a scrip with a few dry crusts in it. Food was going to be a problem at this time of year. The empty sensation in her stomach gave her notice that it was a problem already.

Through a break in the leaves she spied a little glade bisected by a narrow brook. Descending, she washed and drank deeply. Feeling refreshed, she seated herself on a knoll by the water, took out a crust about the size of a child's thumb, and began to breakfast.

She ate slowly, savoring each nibble, chewing deliberately, making every crumb count. When she finished, she was as hungry as ever. Three small morsels of very hard dry bread remained, along with a hard, brownish-yellow chunk of what was most likely cheese. And that was that. There was no hope of foraging. It was too early for berries and fruit, too late for nuts, and there was not an inn, a hamlet, or a farmhouse for days. She was not yet sufficiently skilled in her wand-wielding to conjure up a magical meal. Lean days lay ahead. She closed the scrip and knelt by the brook. At least there was abundant water, and it was cold and fresh.

As she bent forward to drink, she heard a sound that alerted her: a human voice, she was certain of it. Whether male or female, adult or child, she could not tell, for it was faint and faraway, but it was a voice. She drank hurriedly and retreated to the shelter of the trees edging the glade, to listen.

For a time, no sound reached her ears but the ordinary morning noises of the wood, and then she heard the voice again, soft and distant. Whether it was coming closer or moving off she could not determine, nor could she determine the source, nor the tone. It might have been a hunter's call, a cry of alarm, a shout of joy, a plea for succor, or a warning to keep away; she simply could not be certain.

When the voice came a third time, still no clearer, Princess took to the air. The next time she heard it, she knew that it was a woman's voice. The time after that, she recognized it, and called out, "Berzel! Stay right where you are, dear! I'm coming!"

In a minute she was at Berzel's side. Berzel sprang from her horse and welcomed her with open arms. They embraced, Berzel laughed merrily, and then they embraced again.

"Princess, dear Princess. I'm running away with you," Berzel announced. "Daddy behaved like a beast. I will never return to Othion and never see him again."

"Who told you?"

"He did! He burst into my room and accused me of putting you up to whatever it was you did. What *did* you do, Princess dear?"

"I told your father that he ought to remarry. He seemed to think I was proposing."

Shocked, Berzel cried, "But you're married!"

"He was willing to overlook that."

"He must be punished severely. Do you plan to do something terrible to him?"

"Yes. I'm not sure what. I want to discuss it with Kedrigern. But your father will be punished. I'm afraid there's no way around it."

"Oh, good," Berzel exclaimed, hopping up and down and cutting a caper. "And we'll run away, and I'll live with you, and you'll teach me all the things you know, and when you decide I'm ready to marry you'll find me a handsome prince, and he'll build us a castle right next door to you, and you and I will be together every day for the rest of our lives! Won't it be wonderful?"

"Wonderful," Princess said faintly. "Tell me, dear, what did you bring?" she quickly asked.

Berzel gestured triumphantly to the two well-laden horses that rode behind hers. "Everything we need! I have all your gowns, and your shoes—even the one that Daddy took—and your cloaks. I only brought a few of my own things, because you're going to teach me how to dress like a real princess and get me a proper wardrobe."

"Where's the food?"

Berzel looked puzzled. "Food?"

"Things to eat, dear. We must eat. Even princesses eat."

"I don't know anything about food. The servants see to all that."

"We don't have any servants out here, Berzel dear."

Berzel's eyes widened. She looked at Princess in bewilderment. "But I *always* have servants," she said.

"Not in the woods, I'm afraid. When you left Othion, you left the servants."

Berzel frowned, concentrating on the problem. After a time, her face lit up. "I'll go back and get some servants!" she said.

Princess took her by the arm and led her away from the horses and into the shade, saying as they walked, "I don't think that would be a good idea. Your father must know you're gone, and he'll be very angry. You'd never make it into Othion unnoticed."

"All right, then, I won't go back," said Berzel with a defiant pout. "I'll stay out here and starve. We'll starve together, dear Princess, like the sweet little children in the story. Daddy will find us under a tree, with our arms around each other, dead and wasted, with lovely peaceful smiles on our faces, and he'll feel awful."

"I sincerely hope not, dear Berzel. We'll be very hungry, but I don't intend to starve. First, let's unload these horses."

"Are we going to change?"

"We're going to leave everything right here, and ride as fast as we can after Kedrigern and Traffeo. They have enough food for all four of us. Then we'll spend a night at the abbey —the monks don't encourage female visitors, but they won't refuse us shelter for one night, and plenty of good wholesome food—and then you and I will go to Silent Thunder Mountain and wait for Kedrigern to bring back the cure. After that, we'll see."

"You're so *organized*, Princess dear! You have everything planned out so neatly—will you teach me how to plan things out like that?"

"At the earliest opportunity."

"But what about all your lovely clothes?" Berzel asked in sudden dismay.

"I'll take a spare cloak, and put a spell on the rest. They'll be safe here."

"Do you do *spells*, too?"

"Now and then, dear. Come, give me a hand. You start putting things into nice neat piles. I'm going to fly up and get my blankets. There's no time to waste."

Goaded by their ever-growing hunger, they covered considerable ground before the fading light forced them to halt. After dining on a shared morsel of bread that allowed each of them a portion the size of a crouton, washing each nibble down with liberal quantities of water in a vain attempt to create the illusion of surfeit, they rolled themselves up in layers of cloaks and blankets.

Berzel was unwontedly reticent. She had spent much of the meal staring moodily into the fire, and Princess suspected that the full impact of her flight was beginning to dawn on the girl. No father to turn to; no servants to cater to her slightest whim; no guardsmen to protect her from harm; no castle to shelter her from the weather; worst of all, no snacks from the kitchen at any time she chose—no roast meat, no poultry, no fish, no sweetbreads or sausages or ragouts, no breads, cakes, pies, tarts or cookies, no soups or sauces, no puddings or syrups or jellies or jams, no clotted cream and berries. Only bread crumbs and water in a dark wood.

And all for a gesture of friendship and devotion. All for me, thought Princess, and her heart went out to the poor child sleeping at her side. A feeling of responsibility enfolded her like a heavy, clinging mantle. She looked at Berzel, a homeless waif afflicted with magical evil, and thought of herself, scarcely older than this child, struck down by a bog-fairy's cruel vengeance. She shuddered at the memory of those dreary days, months, years—perhaps decades, perhaps longer—in the Dismal Bog. It might have been quite a long time—centuries, even—because all memory of pre-bog life, except for tiny vignettes (father's beard, mother's hair, the dress she wore to the fateful birthday celebration), was gone and showed no sign of returning. Kedrigern blamed her loss of memory on overexposure to magic, and assured her that it was a temporary condition. He knew about these things. All the same, it seemed to be hanging on for a long time. Years after her initial disenchantment, she remembered little more than she had on the day she regained human form.

Ithian's words came back to trouble her. Would she really grow older and older while Kedrigern aged at the wizardly rate? So far, she seemed to be holding up quite well. Would the years fall upon her all of a sudden, like some temporal avalanche? That was an appalling prospect.

On the other hand, overexposure to magic might have its positive side. She might be already as old as Kedrigern, perhaps even older, her aging slowed by the huge amounts of magic she had undergone. That was possible. It would be some time before she could be absolutely certain, but the thought was the most pleasant and consoling in recent days, and she clung to it. And might it not apply also to Berzel? Werewolves who embraced their lycanthropy were reputed to enjoy enormously long lifetimes. That benefit might apply equally to those who reversed their condition. Magic worked in strange ways.

It would be suitable recompense for Berzel to know that her youthful beauty and freshness would last a century, and for another century or two she would ripen into a magnificent maturity. That was worth a few nights of howling at the moon and gnawing on soup bones.

Of course, that might complicate marriage arrangements. Most men are happy to find a young and pretty woman for a wife, but if she is still young and pretty when her husband is bent and toothless and doddering, there is talk.

Princess sighed and turned on her side. Magic was a complicated business, whether one practiced it, experienced it, or merely thought about it. She put it from her mind, and drifted off to sleep amid fantasies of food.

They finished the last crumb of bread and the last tiny morsel of cheese on the second evening. As darkness fell, Princess went aloft to scan the woods for the wizards' campfire. She could see no trace of it, or of anything else to suggest the presence of human beings.

When she landed, she was weak with exhaustion. She staggered to her blanket and threw herself down, drawing long sighing breaths. She lay unmoving for a time, then propped herself on one elbow and gazed vacantly into the fire.

"Are we going to starve to death, dear Princess?" Berzel asked.

"We are not. At worst, we're going to be very hungry for the next few days, but we won't starve."

"I'm starving now. I've never been so hungry."

"Drink some water."

"That just makes me hungrier."

"Be patient, Berzel. With luck, we'll find Keddie in a day or two. If we don't, we'll be at the abbey soon after, and the monks will feed us generously. They're obliged to feed travelers."

"Do you know a lot about the abbey? Tell me all about it. Tell me about the meals."

"Well, I've never actually been there. Keddie has, though. He was very pleased with the food."

"Do you know the way? We won't get lost, will we?"

"It's five days' ride west of Othion, in the mountains. We can't miss it," Princess said confidently. Berzel looked unconvinced. Princess added, "Remember, Berzel dear, I can fly. I'll find it."

"But what if you're too weak to fly?"

This thought had occurred to Princess, but she had driven it from her mind at once. Hearing it from Berzel, she felt a surge of doubt, and some fear. This evening's flight had exhausted her. After two or three days of nothing but water, she might not be able to make it above treetop height.

"Don't be silly, child," she said impatiently, turning her back on Berzel.

For the next two days, they scarcely spoke at all. Berzel made little sad hungry noises halfway between a sigh and a groan, but Princess was silent, from weakness and weariness as much as from irritation.

When, at the end of the fifth day, they had seen no sign of the wizards or the abbey, Princess began to fear. She flew until her wings ached and her head spun, and saw nothing but trees and barren mountaintops: not a glimmer of light, not a wisp of smoke, not a stir of movement. They had come five days from Othion, they were in the mountains, and the abbey was nowhere to be seen. Somehow, it had gotten itself lost. Or they had. West did not always seem to be where it ought to be, and mountaintops all looked much the same.

That night Princess was awakened by the sound of Berzel's sobbing. She went to her and put her arms about her, whispering gentle consolation. As Berzel clung to her, weeping, she remembered the child's own prediction of their fate, and her heart sank.

They woke when the sun was above the treetops, and rose sluggishly. Princess found her mind clear, though her body was weak and aching. They had to get to a peak, and from there she would fly until she found the abbey or . . . or some other source of food or shelter, she quickly told herself. It had to be today.

The forest trail rose gently, and Princess's spirits rose with each step. There was no danger of losing their way, so she had let Berzel take the lead. They would be at the peak by midday or not long after, at this rate, and she would be able to conduct her aerial reconnaissance in full light. Things were looking better. They would dine this night at the abbey, and all would be well.

"Princess! I smell food!" Berzel cried from up ahead.

The poor dear child was having hallucinations, thought Princess, riding to her. But the air bore the unmistakable aroma of fresh-baked bread. She inhaled more deeply, and caught the savor of spicy stew, and rich pastries, and roasting meat. It was not a hallucination. It was very real.

"You found it, you found it! Oh, Princess dear, I knew you would! You're so clever!" Berzel rejoiced, clapping her hands, her mood and her speech restored at once. "You took us all the way, and I was sure we were lost and you were too kind to tell me so and plunge me into despair, and all the time you *knew*, and you were leading us right to the gates! Oh, Princess, it's so lovely, and it smells so good!"

"Well, I did promise," Princess said as she drew up at Berzel's side. The road curved sharply, and just ahead rose a sizeable building of dark gray stone. It was smaller than she had anticipated, more the size of a manor house than an abbey with a famed library; but it could only be the abbey.

They rode up an avenue of yew trees, past a dark pond ringed with willows. The doors of the house stood open, and a host of servants in dark livery emerged. Two of them led the horses off, after another had removed their skimpy possessions. An older servant, wearing a long black cloak with black braid, gestured within and led the way, while the rest fell in behind them.

"Thank you very much," said Princess to the servant in the lead. He bowed his head, but did not speak.

They went down a wide corridor that led to a broad staircase. At one side was a great hall, where a table was set. The air was filled with the aroma of food. The servant paused with one foot on the first step and gestured toward the upper story.

"I think he's inviting us to freshen up before we dine," Princess said.

"I'd rather dine first," Berzel said, gazing longingly into the great hall. "That would freshen me up no end."

"So would I, but we must remember that we're princesses."

They were shown into a spacious chamber that held a large, soft, canopied bed. The walls of the chamber were of dark wood, hung with dark tapestries. The bedclothes were black.

"Everything is so dark. It's like a tomb," said Berzel with a little moue and a delicate shudder.

"Well, it *is* an abbey. Hardly a setting for gaudiness and frivolity."

"And nobody speaks."

"They've probably taken a vow of silence. We're among holy men, Berzel dear."

"How long must we wait? Will they go off and pray for hours and leave us up here starving? What about all that food downstairs?"

"Let's freshen up, and shake the dust out of our clothes, and I'm sure they'll announce dinner in no time at all."

Scarcely had they completed a hurried toilet than a dull clanking sound came from below. It was a bell, the summons to dine; it could be nothing else, but it sounded like a bell made of lead. Neither Princess nor Berzel paused to comment on the curious dull tone. They hurried downstairs as fast as decorum and their strength permitted.

Princess had anticipated a meal of plain but wholesome food, simply prepared and unpretentiously served. This was a banquet. Dish followed succulent dish, all so judiciously ordered that each new flavor enhanced the one still lingering on the palate and prepared the diner for the next. The soup, a clear broth flavored with tarragon and chervil and accompanied by cold sliced beef and sausages, was followed by meats roasted, broiled, fried, or simmered in court-bouillon, and by hot pâtés and salad. Next came fowl, leveret, and lamb roasted on a spit and garnished with lemons, oranges, olives, and herbs. The fourth course consisted of smaller roast fowl —ortolans, thrushes, snipe, and larks, for the most part—and a variety of small fried dishes. After this came fish cooked in pastry. Fruits in syrup and cream followed, and then, to end the meal on the proper note, light sweet pastries, rose and jasmine pastilles, and sugared almonds. The wines were incomparable, the napery immaculate, the service impeccable. Princess savored her very last pastille with the feeling that her life, and Berzel's, had not been merely saved, but enriched and exalted by the silent solicitude of these generous holy men.

And silent it was. Dish did not clatter against dish, nor did goblet clink against goblet. Not a footfall was heard, not a door creaked, not a word was spoken.

At first, the quiet made no impression on either of the ladies, preoccupied as they were with the aroma, the sight, and above all, the taste of such exquisite fare. But as dish followed dish and course succeeded course, all without a sound, Princess became acutely aware of the hush that lay all around them. Every bite began to sound like a rending, every swallow a torrent, and her eating became daintier and daintier in consequence, as did Berzel's.

When the meal was done they looked tentatively at one another, each of them reluctant to break the silence. At last, Berzel leaned toward Princess and whispered, "We've never had a feast like this in Othion. Is this how princesses usually dine?"

"Now and then," Princess replied *sotto voce*.

"I like it. When I'm married and have my own castle, we'll dine like this all the time."

"You'd better have wide doorways," Princess said. She felt very full.

Berzel went blithely on. "Only we won't be so quiet. Isn't it terribly quiet here? We'll have poets reciting between the courses, and troubadours and minstrels playing, and jugglers and buffoons and a jester. You and Master Kedrigern can come to dinner every day. Won't that be lovely?"

"It sounds delightful. I wouldn't count on seeing us every day, though. Keddie really prefers to dine at home."

With a subdued, almost soundless clapping of her hands, Berzel said, "Then on the nights he wants to eat at home, we'll come over to your house and bring the minstrels and jugglers and poets and troubadours and buffoons and jester! Won't he just love that?"

"I'll discuss it with him," Princess said, reaching over to pat Berzel's hand reassuringly, reflecting that there was probably no surer way to find oneself in an enchanted thousand-year sleep, or magically whisked away—castle, entourage, and all, jester included—to the antipodes, than to appear at the cottage on Silent Thunder Mountain with a troop of pantaloons and merry-andrews.

The servants had withdrawn. Princess and Berzel were alone in the great hall now, and Princess took the opportunity to inspect their surroundings. The furnishings were similar to those in the upper chamber: the wood heavy and dark, the hangings dark and heavy, the windows curtained in black. The monks, she assumed, were members of a rigorous penitential order, living in profound silence a life of mortification and sacrifice. They very likely slept in coffins, or on cold hard slabs, and dined on crusts and ditchwater. The comfort of the accommodations they offered to wayfarers, and the opulent table they set before them, were in all likelihood a form of atonement for their own past self-indulgence. The thought of these good and holy men living their austere lives plunged her into a reverie from which Berzel's repeated tugging at her sleeve aroused her. She turned and saw a cowled black figure in the doorway.

The figure stood unmoving for a moment, tall and thin and slightly skewed in posture. Then, raising a pale hand in welcome, he approached the table at a rocking gait and paused at the head.

"We are honored by the visit of two ladies of such beauty and distinction," he said in a hoarse voice just barely above a whisper.

"You are most kind and generous," Princess replied. "Are you the abbot?"

He extended his hands. They were grayish-white and skeletally thin. "I am in charge here. Was your repast satisfactory, my ladies?"

"Words cannot do it justice," Princess said. "It combined the refinement of the East with the dispatch of the West, the abundance of the South with the vigor of the North, the elegance of the palace with the fastidiousness of a private table. It was imaginative in conception, painstaking in preparation, graceful in the serving, delectable in the consumption, and timely in the removal."

"You are most gracious. My cook is an unsightly old fellow, but he is not without a certain flair."

"I liked it, too," Berzel added, smiling brightly. "I'm going to eat like this all the time when I've married a handsome prince and live in a lovely castle next door to my dear friend Princess."

"May I take it that you are both princesses?"

"That is correct. I may even be a queen one day," Berzel announced.

"Indeed you may, dear lady, and sooner than you think. But since you are both of the blood royal, you might allow me to entertain you with the pastime of kings and queens, the noble game of chess," said their host.

"I am no more than a fair player," Princess confessed, and Berzel said, "I'm terrible at chess. Daddy refuses to play with me anymore. All those pieces, and they all go different ways. . . . It's too much for me."

"One may play for both. I assure you, ladies, my skill at chess is modest." Turning with a slight dipping motion and starting toward the door, he added, "If you will follow me, we will adjourn to the chess pavilion."

They crossed to the opposite wing and entered a room the size of the great hall, with a much higher ceiling. Their footsteps echoed as they followed their host up a narrow staircase to a balcony that encircled the room. When they reached the balcony, he stopped and gestured to the floor below. It was a huge chessboard, with pieces proportionately large. Each square was, Princess estimated, three full paces across. The pawns were human sized; the castles were the size of small watchtowers; the king and queen sat on lofty thrones.

"Magnificent. But how does one move a piece?" Princess asked.

"No need to concern yourself with such matters, my lady. Your pieces will move as you wish them to move. Will you be seated?" the host said, indicating two deeply cushioned chairs by the balcony rail, overlooking the chessboard just behind the royal thrones. "You will play white. I always play the black."

"Very sporting of you, Abbot," Princess said.

She and Berzel made themselves comfortable, settling into the chairs and drawing rugs over their feet and legs against the slight chill of the room. Their host regarded them, unfastened his hooded cloak, and tossed it casually aside. His face, revealed for the first time, was as pale and gaunt as his hands.

On his head was a three-pointed foolscap of black, with leaden bells at the points. He wore fool's motley of a curious kind: Instead of alternating patches of gaudy color, his was black alternating with blacker. He carried a fool's wand of ebony with a tiny skull at the head.

"I am not an abbot, my lady, and this is not a monastery," he said in his harsh whisper.

"Who are you, then, and where are we?" Princess demanded, rising angrily from her place.

"I am the Black Jester, and you are in my power," said their host with a repulsive smile. "The first move is yours, my lady."

···❧ Ten ❧···

a revoked resolution

THE TWO WIZARDS broke camp at dawn and set out for the abbey, joining the main road by the spring where Kedrigern had replenished his water supply on his earlier visit. They stopped to rest and water the horses, and Kedrigern spoke for the first time of the peculiar circumstances of his departure, describing in some detail the odd behavior of the abbot and the curious incident of the wolf in the nighttime. Traffeo listened with interest, making no comment, uttering only a monosyllable every now and then to demonstrate his continued attention and his occasional surprise.

"I haven't thought about the abbey for months, but do you know, I shouldn't be surprised to learn that something is afoot up there," Kedrigern concluded somberly.

"You've been there and I haven't, so my opinion in the matter may not be worth much, but I think you ought to remember that people living such isolated lives are apt to fall into peculiar ways," Traffeo observed.

"They're not totally isolated. Travelers come from time to time, and there are servants who have contact with the outside world. I'm sure the monks have their idiosyncrasies, but I can't get over the feeling that the cellarer wanted very much to let me in on a secret, and the abbot was afraid that I'd stumble upon something. It bothers me." Kedrigern was silent, frowning and fussing with his blanket roll, and then he looked at Traffeo and shook his head. "I suppose you're right, though. I mustn't imagine problems. The real ones are quite enough. We have to concentrate on finding *The Book of Five Blue Snails*, and finding it soon."

"Absolutely. That's the important thing."

"Still, let's keep our eyes open."

"Of course. You may be right, you know. We should be circumspect, in any case." At a sudden thought, he added, "Tell me, what order do these monks belong to?"

"I can't say. That's another odd thing about them: They don't wear a distinctive habit, and the abbey doesn't seem to have a name."

"Perhaps they're not a regular order at all. You do come upon groups of men or women banded together for some pious purpose or another. These monks might be survivors of institutions that have been destroyed or broken up. It's hard times for holy men."

"It's hard times for everyone," Kedrigern said gloomily.

"That's true," Traffeo said, "but holy men and women have it tougher than most. It seems as though someone's always attacking a monastery or an abbey or a convent, or burning down a church. If they're not doing it to eradicate heresy, they're doing it for loot, or just a chance to get some exercise."

Kedrigern thought that over, and finally nodded in reluctant agreement and said, "Whatever their order, it's unlikely that the people at the abbey take a friendly view of wizards. Last time I was there I identified myself as Siger of Trondhjem. I said I was a student."

Traffeo regarded him dubiously. "A bit long in the tooth to pass yourself off as a student, aren't you?" he said.

"I don't think so. I'm not even a hundred and seventy, and very fit," said Kedrigern huffily.

"I meant no offense. My point is that you're obviously a

mature and experienced man, and widely traveled. It's hard to see you as a student."

"I could be a graduate student," Kedrigern suggested.

"If you're asked, I'd suggest that you say you study the law. It's possible to spend one's entire life studying the law."

"What if they ask me questions?"

Traffeo dismissed all such apprehension with an easy gesture and a knowing smile. "If people think you're a man of law, you can tell them anything. They won't expect to understand a word you say."

"An excellent suggestion, Traffeo. What about yourself?"

"At the period of my life when it was advisable to travel incognito, I used the name Hamish of Northumbria, a doctor of physic."

"Do you know anything about medicine?"

"I can discourse on astronomical influences and the humors, and go on at great length about physiognomy. If anyone looks suspicious, I quote a bit of Galen or Dioscorides. That's always been enough to get me through."

Kedrigern rose to his feet and brushed himself off. With a courtly bow to his companion, he said, "Shall we proceed, my dear Hamish?"

"At once, my dear Siger," said Traffeo, climbing to his feet and returning the bow.

The sun was just topping the trees when they reached the abbey. They were admitted by a stocky, rosy-cheeked young monk who welcomed them with a smile and a blessing and summoned a groom to take their horses. As they walked to the kitchen, Kedrigern casually inquired after the health of the former doorkeeper.

The young monk's cheery manner vanished. "Brother Ian is with us no more," he said, lowering his eyes.

"I'm sorry to hear that. Where did he go?" Kedrigern asked.

"He is dead."

"Dead?" Kedrigern stopped and stared at the young monk in shock. "He looked as healthy as any man I've ever seen, and stronger than any two."

"Brother Ian was the strongest man in the abbey. Nevertheless, he is dead."

They walked on in uncomfortable silence. On a sudden hunch, Kedrigern asked, "How many deaths is that since winter? Five? Six?"

"Oh, no! We have lost only four brothers," said the young monk quickly.

"Ah, only four. I see." Kedrigern said no more until they were almost at the entrance to the kitchen, then he murmured, as if thinking aloud, "Still, to have four men die in unusual ways . . . under strange circumstances . . ." He shook his head slowly and said no more.

His words were sufficient to put the young monk in a high state of agitation. When they reached the kitchen, the doorkeeper poked his head in, shouted, "Visitors to the abbey, Brother Cellarer!" and dashed off at once. Kedrigern was fairly certain where he was headed.

"Siger of Trondhjem! You have returned!" cried the cellarer happily.

"I have indeed, Duodecimo of Ardua. And this is my friend and associate, Hamish of Northumbria."

The two men exchanged greetings. Duodecimo led the way to a table in a shaded corner, by a window overlooking the herb garden, then left them with assurances that he would return posthaste.

"Did you mean to frighten the doorkeeper?" Traffeo asked in a lowered voice.

"It occurred to me that we don't have much time, and that might be the best way to get the abbot's attention."

"I hope you're right. What if he sends us packing?"

"Then we'll find a way to get back in. But I don't think he will." Kedrigern leaned forward and glanced about the room before speaking in a voice hardly more than a whisper. "I told you that I had a feeling something strange was happening in the abbey. Well, we've learned that four monks have died in the past few months, and that mere mention of the fact makes people nervous."

"Four deaths would make anyone nervous," Traffeo observed.

"I don't think it would make monks quite as nervous as it might make other people; and it shouldn't make them behave in a furtive, guilty way unless there's some mystery to it all. And if that's the case, and we solve the mystery, the abbot will owe us a favor."

Traffeo frowned. "That's all very logical, but it does seem to be pressing things a bit."

"The next full moon is in thirteen days, and it's a five-day ride back to Othion. We have to press."

Traffeo grunted in grudging acquiescence. Before he could augment his opinion verbally, Duodecimo returned, followed by a young monk whom Kedrigern recognized from his previous visit. The two monks were a sight to make a hungry traveler cry out in joy and clap his hands.

Balanced on their arms, from palm to just above the elbow, was a train of platters, plates, and dishes containing foods beautiful to behold and tantalizing to smell. There were bowls of pâté; platters of sliced beef and ham and sausage and chicken; a bowl of green salad dotted with the white flesh of sliced radishes; boards of cheeses, gold and sage-green and wheat-white and orange and mellow chestnut-brown; a basket of breads; a crock of butter; and two pitchers of wine, one white and one red. As he laid the dishes before them, Duodecimo uttered a hurried apology for having forgotten the fruit, and the young monk dashed off to fetch it as soon as he had unburdened himself.

"William of Primofolio is a good lad," said the cellarer. "In his haste to serve, he sometimes overlooks things, but he is learning."

"Is he your assistant?" Traffeo asked.

"Yes. We are fortunate to have him with us. But I'm prattling away, as I always seem to do, and you are too polite to stop me! Eat, my friends, eat all you will, with our blessing."

They fell to with appetites that surprised them. The feast that had delighted eyes and nostrils pleased the other senses with its varied textures, its crackle of crusts, and its spectrum of flavors. As he took up morsel after morsel, Kedrigern thought back to the numberless foul and skimpy meals he had endured at dirty, bad-smelling inns, and his heart filled with

gratitude toward the good monks for their hospitality to wayfarers.

Young William came back bearing a great earthenware
bowl of fruit that glowed with the gold of apricots and the
inward ruby light of grapes. When he had left them, to return
to his kitchen duties, the cellarer said, "A fine boy, that William. He grew these fruits himself. He is also a very good
baker."

"A man of many talents," said Kedrigern, choosing an
apricot.

"Indeed, indeed. I have been blessed with good assistants.
My other helper, Francis of Gorhambury—you have not met
Francis, I think."

"We have not had that pleasure."

"Francis is a brilliant and promising youth. His strength is
his intellect and his power of organization. William's is his
energy and feeling. They complement each other," said Duodecimo, like a proud parent.

"You're a fortunate man. It's difficult to find good help
these days," Traffeo said, reaching for a bunch of grapes.

They sat in amiable and satisfied silence for a time, during
which Kedrigern treated himself to a second and third apricot.
At length, he observed, "I'm glad to find that the problem
with the smokehouse has been solved. The ham and sausage
were delicious."

Duodecimo gave a start. "The smokehouse? What about
the smokehouse? Who told you?" he asked, his face suddenly
pale.

"When I was here last winter, you apologized for being
unable to offer me smoked meats, saying there had been some
misfortune and they were spoiled. Surely you remember."

"Yes. Yes, of course." Duodecimo sighed with relief and
smiled a weak and unconvincing smile. "Yes, the smokehouse
is . . . is in order once again."

"What was the trouble?"

Duodecimo squirmed like a rabbit in a snare. He wet his
lips, darted desperate glances in all directions, and stam-
mered, "It was . . . it seems . . . something got into the
smokehouse . . . terrible . . . not what one wants to discuss after

a meal . . ." He pressed his lips tightly together and shook his head, but the expression on his face and the look in his eyes betrayed his desire to speak, a desire that might have overcome his discipline had not an unfamiliar young monk approached the table and stood silently awaiting the cellarer's attention.

He was about the age of William of Primofolio, but had an air of years and sobriety that the eager, energetic William lacked. His quick eyes and wide forehead suggested a keen intellect, while his silent attendance bespoke self-possession. He seemed a man more suited to assist a monarch than a cellarer, and Kedrigern wondered what had brought him to the abbey rather than to some royal court.

"Yes, Francis?" said Duodecimo.

"The abbot would speak with our visitors, Brother Cellarer. He has sent me to conduct them," the young monk said.

Kedrigern and Traffeo exchanged a glance. Kedrigern winked. Duodecimo rose, reprieved, and said, "You are timely, Francis. They have just finished their meal." Turning to the two wizards, he introduced the messenger. "Siger of Trondhjem, Hamish of Northumbria, this is my other assistant, Francis of Gorhambury. He is one of the best minds in our abbey. We expect great things of Francis."

Francis acknowledged the compliment with an almost imperceptible inclination of his head. His eyes glittered with triumph, but his expression did not change.

Rising, Traffeo said, "As you say, Duodecimo, you have been blessed with good assistants."

"Yes. Very different young men, I should say, but as you pointed out, complementing one another," Kedrigern added.

At his ease now that a safe topic was under discussion, the cellarer was expansive. "But would you believe, Siger, that one of our brothers cannot tell them apart? Indeed, he sometimes seems to believe that Francis and William are the same person—he will not be dissuaded!" Duodecimo gave a little wondering laugh and went on, "Good Brother Filigrane is wise in the ways of books and letters, and a scribe without peer, but try as he may, he cannot tell Francis from William."

Shaking his head and chuckling, he walked before them, leaving them at the door.

With Francis in the middle, the three crossed the abbey grounds. Though it was still morning, the sun was hot and they walked at an unhurried pace, and Kedrigern took the opportunity to study the layout of the buildings. The towering library was still veiled in scaffolding, but no work appeared to have been done on it so far. It was a forbidding structure, more like a prison than a repository of wisdom and learning; worse still, for the visitors, it looked like a building of inordinate capaciousness. If the abbot could not be persuaded both to admit and to guide them, delay was inevitable.

As they neared the chapter house, where the abbot awaited, a bent and aged monk made his halting way toward them. One hand shielded his eyes; with the other he clutched a stout staff. Kedrigern heard Francis sigh as they came near the old monk.

"Good morning, Brother William and your honors," the monk said in a faint rustling voice, stepping in their path. They halted.

"Good morning, Brother Filigrane. In this bright sunlight, you have mistaken me. I am Brother Francis," said the young monk patiently.

"The cellarer's assistant?"

"Yes."

"Ah, yes. The cellarer's assistant. And who are these men, Brother William?"

"Brother *Francis*," said Brother Francis, a bit less patiently.

Filigrane peered closely into their faces, then stepped back, shaking his head. "Neither of these men is Brother Francis," he said. "I know Brother Francis when I see him. He is the cellarer's assistant."

"I am Siger of Trondhjem, and this is Hamish of Northumbria. We are travelers," said Kedrigern.

"The abbot awaits our visitors," Francis said, edging away.

Still shaking his head, Filigrane moved aside to allow them to pass. Neither of the wizards could think of a comment both appropriate and tactful, and it was only when they were within the shadow of the chapter house that Francis broke the silence by saying in a low, dispassionate voice, "Brother Filigrane spent many years in the copying of books. If a man write much, he need have only a little memory."

"Very true," Traffeo murmured.

"Brother Filigrane has also walked much in the sun with his cowl down," Francis added through clenched teeth.

The abbot received them at the door of the chapter house and dismissed Francis at once. He smiled unnervingly. Rectoverso's gaunt predator's face was not framed for expressing welcome, and his deep, solemn voice was more fitted to the intoning of dismal portents than words of greeting, but clearly he was trying his best to be jovial.

"Siger of Trondhjem, we welcome you and your companion!" said the abbot.

"Thank you, Abbot Rectoverso . . . but are you *sure* we're welcome?" Kedrigern asked, taken aback by the warmth of their reception.

"We had hoped for your return."

"You have? That's very nice of you. I thought . . . well, I had the impression that I was not wanted here."

"When last we spoke, Siger, I was much troubled, and I foolishly sent you away when I should have sought your help. But now you are back. Your talents may yet save us, and preserve our great work."

"My talents . . . save . . . your great work?" Kedrigern said faintly, in genuine bewilderment. He looked at Traffeo, raising his open palms in a gesture expressive of his confusion.

"I should have realized then that your powers of observation and deduction were sent to us, but I was afraid. But now you will use them on our behalf, will you not? Of course you will, good Siger!"

"What am I to observe? What should I deduce?"

The abbot raised a finger to his lips for silence. He looked warily in all directions—even up and down—and then drew his visitors closer. "May I speak in confidence?" he said in a strained whisper.

"This is my friend and colleague, Hamish of Northumbria. You may speak freely before him," Kedrigern said.

"Very well," said Rectoverso, with one last glance around.

"Four monks have died, and I believe that their deaths were not accidental, though they were made to appear so. I fear that they were slain by the hand of one of their brothers, and this suggests to me that a terrible wickedness is loose within our walls."

"You suggest murder. Can you be sure?"

"You may judge for yourself. Two weeks before you came here in the winter, an aged monk, Brother Vinet, suffocated in the smokehouse. Ten days later, a young monk drowned in the well."

"An unusual coincidence, I agree, but could they not have been accidents?"

Rectoverso shook his gaunt head in a slow gesture of negation. "I, too, observe things, Siger, but until now I have kept my observations to myself. On the evening of the first death there was a light snowfall that melted by next midday. The soles of the dead man's feet were dry when we found him in the morning."

"Could he not have been in the smokehouse before the snow began?"

"I spoke with him in the refectory while the snow was falling."

Kedrigern raised an eyebrow. "And the second?"

"Colophon of Canevari was our youngest brother. He was found in the well with a book clutched tightly in his hands—as if he had fallen in while wholly preoccupied with his reading."

"Such a thing is possible, surely," said Kedrigern, and Traffeo nodded in agreement.

Again, Rectoverso gave that slow irrefragable shake of the head. "Not for Colophon. His eyes were weak, and he could not read in faint light. He must have fallen in during Vespers, when the sun was nearly set."

"If his eyes were weak, pehaps he did not see the well," Traffeo suggested.

"A wall as high as my waist encircles it. Colophon was a very short man. He could not have tumbled over accidentally."

"Perhaps . . . perhaps he came up against it unexpectedly, while he was deep in thought, and dropped his book, and in reaching for it . . ." Kedrigern began, and then paused glumly.

"I believe I mentioned that we had to pry the book from his dead fingers," the abbot concluded.

Kedrigern rubbed his chin. "What about the other deaths?"

"Esparto of Semé, the baker's assistant, died suddenly in the spring. He had long suffered from stomach pains, and one day they became serious. He died that night."

"Could it have been from natural causes?"

"I do not think so. He turned a bright blue and died screaming for milk."

"That makes three," said Traffeo.

"And one month ago, our doorkeeper, Brother Ian, was crushed by a stone fallen from the library wall."

"Pried loose?" Kedrigern asked.

"Yes."

A profound silence followed the abbot's monosyllabic reply, and at last Kedrigern said thoughtfully, "The situation has its interesting features, but I fail to see how my assistance is crucial in solving the mystery. Your own powers of observation and deduction are considerable, and you know the abbey and all within its walls. What can I, a stranger, do that you cannot?"

"You would view everything and everyone with a fresh eye, free from the preconceptions of long familiarity. You would read the signs for what they truly convey, not for what you are accustomed to having them convey. You might see the detail we all overlook, the sign that points the way to the man or the power behind these deaths."

"Power? What power do you mean, Abbot?"

"I cannot believe that one of our community could take the lives of his brothers unless something evil—perhaps the ultimate Evil—forced his will," said Rectoverso in a harsh whisper.

"Oh dear me," said Kedrigern, going pale.

"So you must help us. It is your duty."

Kedrigern looked to Traffeo, who seemed benumbed by the abbot's revelations. "We must confer before we decide," he said. In truth, his mind was already made up. However much he needed *The Book of Five Blue Snails*, however eager he was to inspect the library, however willing he was to help the good monks solve the mystery of these grisly deaths, there were limits. He had confronted dragons, demons, fiends of various kinds, even had an encounter with Death himself; but he was unwilling to grapple with the Prince of Darkness. Before he and Trafféo could draw apart, the abbot seized each of them by the wrist, and holding them with his skinny hand, went on.

"Our work is holy work. Though some revile us, call us fanatics, madmen, even heretics, we do God's work. His enemies are our enemies, and the battle is unending and without quarter."

"What is your work, Abbot?" Kedrigern asked.

"We create books."

Kedrigern and Trafféo exchanged a look of disbelief, and both turned to Rectoverso. Simultaneously, Trafféo asked, "How does one create a book?" and Kedrigern said, "But books are copied, not created."

Rectoverso released his grip. He held them for a moment with his glittering eye, then lowered his gaze and said, "Let me rephrase: We write books. That is what one expects of monks, is it not?"

They nodded. Though outwardly complaisant, Kedrigern was reaffirming his decision to leave the abbey at once, and was certain that Trafféo would agree with it wholeheartedly. The prospect of dealing with fanatics and madmen was almost as distasteful to him as grappling with the devil.

The abbot seemed to sense his visitors' feelings. With a thin, grim smile that was apparently intended to reassure them, he said, "But of course you wish to confer in a quiet place. I suggest that you walk in the herb garden, or sit in the shade of the arbor. Or perhaps you would prefer to circumambulate the walls as an aid to thought and digestion. At midday, tell me whether you will stay to help us, or ride on. Until then, the abbey is yours."

"May we visit the library?" Kedrigern promptly asked.

"That is impossible at present. Perhaps at some later time —when the mystery of these deaths is solved."

The abbot left them, and the two wizards remained in the

shadow of the chapter house for a time before deciding on a walk around the walls. Outside the abbey, they agreed, they would be able to discuss the situation more freely.

Discuss it they did for the rest of the morning, from every conceivable angle, and arrived, in mind as well as on foot, back where they had started. To stay was essential, if they were to have any hope of finding *The Book of Five Blue Snails*; but perilous beyond imagining, if they were to confront a diabolical enemy. To leave posthaste was the only way to preserve body and soul from transcendent horror, but it might well entail professional disgrace. If they stayed, there was no absolute certainty that they would face the devil; this might all be the work of a common murderer, perhaps the dénouement of some generations-old vendetta; but neither was there any assurance that they would be permitted to study *The Book of Five Blue Snails*. Rectoverso was still unwilling even to admit them to the library; there seemed small likelihood that he would allow them to browse at will, despite the tantalizing hope—or, more properly, bait—that he held out to them.

And yet, clear as it was that this had been a fool's errand and any sensible man would even now be galloping down the trail with the abbey receding at his back, something in Kedrigern urged him to stay. No man should be allowed to murder innocent monks in bizarre ways and go unchecked, undetected, unpunished. But if the murderer is not a man . . . well, that put a very different face on the matter.

They re-entered the abbey, and as they walked up the path toward the chapter house, Traffeo said, "We mustn't stay here. If we leave today and ride fast, we'll have time to comb my library carefully. We're bound to find a cure for Berzel."

"Do you really think so?" Kedrigern asked listlessly.

"No. But we can't stay here."

Kedrigern sighed and said, "I suppose you're right. It's maddening to be this close, though."

"That abbot's not going to let us get any closer."

"No. He's too protective of his precious library. One would think . . . Oh, what's the good of going over it, and over it, and over it? We'll never get our hands on *The Book of Five Blue Snails*. We just have to face that fact."

"Maybe it wasn't even here to begin with. Your servant could have been mistaken."

"No, Zorsch is reliable. He said he saw it, and held it, and he tells the truth."

"Well, then . . . maybe these monks destroyed it. Maybe they sponged the pages clean so they could use the vellum again. They do that, you know."

"Yes, I know, I know," Kedrigern said despondently.

"Maybe rats ate it."

Kedrigern groaned, then walked on in silence until they were passing the kitchen, when he said, "You go on and get the horses. I want to thank Duodecimo for his hospitality."

"I'll wait for you at the stable," Traffeo said.

The kitchen was filled with aromas of good food, but otherwise empty. Kedrigern entered, called the cellarer's name several times, but received no response. Rather than keep Traffeo waiting, he decided to stop back in the kitchen on their way out.

As he reached the stable, he noticed the abbot walking in the direction of the library. Wanting to get the meeting over with and be on his way, he called to Traffeo, and the two men set out to catch up with Rectoverso. They were still some distance away when two servants burst from the door of the library and ran at great speed to the abbot, waving their arms excitedly and shouting words Kedrigern could not distinguish in their overlapping uproar. The servants threw themselves at the abbot's feet as others, equally agitated, emerged from the library.

"Compose yourself, and speak," said Rectoverso to one of the servants just as Kedrigern reached his side.

"Brother Cellarer! In the pit!" the man cried breathlessly, and his companion, nodding frantically, said, "Duodecimo of Ardua is dead, smothered under the earth of the excavation!"

"*Requiescat in pace*," murmured the abbot. He stooped to raise the servants, who stood quaking before his gaze. "Tell me how you learned of something that took place within the inner walls," he said.

"The librarian!" one cried, wild-eyed.

"He told us! He sent us to bring word to you," said the other. "We came at his order."

"We saw nothing. We did not pass the bounds," said the other.

"Very well. Is that all you have to tell me?"

They nodded, and loudly reassured him, and he dismissed them with a gesture. They backed off a few steps, then turned and ran. The abbot looked to Kedrigern, who stood transfixed, shocked and horrified at the news.

"Our enemy is active," said the abbot.

"I spoke with Duodecimo this morning. And now he's dead," Kedrigern murmured in a muted voice.

"Will you stay and help me find the one who slew him?"

"Yes," said Kedrigern, putting aside all prudent resolve at the thought of the good man's death.

"Then come with me," said the abbot.

···✂ *Eleven* ✂···

princess in search of a mate

PRINCESS FOLDED HER arms and looked the Black Jester in the eye. Berzel rose and stood behind her, doing her best to look equally bold.

"We are not impressed," said Princess coolly.

The dark figure bowed graciously. "Perhaps, in time, you will be, dear ladies," he rasped.

"I think not. While we are not ungrateful for your hospitality, we do not take kindly to those who inform us that we are in their power," Princess said, and Berzel, setting her jaw, added, "We certainly don't."

"I was merely informing you of your status. This is my stronghold. All who dwell herein, and all who enter, are in my power and remain in my power for as long as I choose to keep them. My power is considerable."

"It is only fair, then, to inform you of *your* status," said Princess, reaching for her wand. "I have powers of my own, and if you attempt to mistreat us in any way, you may have a taste of them."

"My gracious lady," said the jester, his harsh voice taking on a wounded tone, "ladies both, have you been mistreated?

Have you been threatened? Have you experienced anything but hospitality, generosity, courtesy, and respect within these walls?"

"No. Not so far," Princess admitted. She glanced at Berzel, who shook her head grudgingly.

"Then forgive me, I beg you, for an unfortunate choice of phrase, and let us continue our game of chess. Your move, my lady," said the jester. He bowed once again and withdrew, at his uneven gait, to the balcony opposite them.

"You certainly put *him* in his place," Berzel whispered. "If that's what jesters are like, I'm not having any in *my* castle."

"I don't think he's your typical jester," Princess said. She and Berzel resumed their seats, and Princess looked down on the great chessboard below. "This certainly is no ordinary chess set. It will take three strong men to move those rooks."

Even as she spoke, the Black Jester was at the opposite rail, looking down at the thirty-two pieces arranged before him. His mien was magisterial as he extended his hands and gestured smoothly over them. At the gesture, the white king and queen favored Princess with a dignified nod while all eight white pawns bowed low to her. She gave a regal wave in return.

"My lady need only announce her move. The pieces will obey," said the Black Jester.

"Very well, I open with pawn to king four."

The white king's pawn drew itself up and marched two paces forward. There it stopped, with a loud, emphatic stamping of unseen feet. Princess and Berzel exchanged a covert glance of astonishment. Berzel's eyes grew round, and she leaned close to speak; Princess squeezed her hand and whispered, "He's just showing off. Pretend you don't notice."

She fixed her eyes on the pieces, and as she watched, she heard voices. They seemed to be coming from below. The words were not spoken aloud, but she was hearing them inwardly, as clearly as if she were down among the pieces.

King's pawn gets first move again. Always one of those two, king's pawn or queen's pawn, never one of us. It's not fair, said one pawn.

Of course it's fair, said another. *King's pawn is senior pawn.*

Besides, who ever heard of opening with a rook's pawn? a third inquired scornfully.

With a bitter laugh, the first speaker retorted, *That shows how much you know. Spulsifer opened with pawn to king's rook four in the great tournament at Narbonne, and he won in nine moves.*

Spulsifer was lucky. His opponent died making his eighth move.

That's beside the point! It was a brilliant opening. Took everyone by surprise. They all said so.

What does a rook's pawn know about brilliance? a fourth voice demanded.

A lot more than a bishop's pawn, came angrily from the queen's rook's pawn.

At ease, you pawns, at ease, the queen's knight bellowed, rearing his head and tossing his mane. *No time for bickering in the ranks. We've got a game to win. Look smart, there. Straighten up. Get yourselves centered. Move along, there! You look like a mob of checkers!*

Amid low, indistinct mumbling, the pawns teetered sluggishly until each was precisely centered on his proper square. The knight looked them over one by one.

That's better, he said. *I don't want any more of that arguing among yourselves, do you hear me? We're facing a tough set of chessmen, and we won't have a chance against them unless we work together.* A bit of murmuring came from the ranks. He paused until it had died out, then went on. *Their majesties expect every pawn to do his best. Remember, there's promotion for any one of you who can break through to the black rear echelon. Tom's halfway there already, and every one of you has a chance to make it.*

Who's in command this time, sir? a pawn asked.

Never you mind. She's a lady of noble birth with hair like a raven's wing and eyes any pawn would die for. Knows her magic, too, I'm told. You're lucky to serve such a fine lady, and if one of you lets her down, I'll personally make him wish he'd been sacrificed!

A voice muttered, *Big talk for someone who can't even walk three steps in a straight line.* His words were followed by furtive laughter.

I want that pawn's name! the knight howled. *Who said that? I'll trample him!*

Peace, peace, my son, said a gentle voice at the knight's side. *Let us not give way to anger. Rather let us dedicate ourselves to our duty, and in a humble spirit place ourselves at the service of this noble lady who has risked so much to lead us.*

Yes, Your Excellency. Sorry about that. It won't happen again, said the knight, abashed.

Once the queen's bishop had spoken, the pawns were silent and orderly. Princess was curious about the import of his words, for she was aware of no risk, and none had been suggested. The voice of the Black Jester broke into her musings.

"The pieces are a talkative lot, my lady. Do they distract you?" he asked.

"Not at all. The queen's bishop said something about my taking a risk in leading them. Do you have any idea what he meant?"

"The risk of losing to one so lowly as myself, my lady. What else could he mean? And now I, too, will open with pawn to king four."

The black king's pawn glided forward smoothly and silently and came to a stop facing the white king's pawn. The two glared at one another.

Don't take nothing from him, Tom! a pawn called out in encouragement from the queen's side.

That's right, Tom! If he looks at you sideways, bash him one! shouted another.

All right, pawns, settle down, settle down. Save it for the endgame, said the white king's knight.

The pawns obeyed, and the other pieces remained silent. Princess was now better able to concentrate on her plan of development. She and Kedrigern played an occasional game of chess, and she had a vague memory of tactics and strategy —presumably from the days before her transformation—but she was not an expert, and she knew it. She had to think out every move carefully. Princess did not like to lose—especially to a jester.

It occurred to her that in all the chatter by her pieces she had not heard a word from the black side. Were the black pieces mute? Did they communicate only among themselves and with the Black Jester? Was their silence a strategem to disturb her concentration—as it was clearly doing—or a courtesy to permit her time for reflection? She wondered at these possibilities, weighed them, and at last, with a frown at her opponent, turned her thoughts to the game.

Boldness, she decided, was the key. Judging from his dress and manner, the Black Jester was a man who believed in intimidating people, or at least making them uncomfortable. Well, she would not be intimidated, and if anyone was going to be uncomfortable, it would not be herself. She would go on the attack and not let up for an instant. Decisive, aggressive moves would show the Black Jester that he was not dealing with a pair of timid, woebegone lost princesses. A hard game, a quick victory, and they would thank their host politely and be on their way.

"Queen to rook five," she said.

What? What's that? Rook's fifth square? Must dash, then. Have to run, said the queen. She gathered up her voluminous skirts, stepped down from her throne, and turning to the king, said, *I'm off, dear old thing. Be back when I can. Take care, now. Mind your castle as soon as you're able, and watch out for pins and forks.* Raising her voice, she called out, *The rest of you see to it that nothing happens to His Majesty while I'm gone. I'll be popping by from time to time. Look sharp. Chin up.* And off she sped to her destination.

"Look at her go!" Berzel said. "What an energetic woman! That's the kind of queen I want to be!"

Princess did not reply. She was listening to a long yawn followed by a deep, dozy voice saying, *Blasted woman . . . always haring off somewhere. What's the good of all the rushing and dashing and chasing about? Ought to learn to take things one square at a time.*

A penetrating observation, Your Majesty, a genteel voice at the king's side responded.

You're a fine one to talk, Bishop, the king said grumpily. *You're as bad as she is.*

With a soft, self-deprecating laugh, the bishop said, *Ah, but I have not Her Majesty's responsibilities, nor her power. I must go at things obliquely, while Her Majesty may move as she desires.*

Ought to learn to sit still, the lot of you, the king muttered.

"An aggressive move, my lady," said the Black Jester. "I will answer it with knight to queen's bishop three."

The black knight sprang forward over his own pawn, twisting to the side so as to land one square ahead of the neighboring pawn. Princess studied the disposition of pieces. She saw a possibility. Her third move was bishop to bishop four.

Well, what did I say? I knew it. He's as bad as she is, the king grumbled as the bishop moved off.

Princess politely covered a yawn, and tried to look calm and unconcerned. This was difficult to do, since she was within one move of a possible checkmate. If the Black Jester chose to develop his knights and if he used the king's knight to threaten the queen, then it was all over on the fourth move: queen takes pawn, mate.

"You are indeed a combative opponent, my lady," the Black Jester said.

"The object of the game is to win. One tries not to waste time," Princess replied coolly.

"An admirable attitude. I share it wholeheartedly. A short, fierce game can be so invigorating."

"Quite. Your move."

"And my lady is not averse to bloodshed. That is the sign of a true player: the willingess to exchange—to sacrifice, when necessary. However, at the moment, I am unwilling." The Black Jester smiled and the king's knight's pawn glided forward one square. "I am a bit too experienced to fall victim to a Scholar's Mate. Your queen is in danger, my lady."

Princess saw that she might have been a bit too aggressive. She brought her queen back to the bishop's third square, where Her Majesty was hailed by the pawns all around.

Brave lads! she said, a bit out of breath from her sudden

withdrawal. *Good show. You're all nicely centered*, she added with a regal wave.

It was obvious to Princess that her queen was shaken by the pawn's attack and relieved to be back among her own pieces. She was being brave, but it had been an unnerving moment. The Black Jester's next move came quickly, as his king's knight crossed the empty square before him and settled on the bishop's third, threatening the white king's pawn. Tom glanced about uneasily, then stood tall and squared his shoulders.

Courage, my son, the bishop called from his place two squares to Tom's side.

Buck up, Tom! We're all behind you. Stout lad! the queen reassured him.

The bishop was out there with no one at his back. Princess sent her queen's knight to the square directly behind him. Tom breathed a great sigh of relief at the sight of the knight, who now guarded his square.

Here, now, eyes front! Look smart! the knight snapped.

The black bishop stirred at the king's side and glided at a dignified pace to his fellow bishop's fourth square, a position that put him face to face with the white king's bishop. They bowed respectfully to one another. The black bishop gazed down the black diagonals to the right and the left, and his gaze lingered on the pawn who stood at the queen's back. The bishop smiled, but did not speak.

He gives me the creeps, that one, the pawn whispered.

From behind his shoulder, the king's knight said, *None of that, now, lad. Mind your manners*.

Princess advanced her queen's pawn one square. The Black Jester countered with the identical move. Princess took stock of the situation, and was not pleased. Her rapid deployment of major pieces had been stopped cold. She had been rash, thinking she could trap a seasoned opponent into an easy mate, and now she was paying for her rashness. It was all very well to shrug things off and say "It's only a game," but losing is never as nice as winning, and losing to an arrogant, smarmy jester —especially when one is a princess—is hard to take.

Her queen appeared safe for the time being, in her own

third rank. A bishop, a knight, and two pawns were near, but her right side was undefended. The unfortunate pawn at her back was under the baleful eye of the black bishop, and needed moral support. Princess decided to strengthen her right-side position by moving her king's knight to rook three.

"Interesting. I had not anticipated that move," the Black Jester said thoughtfully.

"Well, there it is," Princess said.

"Indeed. And I am happy to respond." The black queen's bishop moved gravely across the center of the board to come to a halt at king's knight five. He turned to face the white queen and bowed with great dignity. She looked about for a protector. No one was in position. Things looked bad:

"My lady must prepare for an exchange. A bit of bloodshed might clear the air. Don't you agree?" the Black Jester asked.

Princess pondered the options, and saw that the proper term was *option*. She had one choice: queen to knight three, after which her opponent could either withdraw, or lose his bishop in exchange for her knight. And then what? The black queen's knight appeared to be be planning something . . . and that sinister king's bishop . . . She could only make her move, save the queen, and see what opportunities presented themselves.

The queen stepped gracefully to the adjoining square and took a moment to arrange her train properly. The black bishop lowered his eyes. Princess heard the voices of pawns, very somber and angry.

We'll make them pay, sir, said one, and a second added, *We'll win this one for you, sir, that's a promise.*

Cheer up, lads. I'm not gone yet, said the king's knight.

If he does you in, sir, he's for it. We'll fix him, a third pawn said, glaring at the black bishop, who looked on silent and impassive.

Now, lads, show respect for the cloth, the knight admonished.

Cloth? Him? The only cloth he knows is what he steals off people's backs. He's no more a real bishop than I'm the Pope, and we all know it, the pawn cried angrily.

Steady, steady, now. We don't want anyone saying we can't play the game, do we? As long as we're on this board, that chap's a bishop, and I don't want any of you pawns forgetting that, whatever becomes of me, said the knight.

"Can you hear the pieces talking, Berzel?" Princess asked in a very soft whisper.

"No. I don't hear a thing."

"I do. It's very touching. They talk as though they're actually going to die."

We are, ma'am! Hasn't that devil told you? the rook's pawn blurted.

Quiet, you! None of that, now! the knight commanded, and the pawn just as loudly, cried, *She ought to know, oughtn't she? Someone's got to tell our commander, or she might wind up like us!*

Here, here, what's all this shouting? Do be quiet out there, the king said in a peevish, sleepy voice. *All this running and leaping and rushing about, and now a lot of yelling . . . how's a king to get his rest?*

See what you've done now? You've gone and disturbed His Majesty's nap, said the knight.

She's got to be told!

Not by a pawn, lad. Time enough to talk to our commander when you've made it to the eighth rank. You don't know your place, that's your trouble.

Then tell her yourself! Someone has to do it! the pawn snapped angrily.

Let's all get hold of ourselves, said the queen sharply. *Pawn's right, you know. If our commander hasn't been told the truth about this game, it's high time she was. Bishop, would you mind?*

The queen's bishop, who had not yet moved, said, *As Her Majesty wishes.* Clearing his throat, he called out, *My honored commander—can you hear me?*

"Yes, Your Excellency. I've heard everything you've all been saying," Princess replied, thinking the words but not speaking them aloud.

Yes, yes, of course . . . I should have remembered. And am I correct in assuming that you are uninformed as to the true nature of this match?

"All I know, Your Excellency, is that our host, who calls himself the Black Jester, invited us to play a game of chess after dinner. I have never played with such large or talkative pieces before, but otherwise it seems to be an ordinary game of chess."

How did you come to visit this place, if I may ask?

"We were looking for the abbey, and we thought this was it. We were quite lost, you see, and we don't know the abbey by sight. Only after dinner did we learn that it was the household of the Black Jester."

I was captured in the same way, my lady. I played a game of chess and lost, and now I am as you see me.

For a moment Princess was speechless. She looked down at the pieces, wide-eyed, and swallowed audibly. Berzel looked at her with growing curiosity.

"Is something wrong, Princess dear?" she asked tenderly.

"Yes," was the all but inaudible reply.

"Did you make a bad move?"

"A very bad move, I think."

It was so with all of us, my lady, the bishop continued.

Their majesties were out hunting and sought shelter from a sudden storm. Sir Roger was returning from a tournament and Sir Evan was on his way to the war . . . I am not certain which one.

"And do you just go on being chess pieces . . . forever?"

Not forever, my lady. Only until we fall in battle.

"That doesn't look like a bad move, Princess dear," Berzel broke in. "I don't see anything else you could have done. Of course, I'm not half as good a player as you are, but all the same, I think—"

"I didn't mean *that* move," Princess said impatiently.

"Oh. Well, it's too late to worry about the others," said Berzel cheerily. "We just have to get on with it."

Those who survive a game play on. Those who fall are replaced. His Majesty has been here longer than he can recall. Her Majesty is certain that they have been here for more than a decade. The mortality rate among the rest of us is somewhat higher.

"That's terrible! Who is the Black Jester? How can this be stopped?"

The one who calls himself the Black Jester is a sorcerer whose power is surpassed only by his wickedness. If he is defeated in a game of chess, the player and winning pieces are set free. What it will take to overcome him completely and end his depredations, I cannot say, the bishop confessed.

"But if I can win this game, you will all go free—is that right?"

Those who survive will go free. Some will fall. That is inevitable.

"And those who fall . . . ?"

Those who fall, die, my lady.

It's all right, my lady, said the king's knight, looking the threatening bishop in the eye. *I don't mind so much, as long as I can go down fighting.*

"But how can I send you to your deaths?"

Have to, my dear, said the queen. *If you don't, we're all lost, and you two with us. No choice in the matter. If you hesitate, that only plays right into his hands.*

Just give the orders, ma'am. We'll do what we have to, said the king's pawn.

Tom's right, ma'am, said another pawn. *If we have to go, we'll take a few of that lot with us.*

"How do you feel about this, Bishop?" Princess asked.

Evil must be resisted, my lady, and the Black Jester is a very evil creature indeed. As for myself, I am prepared to face my Maker, and I think He will judge me the more leniently if I fall in a good cause. We are at your service in this struggle, I assure you.

"You're all very brave. I'm proud to command you," Princess said, her voice quavering with feeling.

Loud cheering went up from the pawns, and the knights joined in with *Hear, hear!* The queen waved to her, and the king made a deep grumbly noise that was not altogether disapproving. Princess rolled back her sleeves a couple of turns and looked staunchly at Berzel.

"You're right. We just have to get on with it." Turning to face the Black Jester, she said fiercely, "Your move, clown."

·····{ Twelve }·····

through the mill

THE ROYAL PALACE of Othion was in such an uproar that half the morning was gone before Zorsch was able to determine that (a) Princess had departed during the night, (b) Berzel had followed her in a very short time, (c) no one appeared to have any idea why either of them had left or where they might be headed, and (d) Ithian was in a rage, threatening serious inconvenience and eventual death of an unpleasant kind to anyone involved in any way in the disappearances. Zorsch was not slow-witted. As the only member of Princess's entourage on hand, he was the likeliest object of Ithian's attention and he wanted none of it. Minutes after learning of Ithian's mood, Zorsch rolled his few belongings in a blanket and stuffed his tunic with foodstuffs. Stealthily he led his horse from the palace stables, slipped out of the gates, and made his way from Othion.

He had no idea where to seek Princess, but he knew that the monastery that was Kedrigern's destination lay to the west, and if he could find Kedrigern, Kedrigern would find Princess. He turned his horse's head westward and urged it to great speed.

Zorsch rode steadily until Othion was well behind him, then he stopped to listen for the sound of pursuit. He heard only the noises of the woodland. Pausing to rest his horse while he gnawed on a very hard piece of dried beef, he sat down under a tree and tried to puzzle out what was going on. It was, he decided, impossible. Kings, princesses, and wizards seemed to operate by rules all their own, indecipherable to the uninitiated and usually awkward, if not downright dangerous, to them, as well. It was bad business to get mixed up with such folk; nothing but trouble in the long run. True, Kedrigern had offered his help, and Princess was as sympathetic as one could wish, but what good had they done him? Here he was, a fugitive in a strange land, with the moon nearly halfway through its cycle, and no closer to a cure than he had been in his own dooryard. He let out a long sad sigh. Maybe the wisest course was to make his way home and accept the fact that one morning a month, for the rest of his life, he would awake in torn and muddied garments, covered with minor abrasions, bereft of memories. At least he would be home.

As he thought about home, and the old days, he realized that quite a few of his companions underwent exactly the same experience at regular intervals, even though they had never been bitten. What is more, they boasted about these mornings after, and considered them proof of a high old time the night before. His predicament was not really so unusual, except for that one little detail of becoming a wolf. And there was no need to reveal that detail to anyone.

He sighed again, more gently, and smiled as he thought of Meerla, the miller's daughter. Of her long hair, the color of chestnuts, swaying as she walked; and of her wide eyes, the color of violets, looking up at him in loving admiration; of her lovely little nose, and those rose-petal lips; of all these things he thought long and longingly. His secret could be revealed to Meerla. Perhaps he could go back and explain everything, and make her understand. She was ever a kindhearted girl, and very fond of pets. Her preference had always been for fuzzy baby animals, true, but surely she could learn to love a wolf

. . . or at least put up with one for a single night every month. It was little to ask of one who truly loved. And Meerla had often spoken of her own desire to settle down and have a home and children.

Zorsch pondered that for a time, and cold reason began to assert itself. A home and children was not the same as a den and cubs, he thought, and his dream crumbled. There was no running away; he had to be cured, permanently, or his future was blighted. And the only hope for a cure was Kedrigern. He hauled himself wearily to his feet, remounted, and headed west.

When the sun was halfway between the treetops and the ground, Zorsch began to look for a campsite: a dry place, but not too far from water; secure and hidden, but near the road and with alternative avenues of flight. Best of all would be to come upon an inn, but these woods were said to be uninhabited. He pressed on, scanning the road on either side, seeing no promising spots, and as the sun sank ever lower and the terrain became ever more obscure, he had a glimpse of light among the trees to his left. A cottage, he thought with a great surge of relief—perhaps an inn, with a cheery fire, and corny ale, and hot food, and a soft bed, and a stable for his weary horse. Grinning in anticipation and humming softly to himself, he guided his mount toward the light.

The horse picked its way cautiously over the uneven ground, making scarcely a sound. Soon, Zorsch could hear voices, and what sounded like song. He smiled and chuckled to himself—not just any old inn, but a merry inn, a place of song and game and joy unconfined, the very thing a traveler craved after a long day on the road. He was about to call out a hearty greeting, when the light suddenly flared up, and the voices rose in cackling laughter. The song resumed—not so much a song as a chant, really—and now he was able to distinguish the words. They froze his blood.

> "Witches of the Burning Well,
>   Form the circle! Weave the spell!
>   Cast him in the fiery mud,

Bake his brains and boil his blood!
Fry his liver, roast his bones!
Make a dinner fit for crones!"

An agonized scream followed. It was cut off sharply by a
great hollow roar and a skyward spurt of flame, and then a
long arpeggio of delighted cackling. Zorsch eased his horse
around. With his heart pounding, he made his way as swiftly
and quietly as possible back to the trail and rode on, heedless
of the gathering dark.

Soon he could see nothing but occasional glimpses of the
stars. The waning moon gave no useful light, and the wood
closed in on both sides and overhead. He could not ride on all
night, but he was not ready to stop. The horse picked its slow
way onward. At every moment, Zorsch expected to see the
infrequent stars blotted out by hungry witches flying over, in
search of him, and feel strong bony fingers clawing at him to
carry him off and make him an entrée at a witches' feast. It
was horrible. These woods were a terrible place; the wrath of
Ithian could be no worse than these sylvan perils. He saw no
hope for Princess and Berzel, and very little hope for the two
wizards. As for himself, he considered it a matter of minutes
before he met some grisly fate.

And then, in his despair, once again he saw a faint glimmer
of light, this time directly ahead. The horse was moving at a
slow walk, making no sound at all. Zorsch let him go on,
holding the reins tight, ready to stop the creature in an instant
and wheel off into the woods. But this light did not move or
change. No song or chant came to his ears, but the sound of
running water and the rhythmic rumble and creak of a mill
wheel. Closer and closer Zorsch came, and no horrors leapt
from the dark, no blood-chilling chants met his ears. He heard
the rush of the stream and the familiar groan of the wheel, and
nothing more. Soon he could distinguish the outlines of a sizeable but quite ordinary building with a mill wheel at one side
and a tidy narrow bridge across the swift-flowing stream. He
thought of Meerla and her father. He thought of home. A

sudden leap of hope overcame his fears and he called out to announce himself.

"Who's there?" said a deep voice from within.

"A traveler. I am weary and hungry, and I crave shelter," Zorsch responded, and waited.

A bulky, irregular figure emerged from the doorway and stood silhouetted by the interior light. "How many?" he asked.

"I am alone."

"I will feed you and give you a place to sleep. It is poor fare this night, traveler, but you are welcome," said the miller.

"To a hungry man, no fare is poor. I thank you," said Zorsch, dismounting and leading his horse forward.

"The stable is over there," said the miller, pointing to a nearby building. "Come in when you're done."

Zorsch saw to his weary mount, then shouldered his blanket roll and proceeded to the mill. He entered a large room illuminated by the light from a fireplace. A table stood at a comfortable distance from the fire, and a rough joint-stool was pulled up to it. The miller stood before the fire, his big form outlined, features shadowed. An old woman who was bowed over a pot half turned to favor Zorsch with a one-tooth-revealing smile, then ladled something from the pot into a shallow bowl and set it on the table.

"Boiled turnips, traveler," said the miller. "That is all we can offer you tonight."

"I love turnips," Zorsch said.

"Tomorrow we eat meat, and the next day I grind flour for baking. But tonight, turnips."

"I have some bread I'd be happy to share with you," said Zorsch, reaching into his tunic and pulling out two small round loaves. He displayed them, one in each hand, and set them down on the table with the sound of dropped stones.

"No need, traveler. In this house, we eat no bread but our own," the miller said.

The crone nodded eagerly, gummed, snuffled, and said, "Oh, yes, yes. Our own bread. Lovely bread."

"Well, if you're sure you don't want these . . . " Zorsch began.

"We do not," said the miller.

"Then I'll keep them to eat along the way. I still have a long way to go, you see."

"Eat your turnips," the miller said.

"Lovely turnips. Lovely turnips," the old woman repeated, shaking her head loosely.

Zorsch fell to and quickly emptied the bowl. No sooner had he finished the last bit of turnip than the old woman whisked the bowl away from under his nose and refilled it with steaming chunks of turnip.

"Eat more," said the miller.

"You're most generous. Are you sure you don't want any?"

"I hate turnips."

The old woman scooped up a ladle of the pot liquor and shuffled to Zorsch's side. "Some lovely gravy. You can dunk your bread in it," she said, pouring the liquid into the bowl.

"Thank you. It's delicious," said Zorsch.

"Give him an onion," the miller ordered her.

"Oh, yes, an onion. A lovely onion. Just the thing." The old woman made her slow, waddling way to the corner of the room, where she rummaged in a sack and returned holding up an onion, displaying it like a great pearl, muttering, "Just the thing. A lovely onion is what we need. Just what we need."

Zorsch accepted the onion with thanks. It was a bit softer than an onion ideally ought to be, but quite edible. He drew one of the loaves from his tunic and held it up for his host and hostess to see.

"Are you quite sure you wouldn't like some bread?" he asked.

"Eat," said the miller.

Zorsch banged the little loaf on the table top until it broke into shards which he then dropped, along with the swept-up crumbs, into his bowl. Alternating bites of onion with chunks of turnip, he soon finished his main course and turned his attention to the now pulpy and chewable chunks of bread. When they were all gone, he drank the last drops of liquid from the bowl, wiped his mouth with the back of his hand, and sighed with repletion.

"Full?" asked the miller.

"Quite."

"Good. Now you sleep."

As if responding to the word, Zorsch flung out his arms, stretched, and yawned loudly and long. "It's been a busy day," he said, blinking and rubbing his eyes. "Very good of you to put me up like this."

"We are happy to serve you," said the miller. "We love to serve the people who travel this way."

"Oh, yes, yes, we do. It's lovely to serve travelers," said the crone, showing her tooth.

The miller took a horn lantern from the chimney-piece and lit it with a coal from the fire. He raised it before him, giving Zorsch his first clear sight of his host's features.

Zorsch gave a start, which he immediately tried to cover by rising, looking about for his blanket roll and taking up his bowl and spoon, then setting them down again and picking up the joint-stool and standing dumbly by the table, staring. The miller's face was a tangle of thick black hair from which disturbing features protruded. The nose was a broad hook bent in the middle. One eye was a tiny glittering ebony bead, the other a projecting dome of dull white the size of a goose egg. Blubbery wet red lips were parted to reveal large irregular teeth resembling lichen-covered stones. Combined with the miller's great size and lopsided posture, his facial features conveyed an air of menace. Zorsch felt a moment of revulsion and a pang of doubt at accepting the man's hospitality; but then he smiled to reassure both his host and himself, and thanked the miller once again. The man was generous, and it would be silly and ungrateful to hold his unfortunate appearance against him. His generosity was all the more touching for his fearsome looks, and his isolation in this unpeopled wood where grain to grind could only be a rarity. He had given freely of his meager store; it behooved Zorsch to return his largesse with civility.

"This way," said the miller, indicating a doorway on the other side of the chimney-piece.

Zorsch picked up his blanket roll and went to the doorway. The miller directed the lantern's beam within, and Zorsch saw a low shed with a thick pallet in one corner.

"You sleep here," said the miller.

"It looks very comfortable."

"Sleep well," the miller said, handing the lantern to his guest.

Zorsch tested the pallet and found it just right. He pulled off his boots and rolled himself in his blanket. For a few minutes he lay still, thinking of his narrow escape from the witches and his good fortune in coming upon the hospitable miller. The man might be distressing to look at, but a hot dinner and a clean straw pallet in a snug dry shed beat dry bread and water and a night on the cold damp ground. He tried to think of ways he might repay the miller. Perhaps Kedrigern or Princess could work a spell to improve the man's facial features. Maybe Ithian—once he cooled down—could do something. Surely there would be work for a miller in Othion. Or Berzel . . . Yes, Berzel was always being praised for her kindness to those in need. Here was a perfect opportunity for her. With that settled in his mind, Zorsch extinguished the lantern and composed himself for sleep.

When he opened his eyes, he sat up with a start. Broad daylight shone through the chinks in the outer wall. He had slept until mid-morning. He rose hurriedly, rolled up his blanket, and pushed through the door.

A huge kettle was hung over the fire, the water in it just beginning to give off steam. The miller entered the room bearing an armful of wood, which he dropped noisily to the floor. The old woman proceeded to feed the fire, nodding and saying softly, "Lovely fire. Oh, yes, lovely."

"I must have overslept. I'll have to run," Zorsch said.

"You stay. Meat today," said the miller, and the old woman looked up, flashed her tooth in a ghastly smile, and said, "Bread soon, too. Lovely bread. Just the thing."

"Thank you, but I really must find my master, so he can find my mistress. I must dash."

"You stay," the miller repeated. He seized Zorsch by the tunic with one hand, and with the other he looped a rope around Zorsch's ankles, jerking it painfully tight.

"But I must go!" Zorsch cried.

"If you go, no meat today," the miller informed him, grinning in a truly hideous manner.

"And no flour for bread tomorrow," the crone added, her head bobbing.

Zorsch's piteous howls of protest and entreaty were ignored. The miller tossed the end of the rope over a beam and drew Zorsch up. He fastened the rope to a peg, then tugged a large wooden basin into place directly under the dangling man.

"Mustn't waste the blood. Makes a lovely pudding, blood does," the old woman said as she peeled a turnip.

Zorsch gave a faint cry and went limp. When he regained his senses, he heard a sharp skritching whine coming from just outside the door. Recognizing the sound of steel against a grindstone, he let out a much louder cry and began to blubber, "No, not me! I'm poisonous! I'm unhealthy! Turnips are a good healthy food, but I'm not!"

"Turnips are lovely, but we like a change every now and then," said the old woman, looking up at him and smiling her unidenticular smile.

"I know wonderful recipes! I can show you a hundred exciting ways to cook turnips!" Zorsch wailed. The miller entered, carrying a long knife, and Zorsch swung around to address him. "You can't eat me! There's something I didn't tell you—I'm a werewolf!"

"That's all right. We like game."

"You're not paying attention! I'm not a wererabbit, I'm a werewolf! I turn into a wolf when the moon is full! I'm indigestible!"

The miller—as far as Zorsch could tell from an upside-down position—grinned. "No fear of that, traveler. By the time the moon is full, you'll be long digested," he said. With his toe, he moved the wooden basin just a bit to the left.

"We'll cook this one a bit longer. Make him lovely and tender," said the old woman.

"That should do it," said the miller, adjusting the placement of the tub by a hair. "Thank you for warning me, traveler. I used to be something of a sorcerer, and I know a spell that will cover any possible complications."

Zorsch groaned and gave way to whimpering. All hope
was lost. The miller took two paces back to study the arrangement, gave one satisfied nod, and then stepped smartly forward and took a tight grip on Zorsch's hair. And just as he
drew back the knife, something astonishing happened.

In the middle of the room, on the instant, with no warning,
a hideous fiend appeared—a horrible sight, all claws and
fangs and talons, with eyeless things squirming all over it,
their crablike pincers glowing. The apparition sank one ta-
loned claw into the table, lifted it as easily as one would lift a
broom, and flung it through the wall. With the other claw it
snatched up the old woman, snipped her neatly in half, and
crammed the pieces into its dripping maw. Then it turned its
five carbuncular eyes on the miller. The rat-like creatures that
swarmed about its body chittered and chattered and snapped
their jaws and clicked their pincers.

"What are you doing here? I put you in the wood! You're
supposed to be lurking by a false trail, not hanging about
here," the miller shouted angrily, waving his knife. The creature gave a low, grinding roar and hissed out a gust of fetid
breath. "Get back where you belong! I'm your master, fiend,
and I say get back!" the miller commanded, a slight quaver
discernible in his voice.

Zorsch wanted desperately to faint, but was too terrified for
even that relief. He hung limp, head and heart pounding, and
was unable even to squeak when the miller and the fiend hur-
tled at one another and fell in a rolling, hacking, slashing heap
on the floor. The parasites clacked their pincers and squeaked
like rats; the miller swore terrible oaths; the fiend roared,
snarled, and hissed. The battling pair crashed into the shat-
tered wall, and the whole structure shivered and groaned. Dust
sifted down, the timbers creaked. They slammed into the opposite wall, and beams crashed to the floor. Zorsch found
himself sprawled under a tangle of debris, and tore the rope
from his ankles just as the fiend hurled the miller into the fire.
While Zorsch wormed his way from the wreckage, the miller,
his garments smoldering, went for the fiend with a flaming
brand, howling execrations.

Just outside the remains of the door, by a sizeable grindstone, Zorsch found his blanket roll. He tucked it under his arm, climbed to his feet, and let out a howl of pain as he tried to stand. Dropping to his knees, he crawled for the stable as quickly as his benumbed legs could move.

His horse was gone. Saddle and blanket were where he had put them, but the horse had vanished without a trace—bolted in terror, eaten, bewitched—there was no telling. An awful crash came from the mill, and Zorsch turned in time to see it collapse upon itself. Along with the billowing dust rose tongues of flame that quickly spread to engulf the dry, splintered wood.

Zorsch had had his fill of horrors. He turned, struggled to his feet, and despite the pain, ran into the woods and kept running until he fell exhausted, unable to go a step farther. He lay gasping for breath, and rested until he was able to drag himself on; then he fled, heedless of direction, wanting only to be away from the monstrous mill and its terrifying inhabitants.

In the afternoon the skies clouded over. A light rain began to fall during the night, and continued through the day. Zorsch wandered on aimlessly, completely lost and unable even to guess at directions.

The rains continued for another day, obscuring the sky. When Zorsch was again able to see the sun and set his course westward, he had no idea how far he had gone from the main road, or in which direction. Amid his confusions were a few certainties: He was unpleasantly damp from head to foot; his food was almost gone; he would forage for himself and sleep in the woods, avoiding all habitations, human or otherwise; he had better find Kedrigern quickly.

He took one sunny day to dry his clothes and boots. He set snares for small game, and made it a point to find a decent campsite before sundown each day. So far, so good, he told himself. But days passed, the moon waxed ever fuller, and he was in the woods still, with no trace of a monastery, or a mountain, or a road.

And then, to his great relief, he came across a trail on a

gentle hillside slope. He was uncertain, for a moment, whether to follow it upward or down; then, remembering that the monastery was on a mountaintop, and hoping desperately that he had chanced upon an alternate route to his destination, he began to trudge up the hill.

···❧ *Thirteen* ❧···

one for the books

THE LIBRARY STOOD at the southeast corner, on the highest point of the abbey grounds. Beyond its outer walls, which joined with the great wall that enclosed the entire abbey, the hillside fell away in a sheer drop of some three hundred feet before sloping out sufficiently to permit the first hardy trees and bushes to take root.

The edifice towered over the men like a cliff of smooth gray stone. Kedrigern estimated a distance of fifty feet from the ground to the eaves and three times that along the length of the inner walls. He tried to make a mental calculation of the number of books such a space might hold, but he was too distracted by the thought of Duodecimo's death, and could only estimate that the total would be enormous—far more than even the great library of Alexandria at its height, under Caesar. It astonished him to think of so many books; there was not enough knowledge in the world to fill them.

"You go ahead, Siger. I'll stay out here and . . . observe," said Traffeo with a wave of farewell as he backed away.

"Come, follow me, quickly," commanded the abbot. Kedrigern followed.

Passing from the bright morning sunshine into the shadowed confines of the library, he was unable to see clearly for a time. He hurried along after Rectoverso at the best pace he could manage, running one hand along the shelves to retain his bearings and to keep track of the narrow openings through which the abbot slipped so surely. He had gone some distance before he realized that his hand had encountered many shelves that were practically empty. He could not stop to check the accuracy of this impression; the abbot was moving too quickly through the labyrinth of darkened shelves, turning again and again until Kedrigern had lost all sense of direction and could only struggle to keep the swift black figure in sight. The abbot stopped at last by the entrance to a barrel-vaulted corridor. He turned and held up an arresting hand. His expression was grave.

"At the other end of this corridor is the inner library. You are to touch nothing—absolutely nothing. Do not attempt to examine any of the books you see. Do not read the titles. Far better for you if you do not even raise your eyes to glance at the bindings," he said. Without waiting for acknowledgment or reply, he turned and entered the corridor.

Kedrigern plunged after him. He could not have found his way back to the entrance unaided; besides, his curiosity was roused to a peak. The reality of this mysterious library was proving stranger than any tale he had heard and any fancy he had concocted.

They emerged into a second library. The light here was as dim as that of the outer building, but by now, Kedrigern's eyes had grown more accustomed to the gloom. He saw shelves packed end to end with books crammed so closely together that they seemed ready to burst forth and engulf him in a torrent of erupting words. In the great outer library there had been room for thousands more volumes than the shelves contained; here in the plain straight aisles of the inner library there seemed to be scarcely room to insert one thinly scraped leaf of parchment. Wherever a book could be placed, two had been forced. It appeared almost as though the abbey truly had acquired a copy of every book in the world, and was trying to distill the essence from them by slow pressure.

The abbot opened a small door. Kedrigern followed him through, and stopped short with a gasp. He took a step back and looked around. He was in a square courtyard, surrounded by walls fifty feet high, blank and unbroken by any opening other than the narrow slits, no broader than a man's hand, which admitted light and air to the building. The courtyard itself was about the same dimensions as the walls, thus creating a cubical area of some fifty feet on each side, but only a narrow track extended around the walls, for in the center of the courtyard was a black abyss. Face down, one arm and one leg dangling over the edge, lay the dirt-covered body of Duodecimo of Ardua. Two monks stood over it. They bowed to the abbot, then turned curious and hostile eyes on the stranger at his side.

"This is Siger of Trondhjem, a visitor who has agreed to help us. Tell him what he wishes to know," said Rectoverso.

The two unfamiliar monks exchanged an uneasy glance. Sensing an advantage, Kedrigern was blunt. "Why are the shelves of the inner library so crowded, and why was I warned not to touch any of the books?" he asked.

"Answer him, Johannes," commanded the abbot.

The smaller and frailer of the two monks said, "The shelves contain—among other works—books that are the fruits of our labor."

"And what is that labor?"

"Our great mission is to prewrite every book that can ever be written," the monk recited.

Kedrigern blinked at this incredible answer. "Why?" he asked, in a voice scarcely more than a whisper.

"For the world's good and our salvation." Johannes turned to the abbot. "Must I say more?"

"It is sufficient answer," said Rectoverso.

With that line of inquiry so deftly closed, Kedrigern asked the monk, "What is the purpose of this excavation?"

"You have remarked the crowding of our shelves. We are digging the foundation of a new tower to contain the books of the inner library."

"Why not put them in the outer library? The shelves aren't filled."

"Impossible. We must build a new tower."

"But why do something so dangerous, when there's no necessity?"

"There is a great necessity," said Johannes.

"It must be great indeed, and I confess I can't understand it. If you were to weaken the foundations..." Kedrigern looked uncomfortably up at the dark walls enclosing them.

"I am librarian of the inner library. I would never endanger our work," said the monk, controlling his anger with obvious effort.

"Not knowingly, I'm sure. But you'll be building a deep structure, and the dirt is soft. Won't you undermine the present library?"

This time the second monk replied. "We have given the matter considerable thought. We will excavate the dirt until we reach bedrock, then fill the pit with stones to make a firm foundation. We will then dismantle the outer library and build the new tower from the old one, stone by stone."

"And what's to become of the books while you're doing this?"

Rectoverso broke in sharply, "The books will be safely stored. Construction will not endanger them."

"Construction?" Kedrigern smiled and shook his head. "Your construction sounds more like deconstruction to me."

The second monk returned his smile coolly. "We prefer to consider our deconstruction a work of construction."

"Or perhaps a transformation?"

The monk ducked his head obligingly. "One might also use that term."

"We can throw words around all day, but that will get us nowhere. What did Duodecimo have to do with the building of the tower?" Kedrigern asked, returning to the attack.

"With the actual building, nothing. As cellarer, he saw to it that the workers' food was brought in."

"Surely he didn't bring it himself," Kedrigern objected.

The abbot said, "Duodecimo was a conscientious man. He checked the servants to see that the work was done promptly and well."

Kedrigern scratched his chin thoughtfully, looked around,

and after a time said, "The food was not carried through the library. There's a passage from the kitchen. I'd like to see it."

"We will return by the passage. Have you any further questions?" asked the abbot.

Kedrigern knelt and inspected the body, turning it over with some effort. Under a thick coating of dirt and mud, Duodecimo's face was peaceful. He seemed to be no more than mildly startled by death. Looking up, Kedrigern asked, "Who found him?"

"Those working below saw him fall," Johannes answered. "I heard their shouts and told the outer librarian, who dispatched men to tell the abbot."

"Did they see anyone else with him?"

"No one else was with him," Johannes said flatly.

"You sound very positive."

"It was forbidden. Duodecimo would only have come here alone."

Kedrigern accepted the answer, thanked the monks, and expressed his readiness to leave. A lantern was provided, and Rectoverso led the way to the passage.

It was a sizeable tunnel, broad enough for the two men to walk side by side, and about six feet high. The abbot was forced to stoop. Kedrigern kept a close eye on the roof, stopping several times to examine the ragged cobwebs that hung in every arch, but he said nothing. The abbot was first to speak, when they were back in the kitchen.

"Poor Duodecimo. It is an ugly way to die," he said with a gentleness that surprised Kedrigern.

Kedrigern looked around the kitchen, and only when he was certain that they were alone did he say, "True enough, but the cellarer was not killed by a fall, nor did he suffocate." The abbot looked at him, startled, and he went on. "He was murdered here, and carried through the passage."

"Duodecimo murdered, too? Are you positive of this, Siger? Could it not have been truly an accident this time?"

"His habit bore traces of cobwebs. There were marks in the passage where his back had scraped the roof."

"But who would slay Duodecimo? And why?"

"Obviously, it's been done by the same hand that slew the

others. The deaths are all related, and I think the connection is the inner library."

"That cannot be. None of the dead men were connected with the work of the inner library," said the abbot.

"Duodecimo brought in food," Kedrigern reminded him.

"Duodecimo was cellarer—an important position in the life of the abbey, but not a part of the inner library."

"And Colophon was found with a book clutched tightly in his hands—a book he could not have been reading. Tell me, what book was it?"

Rectoverso made a vague gesture with one gaunt hand. "We could not determine. It was in the water too long."

"Then it might have been from the inner library. That's at least possible, is it not?" Grudgingly, the abbot conceded the point with a nod and a grunt. Kedrigern pressed him further. "And it's possible that the others might have discovered something and been killed to keep it secret. That's possible, too, isn't it?"

The abbot looked at him, horror dawning in his eyes. He staggered back and sat down heavily on a bench, then leaned forward and covered his face with his hands.

"It's time you told me about the mission of the inner library," Kedrigern said, taking a seat at the abbot's side.

"Johannes of Octavo has already described it to you," said the abbot without moving.

"He evaded my question, and you encouraged the evasion. If you want my help, you must tell me everything."

Rectoverso sat for a time with his face buried in his hands. At last he raised his head, nodded once, slowly and profoundly, and stood, gesturing for Kedrigern to follow. They walked in silence to the herb garden. There, where no eavesdropper could conceal himself and no one could approach unseen, the abbot spoke.

"Johannes of Octavo told you the truth. The workers in the inner library have dedicated themselves to the prewriting of every book that can ever be written in this world, in any language, on any subject, in any age until the end of time," he said.

Kedrigern shook his head in open bewilderment. "But

why? For what purpose? If you write what will eventually be written by others, then your life's work—forgive me for saying it, Abbot, but I must—your life's work is wasted."

Rectoverso laughed. It was an empty, bitter laugh with no trace of humor in it, only mockery. "You do not understand. No one understands."

"What is there to understand? You have chosen to throw away your lives, Abbot. Monks feed the hungry, care for the sick and homeless, do good works. But in this abbey..." Kedrigern frowned and shook his head.

"Before you condemn us, think of what we have undertaken, Siger. We must write *every* book. Every one, Siger. We must set down not only the good and wholesome works, the books of theology and the law, the histories, sermons, meditations, pious lives, works of philosophy and rhetoric and mathematics, and all the healing arts. Were this all we had to write, we would be the most favored of men. But our work requires us to seek in the depths of moral and intellectual horror, for we must copy out every subtle heresy, every foul word of blasphemy, every depraved fantasy of greed, and lust, and envy, every dream of revenge and murder and blood, all things warped and hideous and evil that our wicked race will ever conceive. We must foresee all wild imaginings, discoveries, inventions, arts and sciences and wisdom unimagined in our lifetime, and write of farfetched visions and dreamlike powers—of men who swim in the sky and walk beneath the sea and visit other worlds; of creatures the size of cathedrals, and others too small for the eye to see, to whom a drop of water is as a universe; of voices that call across the oceans and continents, eyes that see clearly at great distances, ears that hear the speech of the dead. We must imagine all possible languages, their laws, their sounds, and their alphabets, and all things that the unborn generations will say and write in these tongues, and how, and what responses they will evoke. We must conceive of all other signs and symbols and structures by which ideas may be communicated. We must foresee everything and exhaust all possibilities, writing everything down for all to read."

Kedrigern digested the abbot's words, and with a gesture of

helplessness said, "If you write of evil and depravity and madness, how can Johannes of Octavo say that your motives are good and holy? How will all that help the world's salvation?"

"If we write down all possible things that may be written, we must write of evil as well as good. Surely that is obvious."

"But why must you write any of these things, if they will one day be written by another?"

"We write what *can*, and *may*, be written in the days to come. Our hope is that because we have written these things, others will not write them, nor do them, nor even think of them," said the abbot with a thin, triumphant smile, as though he had at last made the mysterious work of the inner library clear.

As far as Kedrigern was concerned, he had not. "But I repeat, Abbot, why do it at all? There's no certainty that you'll accomplish anything."

"Ah, but there is."

"There is?"

"Know this, Siger of Trondhjem: Before the end of time, all that can be accomplished in thought, word, or act, will be accomplished by the race of man. The end will come only when the world has exhausted all possibilities. This is our belief. By recording minutely and exactly all evil before it is committed, we make it unnecessary for men to practice such things. We would force the world to become good," declared the abbot.

"But if you record all good things, as well . . ."

"Ah, but we will first record the wickedness and the folly. Then, when the world has been purged of evil by our efforts," said Rectoverso, spreading his arms wide, "only then will we write of the good and holy things. As our work draws ever closer to its end, a great quiet will come upon the world, a universal peace as men cease to act, for good or for evil, because all that can be done is already written down and recorded in our library, and there is no longer any need for action or thought. In the end, there will be only the library, with its rows upon rows of books. And they will be sealed away from all eyes, because there will be no longer a need for them, or an interest in their contents. Only a stillness, and quiet, and a waiting for the end." The abbot smiled benignly and raised his eyes to the heavens.

In a sense, this was all reassuring. One of Kedrigern's first impressions of this abbey was that it was well furnished with lunatics, and here was proof. Though not a theologian or a churchman, he knew enough to be certain that the abbey's mission was of highly questionable orthodoxy; most likely, it was the sort of thing that would set an inquisitor to searching eagerly for dry wood and a convenient stake. And yet such intensity, such total dedication, was moving to behold.

"I confess, Abbot, your ideas are new to me. Are they the views of your order?" he asked, knowing well they were the views of no known order but hoping to learn more of their origin.

"We belong to no order here—not those of us who labor at the great mission. The others follow the Rule, they labor and pray, hiding from the truth like all the rest of the world, but we of the inner library . . . we are outcasts all."

"Why do you say 'outcasts'? You've made a free choice to leave the world, haven't you?"

Rectoverso threw back his head and gave a cry that might have been a laugh or a howl of pain. Fixing his deep eyes on Kedrigern's, he said, "We of the inner library are the most wretched of sinners, men fallen and doomed beyond all but the last, most desperate hope. Heretics, murderers, lechers, thieves, swearers of false oaths, worshippers of false gods, we have come together in despair to offer what remains of our miserable lives in atonement for our past. To save this leprous world we have embraced its leprosy. To cleanse it, we wallow in its filth."

In Kedrigern's experience, holy men were wont to describe their lives in just such terms. The more blameless the life, it seemed to him, the more lurid the self-denunciation. And so he was not greatly impressed by Rectoverso's words.

The abbot seemed to sense this. He gripped Kedrigern by the shoulder and said intently, "Those who are lost may deal in matters that would shrivel an ordinary soul. We who have assumed the burden have gathered in one place all the wickedness of the world: Every horror, every abomination, all curses, spells, sorcery, enchantments, all have been sought out and brought within these walls. All that has been set down, and all that ever will be set down, will one day be gathered here, and on that day all men will be free of evil forever. This has been our belief and our strength."

It was hard to fix upon the proper response to such words. Kedrigern asked solicitously, "Is it only those who work in the inner library who share this belief?"

"Yes. We are the monastery within the monastery, the community within the community. There are scores of us. Most remain within the inner walls." Rectoverso raised his arm and pointed a pale hand at the library. "There they eat, sleep, and work, unseen and unknown to the world outside the walls. They are prisoners of their awesome mission. Enervated by the heat of summer, shivering in the winter cold, they work on. Some write, some catalogue, some dig the foundation or carry stone, some bind the finished pages; all labor at the great mission. Their eyes burn, their hands cramp, their backs ache, food is scanty, the work is hard. They suffer in this world, that others might escape suffering in the next. And we are lost, all of us, lost and doomed and damned." He paused, and his voice softened. With genuine feeling, he said, "But Duodecimo was a good man. He was not one of the lost. He should not have died."

In the days that followed, Kedrigern and Traffeo questioned and probed and sifted and conferred, and got nowhere. They had free access to every part of the abbey except the one building that was their goal: Neither of them was permitted to enter the library unless accompanied by the abbot, and the few visits allowed were no more than headlong dashes through a shadowy labyrinth. But even if they had had the run of the library—which they could easily have enjoyed by a small exercise of their powers—they knew that the sheer chaotic abundance of materials and their ignorance of the system under which the books were shelved—if any such system in fact existed—made their chance of finding *The Book of Five Blue Snails* all but infinitesimal. And time was running out.

Then, on the day before their planned departure, as the two wizards were seated silent and despondent in the arbor, Brother Filigrane approached them. Seating himself on the shaded bench opposite theirs, he peered at them closely, and favored them with a benign smile.

"I greet the solvers of the mystery," he said.

"Then you're greeting the wrong people," Traffeo responded sourly. "We've solved no mystery here, and we must leave at dawn tomorrow."

"Looking foolish," Kedrigern added. "I suppose I'd better get used to that."

The old monk's smile was unchanged. "All is a puzzle, all a riddle. I know what you seek, and you seek what I know. Find the clue and solve the riddle and things will be well."

"We're not having much luck with riddles," Traffeo grumbled.

"I give you one more. You must listen carefully: 'Walk on, walk on, walk on. Levitate for eight; lie for an eye; reconsider, too; then languish in solitude. Go over the treetops, under the toadstool, and find what is not to be seen.'"

Filigrane hauled himself up, still smiling, and tottered off under the overarching vines, leaning heavily on his stick, pausing every few steps to draw a deep breath. The wizards looked after him.

"Extraordinary man," Traffeo murmured, shaking his head.

"Extraordinary riddle," Kedrigern observed thoughtfully.

"Odious things, riddles. Waste of time," Traffeo said with a sniff of disapproval.

"Not at all. They sharpen the wits. Sometimes they make the difference between life and death. I must tell you of the curious adventure of the Green Riddler when we're on our way back to Othion," said Kedrigern. His voice faded, and his brow furrowed in concentration. He rubbed his chin and stared off into the distance.

Traffeo subsided into mumbling, then into silence. Kedrigern leaned back, clasped his hands behind his head, and shut his eyes. He turned Filigrane's riddle over and over in his mind. Walk on. Levitate for eight. Lie for an eye. Nonsense.

For an *I*? Reconsider, too. Two? *Two*! He started up with a shout. "It's a map!"

"What? Who?" Traffeo cried, startled.

"The riddle is a map—Filigrane's given us directions!"

"What directions? Where to? What are you talking about?"

"Just think for a moment. We haven't even attempted to get into the library because we know we'll never find our way around it. But Filigrane has just given us a path to follow. Remember all those *l*'s and *r*'s, and the concealed numbers: We're to walk straight ahead to the third aisle, go left to the eighth, left again for one, then right for two and left for one."

"And then, in the middle of the library, we jump over the treetops and crawl under a mushroom. You sound as dotty as old Filigrane."

"I'm not entirely clear about that last part, I confess, but I'm convinced that we've got a set of directions, and tonight I'm going to find out. It's our last chance. Are you with me?"

Traffeo hesitated for a moment, then grudgingly said, "Oh, all right. We have nothing to lose."

Locks are no barrier to wizards. Late that night, Kedrigern and Traffeo entered the library, relocking the great door behind them. Inside, all was pitch-black.

"Can you give us a light?" Kedrigern asked.

"Certainly." Traffeo snapped his fingers and a glow appeared ahead of them, flowing and fluttering at first, then shaping itself into a ball that floated just over their heads, illuminating their surroundings with a soft white light.

"Thank you. I never really mastered that," Kedrigern said.

"No trouble at all. I'll show you the technique. It comes in handy."

They walked to the third aisle and turned left, down a narrow passage between half-empty shelves. The shelves all reached to the ceiling, but no two seemed to be of the same width. The irregular spaces between them created a confusion of paths, but guided by Filigrane's riddle, Kedrigern made his way with assurance. After the last left turn, he found himself facing one side of a massive stone column. Incised in the stone was an Arcadian scene depicting a forested valley ringed by high cliffs.

"Over the treetops," Traffeo whispered excitedly, pointing.

"And under the toadstool," said Kedrigern, reaching up to a stone toadstool, feeling under the cap until his fingers touched a small knob.

He pressed the knob. Without a sound, the cold pastoral swung inward, revealing a flight of steps.

"My congratulations," said Traffeo.

"Never underestimate a riddle. Or an old monk."

"I shall reconsider my position on both. Shall we descend?"

First propping the door open securely with heavy volumes, they made their way down a long curving staircase that led to a vaulted chamber deep below the library. It was square in shape, with the stairs at the center of one wall. An arch opened in each of the other walls, leading to smaller chambers which led to still others. All of these were low-roofed, supported by heavy corner columns, and lined with bookshelves.

"A room inside a room inside a room," Kedrigern said excitedly, recalling Zorsch's words. *"The Book of Five Blue Snails* is down here somewhere, I'm certain of it!"

"Let's make sure we can find our way back," Traffeo said. He spoke a phrase, and the ball of light divided into two, each the size and brightness of the original. One stayed in place while the other moved ahead to light their way.

They explored for about an hour, sometimes separately, sometimes together, the light dividing at each turning. By Kedrigern's calculation, they were now under the inner library, getting close to the excavated area. They came at last to rooms with no outlets, and separated to examine them. As Kedrigern ducked under one archway, he felt a sudden chill envelop him. The light dimmed, flickered, and then began to burn blue. A foul stench in the air made Kedrigern's stomach churn and his mouth water in a sickly way. His head swam. He felt things pawing at his clothing. Slimy fingers groped blindly for his eyes, and something tugged at his legs. He turned to flee, and all the clutching things tried to draw him back. He broke free, and reached the archway with the sensation of a man escaping a closing trap by the narrowest of margins. Never before had he experienced such a sensation of concentrated malevolence.

He leaned back against the cool stone, breathing deeply, gathering his wits, and when he had pulled himself together, he drew out his medallion and viewed the chamber through the Aperture of True Vision. Traffeo came to his side and started forward to enter the chamber. Kedrigern reached out to restrain him.

"Don't go in!"

"What's in there? What happened to you? You look awful!" Traffeo said at sight of Kedrigern's expression.

"That chamber is awash in evil. Those books . . . every book of foul magic I've ever heard of is in that one room . . . and more, many more. No wonder they're buried down here, where no one can chance upon them."

Traffeo gripped Kedrigern's arm in a sudden spasm. He brought the faintly glowing blue light low and pointed to a trail of muddy footprints ending by an empty shelf. "It appears that someone has," he said.

"But how could anyone endure that room? The evil would suffocate . . . unless . . . Oh, dear. Oh, dear me." Kedrigern shuddered and took several deep breaths, like a man struggling against pain. "Unless they're as evil as the things in there," he concluded.

Traffeo moved the light so as to trace the path of the footprints. They led to a corner of the room where the stones of the wall were tumbled to the floor and a black hole opened above them. "A tunnel!" he exclaimed.

Kedrigern nodded weakly. "From the excavation. Someone's been removing these books. The monks who were killed must have learned of it. Rectoverso must be told at once."

The abbot looked at them with tormented eyes. "It cannot be. It must not be! The work . . . think of our mission! How could a man dedicated to saving future generations from evil commit such wicked deeds?" His words were steadfast and assured, but he spoke with the voice of a general who sees his forces break and fly before the enemy.

"You yourself characterized the workers of the inner library as desperate men steeped in evil. Maybe one of them is even more wicked than you imagined. This might have been planned all along."

"No! Our aim was to sacrifice our worthless souls for future generations . . . to do good, not add to the evil."

Kedrigern tried a different tack. "What if someone started out believing that, but in his gropings came upon the secret of the Philosopher's Stone, or the elixir of life? Perhaps someone came upon something so totally unimaginable that it blasted his mind!"

"They might be possessed!" cried the abbot in sudden horror. "I should have foreseen this. We ventured too far, and now we are damned beyond the last hope of mercy."

"You have to do something. You're the abbot, and it's your duty," said Kedrigern, hauling the unresisting Rectoverso to his feet and pushing him from the cell.

"What can I do?" the abbot said in a dull voice as he stumbled out like a man on his way to the scaffold. "I am more damned than all the rest. You were right to call our plan a mad one. I am steeped in vanity, corrupted by falsehood. I am immersed in heresy, and the fruits of my sin are all about me. I have brought evil and death to what should have been a holy work."

"You can repent, can't you?" Kedrigern snapped impatiently, urging the abbot on.

Rectoverso stopped in his tracks. He turned and gazed wildly on the two men, then embraced them warmly, tears in his eyes as he cried, "I can! I do! I repent all my vain folly, I abjure my heresy! I have done evil, but I can yet undo it!" He wiped his eyes, laughing aloud, a pleased, childlike laugh of sheer joy and deliverance, and then he darted off.

"Where are you going?"

"To the church! The brothers are at Lauds. I will join them, and pray for guidance and strength," the abbot replied without turning.

"But it's almost dawn!" Kedrigern cried, undecided which direction to take, torn between his relief and encouragement at the abbot's regeneration and his anxiety to get at once to the heart of the mystery, his confusion compounded by the night's exertions and his lack of sleep. Rectoverso strode to the church without a backward glance, his hands raised to the heavens as he cried, "Dawn! Yes, it is indeed dawn! Rebirth! A new life!"

With a gesture of surrender, followed by a wrenching yawn, Kedrigern fell in behind him, Traffeo at his side. They dropped on the steps to await the abbot's reappearance, too tired even to groan. Kedrigern turned his thoughts to the night's discoveries. Some of the mysteries had been solved, but not all; by no means all. It was fairly clear in his mind now why the five monks had been murdered, but that brought them no closer to the murderer. And the cause of it all was still obscure. Had the monks indeed been maddened by some creation of their own labors, or had there been a long-standing plot to possess the diabolical books, brought to a head by the excavation? Had a few laborers come upon the buried room by chance, in their digging, and succumbed to the evil that pervaded its atmosphere? Could it be that outsiders had penetrated the abbey disguised as workers, or even insinuated themselves among the monks? And if so... if so... His thoughts became entangled in a web of speculations. What if *The Book of Five Blue Snails* had been stolen? From Zorsch's description, it was an object to catch the eye, even of one who could have no conception of its contents. Perhaps now, with the mystery of the dead monks near a solution, he would finally be given access to those deep chambers, led to the proper shelf by the grateful Rectoverso, only to find... No, no. It was not to be thought of. There was still a chance that he could keep his promise to Ithian, but time was rapidly running out, and he was tired. So very tired...

A touch on his shoulder brought him awake in an instant. He looked up to see the abbot looming over him in the faint gray light of dawn.

"Come. I am ready," said Rectoverso.

Kedrigern drew himself up, stiff in neck, back, and limbs, and groaned at the pangs brought on by movement; stone steps were not the place to sleep on a chilly morning. Traffeo's groans echoed his.

Rectoverso laid a bony hand on Kedrigern's shoulder and

smiled down at him with a benevolence that transfigured his spare features. "It was you who urged me to repent. I thank you, Siger," he said.

"I'm glad I was able to help. But we must hurry . . . the tunnel . . ."

Rectoverso's hand held him in place. "I owe you much. I have been foolish, and suspicious, and treated you ill. But now, Siger, you need only name your reward, and I will—"

"Give us *The Book of Five Blue Snails*!" Kedrigern and Traffeo cried with one voice.

"It is yours. And any other volume you request. Whole shelves of volumes! Now, let us . . ."

Rectoverso paused as the ground shuddered beneath their feet. From the direction of the library came a deep reverberating groan that grew in volume until it echoed from every wall and set trees and vines to swaying. Still it grew, a sound now like the rending of forests, the rush of an avalanche, the grinding of mountain upon mountain. A tumbling column of dust curled into the sky over the library, rolling and churning, geysering upward to darken the still morning air. It spread like a shroud over the astonished monks, who gazed up as if thunderstruck, or fell to their knees, or stared dumbly at one another, and as the roar subsided and the turbulence of the dust cloud slowed, the exclamations of the monks filled the silence.

Kedrigern cleared his throat and swallowed audibly. In a subdued voice, he said to the abbot, "I'm glad you decided to pray."

There was no longer any reason for haste. Kedrigern and Traffeo did what they could to help, but it was obvious that there was little anyone could do. Flesh and bone could not have survived that cataclysm.

The morning sped past. In the afternoon, when the dust had settled, the abbot and the two wizards stood overlooking the ruin. Where there had been a great edifice there was now emptiness. From the raw edge of the new-formed cliff one could see over range after range of hills to the far mountains, beyond which lay Othion, and, for Kedrigern, humiliation. He stepped back from the brink and pulled his cloak close against the fresh north wind.

"What could have brought this about?" Rectoverso asked softly, gazing down into the void.

"A fault in the rock. A subterranean chasm. A flaw in the design," Traffeo suggested without discernible conviction.

"We will never know," said the abbot.

"Never," Kedrigern echoed.

All that they could determine was that the hillside had suddenly burst open to spew a cascade of earth and stone down the steep outer slope. Loose dirt had flowed into the expanding mouth of the excavation, undermining the foundations of the inner library and causing its collapse. This, in turn, accelerated the cave-in, weakening the walls of the outer library and bringing it down. The labor of generations had been reduced to rubble in minutes.

"There's no need to know, is there? It's all over now. At least you can rebuild, and forget the past," said Kedrigern.

"The deconstruction went far beyond our expectations."

"Perhaps the next library should be simpler. A surface structure—no need for all those levels. They just confuse things," Traffeo said.

They turned to make their way to the stables, where the horses were saddled and waiting. The abbot said, "We are grateful to you, Siger."

"I did nothing, Abbot."

"You awoke me."

William of Primofolio awaited them at the stable door. He held a small bundle in his hands. It was wrapped in cloth, and gave off a delicious aroma.

"Our new cellarer has prepared a parting gift for you," said the abbot.

William handed the bundle to Kedrigern, who drew back the white napkin and inhaled deeply. "Onion rolls!" he exclaimed in delight. "Since my childhood, I have had a fondness for onion rolls. You are most kind."

The abbot walked with them to the entrance, and when the travelers had mounted, and the doorkeeper swung the heavy door wide, he said, "Go with our thanks and our blessings, Siger and Hamish."

"Our thanks to you and William. This bread is truly a baker's treat."

"Irregular, perhaps," said the abbot, smiling. "But well deserved."

⋯❁ *Fourteen* ❁⋯

endgame

THE BLACK JESTER did not press his attack. He chose instead to develop his queen's side of the board. Princess, more cautious now, tried to contain his advance while developing her own pieces, all the while worrying about the sacrifices that lay inevitably ahead.

The game could not be won without the loss of pieces, she knew. She remembered all too clearly games that had come down to two kings and a single pawn, and every other piece swept from the board. But how, she asked herself, could she send these brave, unfortunate people to their doom? It was one thing to sacrifice a bit of wood or ivory, quite another to send a man or woman to certain death. And yet, victory in this game seemed to be the only hope of release for the enchanted pieces. Without certain knowledge of the spell placed on them, Princess was loath to attempt a disenchantment. It was too risky. They might be released, but they might, on the other hand, be turned into dominoes. No, she had to play for a win. It was their only hope. But the price was dreadful to contemplate.

And what was she to tell Berzel, and when, and how?

Would the poor girl collapse at the announcement that she was at risk of being turned into a chess piece, and eventually slain *en passant*, or in a fruitless gambit? It seemed inadvisable to tell her, yet cruel to conceal the truth. And what of her own magical powers—should she use them now, or hold them in reserve against a greater peril? If the Black Jester was as powerful as the bishop described him, he might be able to brush her strongest spell aside and inflict some dreadful penalty on everyone. It was yet another dilemma.

Her opponent took the decision out of her hands when, a few moves later, his bishop took her knight. She retaliated at once with a pawn. As the bishop dragged himself off the board, to collapse at the side, a black pawn struck down the avenging white piece.

Settle down, settle down, said the surviving knight when the exchange was over. *They may have come out a bit ahead on this skirmish, but we got that fraudulent bishop.*

He got what he deserved, a pawn said.

No shame at all, that one. Imagine him posing as a man of the cloth! said another.

"Your Excellency, wasn't the bishop really a bishop?" Princess asked her own queen's bishop.

He was not, my lady. We white pieces are what we appear to be. The king's bishop and I are truly bishops. The king and queen are true royalty. The knights are true knights. The pawns are yeomen, pilgrims, servants, itinerant craftsmen . . . I have even known of lost children forced to play.

"Lost children? Oh, how dreadful!"

Indeed it is. But the black pieces are a collection of ruffians, knaves, cutpurses, brigands, blackguards, reprobates, footpads, and picaroons. The deceased bishop, for example, was a notorious robber known, for reasons that are not clear to me, as Freddie the Nose. The black king's bishop is an even more unsavory fellow, and the knights are scoundrels. As for the king and queen . . . I will say no more than that they are persons of a class my lady is unlikely ever to meet by choice.

"What about the rooks?"

*They are castles . . . well, let us call them rather watch-
towers, my lady, constructed by masons who later served as
pawns.*

At the side of the board, the black bishop shuddered and
breathed his last. The Black Jester rose with a desolate cry and
howled, "Fred, old comrade, they'll pay for this! I won't
leave a piece on the board but their king, and I'll make him
hop before I'm done with him, I promise you!"

This was too much for Princess to endure in silence. In a fit
of rage, she sprang to her feet and cried, "You miserable hyp-
ocrite! It's your fault he's dead, and my men, too! It's all
because of your stupid game and your own nasty magic!"

Drawing himself up, the Black Jester said haughtily, "My
dear lady, there is no need for a scene. The game must go on.
Fred knew that, and accepted it like the brave fellow he was. I
will weep for him if I choose."

"What about my knight and pawn? They were decent
men, not like your wretched Freddie the Nose. You should
be weeping and wailing for them, not for some sneaking
villain."

"You are heartless, madam. Fred was a poor unfortunate, a
victim of society, a strayed lamb. It is only a slight exaggera-
tion to say that Fred could steal the saddle from under a rider
on a fast horse, and himself on foot, going the other way. And
this gifted man, this great talent—yes, I dare say this genius
—was besmirched with the name *thief*. He was hounded,
driven, persecuted."

"He's lucky he wasn't hanged," said Princess.

"O heart of ice," the Black Jester said, raising a hand to his
forehead and staggering back a pace. "I cannot let him pass
unsung. I shall compose an epitaph. I shall compose several
epitaphs," he rasped dramatically.

"Go ahead. While you're at it, I'll prepare a eulogy for my
two good men. *They* deserve it."

The Black Jester took up a black lute that lay against the
rail. He struck a chord, cleared his throat, struck another
chord, and announced, "My first epitaph for Fred will be phil-
osophical in tone, a comment on man's fate and the universal

human condition." He began to sing, in a high, thin, grating voice that was very unpleasant to hear.

> "There's really nothing wrong with Fred—
> He merely happens to be dead.
> I know that you (and fear that I)
> And everybody else must die,
> And everything that lives must do it.
> Fred has simply beat us to it."

Berzel, perplexed, turned to Princess and asked, "What's this all about? I don't understand what's going on. Who's Fred?"

"There's something you ought to know, Berzel dear," said Princess, taking her hand. "The Black Jester is lamenting the death of his bishop."

"A bishop named Fred?"

"I'll explain it all later."

"But people don't cry over chess pieces, do they?"

"The bishop was a real human being. Not a very nice one, but a living man all the same. So were our knight and pawn. All these pieces are real people under an enchantment," Princess said.

"Oh, then we can't go on! It would be too awful!"

"We must, Berzel dear. If we win this game, they'll all go free."

Striking another chord, the Black Jester said, "My second epitaph for dear good Fred will be materialistic in tone, rejecting easy sympathy and cheap feeling, looking with a cold eye on life and death and offering a practical course of conduct." He now recited in a dull monotone:

> "Alas, poor Fred. I knew him well . . .
> He lies quite still, and makes no sound.
> Before long, he'll begin to smell.
> I think he should be underground."

Berzel, who had remained politely silent, though fidgety, during the recitation, asked, "What if we lose?"

"Then they don't go free, and neither do we."

As Berzel absorbed that bit of information, the Black Jester said, "My third epitaph for dear departed Fred, a man who enjoyed wit and banter and persiflage, will be light and playful, laughing at death, embracing a gay frivolity in the true *carpe diem* spirit." He strummed a lively introduction and sang:

> "Fred, who used to live nearby,
> Took it in his head to die.
> 'What a thing to do!' we said,
> Shrugged, and thought no more of Fred."

"I hope no one composes things like that about me when I'm gone. Promise me you won't do it, Princess dear."

"I wouldn't dream of it. They're dreadful. Totally insensitive. Crude. Extremely distasteful."

"They do rhyme well," Berzel pointed out. "But dear Princess, what do you mean by saying we won't go free? What will become of us?"

"Don't worry. He's not going to turn us into chess pieces," Princess said, setting her jaw.

"I conclude my epitaphs on a personal note, with a song from the heart, a poignant lament of friend for friend, of tragic loss and manly grief," said the Black Jester. He laid the lute aside, and in a harsh recitative, sang:

> "Fred, they said, is dead. I shed
> A tear to hear. So near and dear
> A chum become so dumb! Now, glum
> And pale, I fail, I wail. So frail
> A lad! How sad! Too bad! Oh, had
> I skill and will, I'd fill the chill
> Bleak air with rare despair, and share
> My pain and bane. Again, in vain
> I try. I sigh, I cry . . . oh, why
> Snuff out this stout old scout? I doubt

My art can chart my heart. Depart,
Then, friend! Ascend! Transcend!
                                  The end."

"He was better when he was being crude and insensitive,"
Princess said under her breath.

"Princess dear, *why* would the Black Jester want to turn us
into chess pieces?" Berzel inquired. She enunciated very carefully, and spoke with the taut, controlled voice of one who
fears her voice will crack at any word.

"I have no idea. But if he tries, he won't get away with
it, I promise you. Now you must excuse me," Princess said,
as she turned to address the bishop. "Your excellency,
would you mind saying a few words over our departed
pieces?"

I am honored to do so, my lady, said the bishop, and delivered an impromptu eulogy of great sensitivity and taste.

With the obsequies completed, play resumed. Other
pieces fell, and were mourned, and as the middle game
progressed, advantage shifted back and forth ever so
slightly. Neither Princess nor the Black Jester could gain a
clear advantage. Before the fortieth move, their forces had
come to nearly exact parity. Each had five pawns, queen,
and rook surviving to protect their king. White had a single
bishop, black a single knight. Then, suddenly, Princess per-
ceived that she was in danger. As she studied the board
closely, she saw, with a sinking heart, that she could not
hope to win. But all was not lost. Her mind was working
furiously, and past games were coming back to her memory.
She saw a chance.

"Your move, my lady. You seem to be in no hurry. Are you
weary? Or are you tasting the inevitability of defeat?" the
Black Jester asked.

"Defeat? By you? What a silly idea," said Princess with a
little laugh, moving her rook to queen's bishop seven.

The Black Jester observed the move, frowned, and looked
at her closely, but said nothing. The pieces were now disposed
thusly:

"You don't seem in much of a hurry, either. Worn out from all that singing and reciting, are you?" Princess asked.

"I am filled with energy, madam," the Black Jester snapped, and moved his own rook to queen eight, pinning the king's bishop.

Princess countered with rook to bishop four, forestalling an attack by the black queen that would have led to further slaughter, and putting black's surviving knight in danger. Her opponent, after a careful survey of the situation, looked at her in unconcealed annoyance. His knight lurched to the edge of the board, landing on the rook's sixth square and putting the white king in check. Princess turned to Berzel and winked. Her plan was working. She brought the white king to knight two. He went slowly, grumbling all the way. The black queen swept along the diagonal and struck down the knight's pawn, an inoffensive chap who had harmed no one and had scarcely spoken a word throughout the entire game. Again, the white king was in check. His bishop moved one square, to king two, and looking down the open file, nodded to his queen, who returned the greeting with a regal wave of the hand.

Not to worry, Your Excellency. We've got our eye on you, she cried.

I am grateful for Your Majesty's protection, the bishop replied.

The Black Jester continued the attack, this time by bringing his rook to knight eight, again placing the king in check. His Majesty moved to one side, quickly and nimbly this time, without a word of complaint. Only when he was safe on his new square did he frown at the black pieces on adjoining squares and mutter, *Where is that woman off to? Who let this riffraff in here? What's it all coming to?*

With a groaning of stone and creaking of timber, the rook pursued the king, moving to rook eight, again placing him in check. Princess heaved a great sigh and wiped her brow.

"Princess dear, our king's in check again. What are we to do?" Berzel asked with just a trace of uneasiness in her voice.

Returning the king to the square he had just vacated, Princess smiled and said, "We are to celebrate, Berzel. We've just managed a draw."

"Is that good?"

"It's a lot better than losing, and for a while there, I thought I had lost. I'll take a draw."

Berzel nodded, looking much relieved. Across from them, the Black Jester frowned down on the board. "If I check with my rook, your king will simply keep skipping back and forth. It's perpetual check," he said peevishly.

"So it is, and that means the game is a draw. Set those people free, and we'll all be on our way," said Princess, rising and smoothing her gown. She began to turn down her sleeves.

"Free? I will set no one free."

"You certainly will. You didn't win."

"Nor did I lose, my lady. We will play again until one of us is victorious. Meanwhile, you are my guests."

"We do not wish to be your guests. Not if you turn your guests into pawns and bishops and knights," Berzel said, her eyes flashing.

"Well put, Berzel dear."

"If my guests are turned into chessmen, my dear young lady, it is no one's fault but their own. They should not play chess if they are not masters of the game," said the Black Jester grandly.

"Neither should you," Princess said with a smile.

"My lady is witty. She would be wise to save her wit for our next game."

"There will be no next game, you evil man."

"There will be, my dear ladies. And in the next game, you shall be either players or pawns. The choice is yours," said the Black Jester. He turned and stalked from the chess pavilion.

Days passed, and Princess and Berzel deliberated over their predicament, going back and forth and back again, weighing every argument, considering every objection, and finding it impossible to decide on the proper course of action. To play was to become a participant—however reluctantly—in this nasty business; to refuse was to become a victim. But perhaps it was better, finer, nobler, to accept one's fate with brave dignity rather than compromise with evil. They were princesses, and *noblesse*, after all, *oblige*.

On the other hand, *noblesse oblige* works two ways: Might not their rank require them to take an active part in overthrowing the Black Jester? Princess had played him to a draw, and in playing, she had observed his weaknesses. If she beat him next time, his power would be broken and his victims freed.

His surviving victims, she quickly corrected herself. Some would fall because of choices she made. Under such conditions, could she play her best game? She pondered this question, and soon was asking herself if she might not play as she had never played before, with so much at stake. It was a quandary.

Sometimes, when she had argued herself into a corner, Princess was tempted to fall back on her magic. But she was still fairly new at it, especially use of the wand, and the Black Jester was obviously a sorcerer of considerable power. His treatment of his guests—prisoners, if he had an ounce of truth in him—was proof of that. There were no locks on the doors, no bars on the windows, no physical restraints of any kind on Princess and Berzel. They had total freedom of the house and grounds. Naturally, the first thing they had done after the drawn game was make for the road; but Princess felt the warning tingle of magic when they were scarcely thirty paces down the avenue of yew trees. It was a one-way spell. Anyone could enter, no one could leave.

She returned to the manor house in a somber mood. To keep up a powerful enclosing spell and at the same time maintain thirty-two people as chess pieces, at least half of them against their will, was very impressive workmanship. And she did not doubt that the Black Jester had a few other enchantments in operation here, as well. Her powers would have to be used very cautiously, if at all.

As the days went by, and the waxing moon brightened the nights, a new hope occurred to Princess: If she could hold off the next game until after the full moon, Berzel's misfortune might be turned to their advantage. How, she did not know; but the sudden appearance of a werewolf was bound to have an effect on things, and any change in the situation was likely to be an improvement.

For eight full days the Black Jester left Princess and Berzel undisturbed. On the ninth he announced his intention of playing chess the following day. Princess, feigning illness, asked for a delay of three days to recover her strength and her wits. The Black Jester refused. She insisted. He stood firm. She pleaded. He relented and allowed an extra day. She reeled, collapsed into a chair, and weakly called for three. He compromised and allowed two, but would yield no further. Princess gave a wan sigh of acquiescence, waved a limp hand, and languished in the chair, with Berzel at her side, making soothing sounds as she chafed a wrist. Once the door closed behind the Black Jester, Princess sprang up and began to pace the floor.

"One day more. That's all we need, just one day more," she said in great agitation.

"Whatever for, Princess dear?" Berzel asked, her eyes wide, lips parted in an expression of sisterly solicitude.

"In three days, you'll turn into a werewolf."

Berzel blinked, startled. "So I shall," she said wonderingly. "In all the excitement, I'd completely forgotten. Shouldn't we tell someone?"

"I don't think that would be a good idea. Let's have it come as a surprise to our host."

"Will that help us?"

"I'm not sure, but it can't hurt." Princess paced the length of the room twice, hands clasped behind her, then paused and flung up a hand, forefinger pointing skyward in a gesture of sudden illumination. "The sight of you as a wolf may be enough to frighten the Black Jester into releasing us and the others."

"I don't like to frighten people, Princess dear. Not even that dreadful man. I just don't have it in me."

"You may feel differently when you're a wolf."

"I don't think so. Everyone says I'm very playful. I just frisk and romp and chase my tail. I'd never hurt anybody intentionally."

"The Black Jester doesn't know that. You could menace him a little," Princess suggested.

"I'm not a menacing type of person."

"Give it a try. Even if you don't scare him into letting us go, you might shake him up enough so that some of his spells will slip, and then I can hit him with a spell of my own."

"What if he tries to destroy me?"

"He wouldn't dare. You're a princess."

"He might consider me a wolf," said Berzel. She was beginning to sound concerned.

"I won't let him hurt you," Princess said, patting Berzel's head fondly. She resumed her pacing, muttering, "If only we could get one more day's delay."

Try as they might, they could not squeeze even an hour's additional time from the Black Jester. Having once granted a concession, he was doubly adamant. On the morning of the appointed day, Princess and Berzel were conducted to the pavilion, where they took their places.

"How kind of you to join me," said the Black Jester with a mocking smile and an exaggerated bow.

"We are still very weak. We need another day of rest," said Princess faintly, as Berzel fanned her with a scented handkerchief.

"Just one more day," Berzel said plaintively.

"Not one more minute, my dear ladies."

"We are princesses. We are frail and ethereal creatures, so delicate and sensitive that we can be dazzled by a moonbeam, bruised by a cobweb, stunned by the brush of a butterfly's wing. Our recent ordeal has left us exhausted, and we require time to recover our powers," said Princess in a voice barely audible.

"No more of this. It is time to play," said the Black Jester.

The pieces saluted her. Princess recognized the king and queen, a bishop and knight, and several pawns. The rest of the pieces were new recruits. Where they had come from she had no idea. Probably the dungeons. She waved to them, feeling a terrible sense of inadequacy, and rose to address them. She hated to make speeches, but anything that would take up time was essential.

"Come, come, let us commence," said the Black Jester.

"I wish to address my pieces."

"How very touching. Be brief, madam."

Brief, my foot, thought Princess. She was determined to draw this game out as long as she could. The moon would be full that night, and if she could last until then, they had a chance.

She delivered a stirring allocution full of references to great heroes of epic and saga, calls to duty and loyalty, examples of camaraderie, hallowed traditions, bold feats, and gallant sacrifices. When at last, with rasping voice, she resumed her seat, the white pieces gave a great cheer. The pawns shouted her name over and over until the knights had to quiet them down, and the queen bawled out *Brave girl!* Even the king mumbled something that sounded like *Bit of all right. Not half bad.*

And then there was nothing for it but to move her pawn to queen four. The Black Jester quickly answered with his own pawn to king four. Princess rested her chin on the palm of her hand and studied the board.

"My lady, you dawdle," said the Black Jester.

"I'm thinking."

"This is overmuch consideration for the second move. If you attempt to waste time, I shall—"

A servant who had entered on silent feet came to his master's side and whispered a message. The Black Jester listened carefully, nodded thoughtfully, and dismissed the man. He smirked at Princess and Berzel.

"It seems there will be a delay after all. A visitor has arrived. Perhaps he can be persuaded to join our game," he said.

"I'm sure you'll do your best to persuade him," said Princess. "Let me see the man. If he's not some low scoundrel, he might make a worthy addition to my forces."

"It is most encouraging to see you enter into the spirit of the game, my lady. He might indeed. Some of your pawns are rather too undisciplined for my liking." He rose and gestured toward the door. "Come, let us examine this newcomer."

They walked to the foyer, and there stood Zorsch. He had a considerable growth of beard, and his clothing was something the worse for travel, but he was a welcome sight to Princess. Judging from his reaction, she was an equally welcome sight to him.

"My lady! You're safe!" he cried, falling to one knee before her.

"Zorsch! You're here!" she exclaimed.

The Black Jester glanced from one to the other with narrow, suspicious eyes. "Is this man known to you?"

"Yes. Zorsch . . ." Princess was about to identify Zorsch as her loyal and trusted servant when she realized that to do so was to doom him to pawnhood and a very chancy future. She hesitated, clearing her throat to cover her confusion.

"Well? Who is the fellow" the Black Jester demanded.

"He's my chess tutor!" cried Princess, in a moment of inspiration. "He's quite brilliant. He could play you a game you'd never forget."

"I could?" Zorsch asked, blinking.

"Don't be modest. You're a master chess player and you know it," Princess said in a no-nonsense-from-you voice.

Zorsch bowed. "If my lady says so."

The Black Jester looked on, lips pursed and brow furrowed as he took the measure of this news. At length, he murmured, "This might prove interesting."

"Oh, fascinating. You must allow me to consult with my tutor. It's only fair," Princess said.

"Fairness is no concern of mine."

"It would also make for a more exciting game."

"*That* concerns me. Yes, it might. Indeed it might." The Black Jester studied Zorsch for a moment, then made his pronouncement. "He may assist you, my lady. Come, let us return at once to the game."

"I cannot allow this," said Princess imperiously. "The man is no pawn, he is a master player. He is hungry and thirsty. He needs a rest and a change of clothing. I will not have him rushed into play in this condition."

"Again you seek to delay."

Princess folded her arms and regarded him icily. "I require playing conditions proper to my rank. If you are unable to provide them, clown, there can be no game."

She was pressing her luck, attacking the Black Jester's pride, trusting to his desire to avenge the drawn game. It was all a grand improvisation. She still had no clear plan, but Zorsch's arrival had given her the chance of besetting her captor with two werewolves instead of one, and made delay of the game essential, whatever the risk.

The Black Jester glared at them, then he leered. "Very well. Let him be fed. Let him bathe in scented waters. Dress him in suitable raiment. And let him be prepared to play this very night, at moonrise."

Princess gestured carelessly. "As you wish," she said.

As they entered the chess pavilion that evening, Princess was composed. She had a plan, to which her companions were agreeable.

In plain dark robes, Zorsch looked quite elegant. Berzel appeared to be very much interested in him, and he in her.

On Princess's advice, Berzel had taken to doing her hair in a different and much more becoming way. The color of her dress was still hopeless, but Princess had put one of the servants to work on it and now it at least fit properly. A colorful sash taken from a table covering made a distinct improvement. All things considered, Berzel was now a very attractive young woman. Though it was hardly a time for sweet dalliance, the glances exchanged between her and Zorsch communicated something more than a temporary alliance.

They took their places. The pawns still confronted one another, queen's pawn glaring sidelong at black king's pawn, the other pieces on their home squares, awaiting the summons to battle.

"Your move, my lady. I trust it will be speedy. You have had ample time to think about it," said the Black Jester.

Princess looked out the window. The moon was full, mottled white in the cloudless sky.

"It's almost time," Zorsch whispered.

"Yes. Only a few minutes now," Berzel said.

Princess rose. "My tutor has reminded me of a tradition among the great masters of the game. He would pay his respects to you in person before I make my move."

"Very well. Let him be quick about it."

"I will accompany him," said Berzel, stepping forward.

They crossed to the Black Jester's place. Berzel curtseyed at his right hand, Zorsch bowed at his left. He acknowledged them with a nod and dismissed them with a wave of the hand, eager to resume play. They stepped back, out of his sight, and before Princess's eyes, very quickly and without fuss, turned into large wolves. For just a moment they remained on their haunches, as if adjusting to their new configuration, and then they padded forward on silent paws.

The Black Jester gave a wild cry of alarm. The pieces on the board wavered. Princess put everything she had into an instantaneous paralyzing spell. The Black Jester froze in his seat, rigid as stone but nonetheless vulnerable as ordinary flesh and blood—and presumably just as appetizing to hungry wolves. Princess took wing and perched on a beam over his

head. She was not certain how Berzel and Zorsch would behave toward her in their wolf mode, and was taking no
chances. She had a feeling that things were going to get pretty
lively in a short time.

"I have a proposition for you, clown. Release everyone and
end the plight of these two werewolves, and I will restrain
them from tearing you to bits," she said. Zorsch put his fore-
paws on the Black Jester's arm and sniffed with interest at his
throat. "I'll let you speak now. If you try any tricks . . . well,
don't," she concluded.

"I won't! I mean I *will*! I'll do as you ask, I mean, only
keep them back!" the Black Jester said in a terrified, hoarse
whisper.

"I'll do what I can. You'd better hurry."

"I'm hurrying! It will take all my power to break a lycanthropy!"

"Then use it. Quickly, now."

"I'll be helpless," the Black Jester whined.

"Good. That will keep you out of mischief."

"Save me from the others! If the wolves don't tear me
apart, my prisoners will!"

"You will be in my custody. Now, get to work."

While the Black Jester attended to Berzel and Zorsch,
Princess watched with amusement and satisfaction the scene
on the chessboard. The enchantment was broken now, and the
two sides faced each other unrestrained by the rules of the
game. Their human outlines began to appear, slowly and
vaguely, but their human faculties returned to them at once.
As soon as the initial surprise had worn off, her queen's pawn
punched the black king's pawn, knocking him down, and several other pawns dashed forward to assist each of them. The
knights were quick to follow. Soon a thorough donnybrook
was in progress in the middle of the pavilion.

"Haul them in! Throw them in chains!" the white queen
bellowed, shaking her fists.

Her counterpart, a flamboyant, bejeweled woman in a
gaudy gown of questionable taste, shrilled, "Shut your mouth,
you horse-faced old harpy!" and the former black king, a great
scar-faced ruffian in a tattered cloak and worn boots, growled,

"Mind your business, you blabby bint, before I blacks your eyes for you!"

"Seize that man!" the white queen howled, and one of the knights lunged for the offender.

"Confounded noise," the white king grumbled, waddling off to a quiet corner. "Bunch of riffraff. Rabble."

"Hop it, lads! The game's up!" cried the erstwhile black king as he made for the door, his doxy clinging to his thick arm and the rest of his pieces close behind, flailing out wildly to cover their flight.

With the white forces victorious, Princess returned her attention to the Black Jester's efforts just at the moment of their successful completion. Berzel and Zorsch stood on either side of him, stunned—but only for an instant. With a cry of triumph, Zorsch rushed to Berzel's waiting arms, and they joined in a passionate embrace. Princess brushed her hands together, pleased with a job so well done, and fluttered down to stand before the vanquished jester.

"Protect me. You promised you would. I'm powerless now," he said in a quavering voice.

"You will be thrown in a dungeon until we decide what to do with you."

"Be merciful!" he wailed, raising clasped hands.

"Merciful? To you? You've behaved like an absolute monster," she replied severely.

"I didn't mean to. I didn't start out to be a monster."

"Well, that's where you ended, and you'll pay for it."

"All I ever wanted was to make people laugh. I only wanted to be funny. I could never get the hang of it."

"The first thing you should have done was get yourself a different outfit. Jesters don't wear black."

"I wanted to be unique."

"You are. But you're not funny."

"If people had only laughed, I would have been nice to them. That's what led me to sorcery—I was looking for a spell to make people laugh," he said bitterly.

"I don't believe there is one."

"Neither do I, now. But by the time I realized, I was a pretty good hand at sorcery. So I decided if I couldn't make people happy, I'd make them miserable."

"Well, you succeeded at that. All right, get along. You can move now, so move," said Princess. She summoned a knight, who took a firm grip on the Black Jester's neck. "Put him in a dungeon, and see that no one molests him. We'll settle his fate tomorrow."

"Right away, my lady. Come on, you," said the knight, hauling the moaning prisoner off.

Princess set the other knight and four husky pawns to rounding up the Black Jester's household staff and making certain that the reconstituted black pieces were off the premises. As they went about their task, the rest of her forces gathered around her, chatting cheerfully, laughing, exuberant at the thought of their deliverance. The pawns thanked her, the bishops blessed her, and then they parted to admit the queen.

"Well done," said the queen, thumping Princess on the back. "Good organizing, too. You'll put this place to rights. Just one thing you overlooked."

"What's that, Your Majesty?"

"Victory dinner! Get them cracking!"

···❧ Fifteen ❧···

salvage operations

KEDRIGERN AND TRAFFEO rode at a slow pace that day, speaking seldom and then only in melancholy monosyllables and disgruntled phrases. Traffeo tried to encourage his fellow wizard, but Kedrigern was steeped in gloom. He had staked everything on *The Book of Five Blue Snails*, and now that volume was forever lost. As was his name in Othion. And everywhere else, once Ithian got to work. There would be joy and gloating among his enemies. Alchemists the world over would rejoice. Kedrigern the Boastful: That would be his title in the profession from now on, for a century, at least. Kedrigern the Failure. Kedrigern the Joke.

There would be no more favors for ingrate kings, that was certain, he promised himself angrily. He realized at once that there would be very few requests, from kings or anyone else, in the days to come.

It would be worse for Princess, he reflected guiltily. She liked making house calls, visiting distant clients, meeting people, seeing things. There would be no more of that for a long time. Their traveling days were over. That was some consolation, and his spirits lifted slightly, but drooped again at the thought of Princess's disappointment. Bad times lay ahead for both of them, no doubt about it, and all because of his rashness.

At Traffeo's insistence, they camped early in a tree-shaded corner of a flowery meadow, with a merry brook of cold sweet water bubbling musically by. They dined on garlic sausages and thick chunks of onion roll spread with a savory butter of pounded chestnuts, all of it washed down with drafts of dry red wine and sips of cold brook water. Traffeo built a cozy fire, and regaled Kedrigern with stories of his stay in the castle of Otranto. Nothing helped. Kedrigern was beyond encouragement. He gazed into the fire, responding to questions with a grunt or a shake of the head or a sigh, and lay awake late into the night, staring up at the gibbous moon.

He rose late next morning, and moved languidly to break camp and pack. They had lost time, and were behind their schedule; even hard riding could not get them back to Othion before the full moon. Kedrigern did not care. He saw no point in exhausting himself and his horse for no better purpose than to witness Berzel's transformation and make himself available for insults. If one is going to skulk through the gates of Othion in disgrace, he reasoned, one may as well skulk through a day or two late and miss a few snide remarks.

They moped and dawdled and plodded on. As they rested by the roadside in the afternoon, Traffeo nudged Kedrigern and pointed to a ragged figure scurrying up the road from the direction they had come. It was a peasant, unspeakably filthy and tattered, and when he saw the two travelers he gave a start and jittered about, uncertain whether to retreat, flee into the woods, or confront them. He clutched a ragged bundle to his chest and made wild, frightened noises.

"The fellow looks absolutely terrified," Traffeo said.

Kedrigern sighed. "Peasants usually do. He's probably fleeing from some shameful situation. Poor soul. I'll give him a coin. I may be a failure, but I can still be generous." He rose and beckoned to the figure.

With hesitant sidelong steps, the man shuffled nearer, watching the two fearfully, wide-eyed, ready to bolt at the first threatening move. Kedrigern smiled a wan smile and held up a bright coin. The peasant sidled closer, making snuffling noises.

"Here, you poor unfortunate. Take this," said Kedrigern, extending his open hand, the coin on his palm.

The peasant leapt back in terror. "Didn't take!" he cried. "Skirp good boy! Doesn't steal!"

"Of course not. No one says you stole anything," the wizard said, gently, in his most reassuring voice.

"Didn't take," Skirp repeated. "Dropped from the sky, they did." He made a wet, blubbering noise, his phonetic impression of a flying sound, and waved one arm overhead. "From the sky." He repeated the blubbering noise, louder this time, and asked, "You buy?"

"What have you got?" Traffeo asked.

"Birds! From the sky!"

"We could have one for dinner," Kedrigern suggested. "How many do you have, Skirp?"

"A hundred!" the peasant cried, holding up three very dirty fingers.

"I'll give you a hundred silver pennies for them," Kedrigern said, counting out three coins.

Skirp made a wild noise of assent, dropped the bundle, and held out his hand. The bundle hit the ground with a flat, unbirdlike smack. Kedrigern gave him the coins and knelt to inspect the bundle. He peeled away the outermost layer of rags, and found a hard rectangular object within, thickly coated in muck. Skirp edged closer, breathing loudly and stinkingly, intent on the wizard's actions.

Kedrigern licked his lips and began to scrape away the muck. When he saw a little patch of leather, his heart gave a jump. The bird was a book. He worked at the filthy covering, more gently now, and his fingers touched something hard. And blue. He drew back his hand, holding his breath. "No. It can't be," he said in a voice hardly more than a whisper.

"Go ahead," said Traffeo.

Throwing caution to the winds, Kedrigern rubbed away the muck with vigorous sweeps of both hands, revealing a pale green cover inlaid with five blue snails. He gasped and softly said, "It is."

Then he sprang to his feet with a whoop of joy, and Traffeo echoed his outburst. The two wizards joined hands and danced clumsily around the book. Skirp took one look at them, shrieked in terror, and fled the way he had come.

They did not notice his departure. Kedrigern, grinning like a child, dropped beside *The Book of Five Blue Snails* and gazed on it in wonder. "It's a miracle, Traffeo. An absolute outright miracle," he said in wonderment.

"It must have shot out of the mountainside and gone skimming through the air. Incredible . . ."

"Wonderful!"

"Marvelous!"

They stared in silence, then Kedrigern said, "Let's look in it."

"What about the others? Skirp said he had three."

"Skirp was as deficient in mathematics as he was in zoology. This is the only bird," Kedrigern said, opening the volume and leafing to the first page of solid print. He stared at it for a moment, then turned to the next page, then the next, and finally, after flipping with increasing vigor and impatience through a score of black-lettered pages, he slammed the cover shut with an angry growl.

"What's wrong?" Traffeo asked.

"It's written in . . . in . . . I don't *know* what it's in! I've never seen this language before!" Kedrigern cried.

Traffeo hunkered down before the book and turned several pages slowly, then stopped and pointed. "Here's something in Latin."

"What is it?"

"How to detect poisons."

Traffeo went on, finding a short treatise on turtles, written in Greek; a remedy for catarrh, in Hebrew; and several Latin antidotes for poison. There were also many pages in what he recognized as Arabic, but could not read. That left about half the book written in a language—or languages—unknown to either wizard.

"Isn't that always the way?" Kedrigern said bitterly. "The very book we need, the one book to solve all our problems, falls into our hands—literally drops from the sky—and half of it is in some language neither of us ever saw before!"

Traffeo murmured something sympathetic.

"We'd be better off if it really had been a bird. At least we'd have a good dinner. But a book in gibberish—!"

"Wait a minute, now. I've seen this gibberish somewhere," Traffeo said.

"You have? Where?"

"I can't quite recall. It was fairly recently, I'm sure."

"Think!"

"I can't force my memory, Kedrigern. It will come back, but I just have to wait."

Kedrigern ground his teeth, but said nothing. He knew the truth of Traffeo's words, but their truth did not make them any more palatable. There was nothing for it but to go their way and be patient.

They went on a way before making camp and eating, and just as dark was falling Traffeo cried, "In one of my books! While we were searching! I've got a dictionary and grammar of that language in my library!"

Kedrigern was on his feet in an instant. "Let's be off at once. There's not a minute to lose."

Traffeo did not stir. "We've already lost the better part of two days. We can't possibly get back to Othion before the full moon."

"A transportation spell! We could be there in an instant!"

"They take too much magic. We'd be useless for days." After a thoughtful silence, Traffeo said, "It will take some time to master the language, anyway. There's just no way you can help Berzel before her next transformation."

"But I promised! I said that before the next full moon had set, I'd find a cure."

"Well, haven't you? You may not be able to make much use of it, but you have found the cure. Probably."

"I can't see Ithian accepting 'probably.'"

"No, I suppose not. Well, revise your prognosis. It's not as though you're defeated, Kedrigern. You've got *The Book of Five Blue Snails*, and I've got the dictionary and grammar. It's just a matter of a few more weeks."

Traffeo was absolutely right, and Kedrigern knew it, but

that did nothing to lessen his frustration. He would help Berzel, as he had promised; but he would not do it *when* he had promised. Berzel would be grateful, Ithian would be generous, everyone would be impressed . . . except Kedrigern, who would know that he had boasted and failed to deliver on the boast.

"All the same, I'd like to get back to Othion as soon as possible," he said after a time. "Is there a shortcut?"

"Yes. Yes, as a matter of fact . . . How's your chess game, Kedrigern?"

"Not much good. Princess always beats me. But why . . . ?"

"Well, we could cut across the Black Jester's land, but there's a risk. He's a sorcerer. He tricks people into playing chess with him, and if they lose, he turns them into chess pieces."

"What if they win?"

"No one seems to have done that, so far. The Black Jester is a pretty good chess player. He probably uses his magic, too."

"If it will save us time, let's cross his lands. He won't trick us into playing chess. We have no time for games."

"He may try something," Traffeo warned.

Kedrigern's voice was like steel. "Let him. Just let him."

They camped in a glen under the full moon, and Kedrigern was as fidgety as a nest of mice. Berzel would be loping and howling this night, despite his promise, and there was nothing he could do to prevent it. Zorsch, too, would undergo the dreaded metamorphosis. It was all very well to say, as Traffeo had said at least a score of times since supper, that by the next full moon they would surely be cured. They were not cured *now*, and that, as far as Kedrigern was concerned, meant that he had failed them. He felt frustrated and very peevish.

Traffeo was no help at all. He spoke reassuring words, and he listened patiently to Kedrigern's outbursts, nodding and sighing and shaking his head and looking sympathetic in all the proper places, but he was clearly more interested in reading such portions of *The Book of Five Blue Snails* as he could, and making detailed notes. Even as Kedrigern settled down for a restless night, Traffeo sat by the fire, absorbed in the book.

Next morning they got an early start. According to Traffeo, they were now in the Black Jester's domain, and they meant to cross it as quickly as possible. To be delayed at this stage of their journey would be intolerable.

"He's a gloomy chap, from what I've heard," Traffeo said as they rode. "Dresses all in black, wears leaden bells on his foolscap, all that sort of nonsense."

"He can wear what he likes, as long as he stays out of our way."

"He has a gloomy house, too. And gloomy grounds."

"If that's what he prefers," Kedrigern said carelessly. "No point in quarreling over a man's taste."

"In fact, his whole domain is gloomy. No one laughs. They don't even smile. There's no singing or dancing or whistling. No merriment in any form. It's positively—"

A burst of raucous laughter came from around the curve ahead. The wizards glanced at one another.

"That's impossible. No one laughs here," said Traffeo.

Another peal of laughter rang out, followed by male voices raised in hearty banter, and a piercing whistle, and more laughter.

"We must be lost," Kedrigern said.

"Impossible. This is the Black Jester's domain."

"But those people sound *happy*."

"It's a trick," said Traffeo darkly.

A very good tenor voice began to sing "Giddy Gay Griselda," and deep basses joined in the hilarious chorus. Kedrigern chuckled at the familiar lyrics, and even Traffeo, uneasy as he was, could not help smiling. Around the turn in the road ahead marched three men, arm in arm, singing lustily. At sight of the two mounted travelers they stopped singing, but their expressions remained jolly. One of them raised his cap in salutation.

"Good morning, your honors. Lovely morning, isn't it?" he said.

"A delightful morning," Traffeo responded.

"Never seen a better," said another of the men, and the third nodded enthusiastically.

"I fear my companion and I have lost our way. Are we anywhere near the domain of the Black Jester?" Traffeo asked.

"This road leads directly to his gates, your honor, but there's nothing to fear. There's no more danger from the Black Jester. Done for, he is," said the first man brightly.

"Done for?"

"Finished and through. He won't be turning decent men into pawns anymore, not him."

"But . . . he was a sorcerer . . . a very powerful sorcerer."

"Well, he met his match, he did. That pretty lady with the little wings, she done him in."

"Princess!" Kedrigern cried in astonishment and delight.

"I believe that title was applied to the lady, your honor," said the first man, and his words were seconded by the others.

"But how did she get here?"

"Same as all of us. She was an unsuspecting victim of trickery and deceit."

"But not for long," said the third man with great satisfaction.

"This is incredible. Princess, here—!" Kedrigern said faintly, gazing from face to face.

"She be at the manor, your honor, just around the bend and up the avenue of yew trees. The nobility and clergy are assembling there to pass justice on old Blackbritches."

"Shouldn't you men have a say in his punishment, as well?"

The three shook their heads in emphatic negation, and the third man said, "Dispensing justice is more in their line, your honor."

"Men of our condition generally doesn't give it out; we gets it," said the second.

"I understand. Congratulations on your deliverance, then, and thank you for the information," said Kedrigern. He turned to Traffeo, his face alight, and snapped, "To the manor!"

The doors of the manor stood open, and sounds of laughter and lively discourse came from within. Kedrigern sprang from his horse, ran inside, and there, at the center of an admiring circle, was Princess.

"Princess! You're here!"

"Kedrigern! You're safe!"

They flew to one another, embraced, kissed, and stood silent in the comfort of each other's arms until a gentle cough awoke them to their surroundings. Princess straightened her circlet and announced, "Your Majesties, Your Excellency, gentlemen, this is my husband, Kedrigern of Silent Thunder Mountain."

A lean, angular woman wearing a gold crown peered hard into Kedrigern's face and barked, "Wizard, aren't you?"

"I am, Your Majesty. But my dear wife is a better one. She's overthrown the Black Jester."

Princess lowered her eyes and murmured, "Well, someone had to do something."

"That she did. Saved us all," the queen declared.

"A brilliant tactician; a woman of great courage and resourcefulness," said the bishop. "She outplayed the Black Jester at chess and then proceeded to outwit him. We owe her our lives and our freedom."

"A fair damsel, and a brave one, too," said a big, burly knight, and his words were greeted with a murmur of general assent.

"What about the Black Jester?" Kedrigern asked.

"In the dungeon," said the queen fiercely. "He'll get what's coming to him. We'll decide over lunch."

The bishop gestured to the doorway. "Gentles all, let us begin our deliberations without. Our commander and her husband must have matters to discuss in private."

Once they were alone, Princess told Kedrigern the whole story of her adventures. He listened with astonishment, and his initial outrage turned to pleasure when she told of Berzel and Zorsch's deliverance. But as he gave his own account, a more sober mood overcame him.

"I'm glad Berzel's ordeal is over. That will make it easier to confront Ithian. All the same, my dear, I've failed," he concluded.

"How can you say you've failed?"

"I made a promise and I didn't live up to it. There's no way of getting around that, my dear. I promised Ithian that I would cure his daughter before the next full moon had set. And I didn't do it."

Princess shook her head and smiled. She took Kedrigern's hand in hers. "That's not what you promised Ithian."

"It's all right, my dear. I can face it. Traffeo tried to be kind, too, and find a way out, but I distinctly remember—"

"No, you don't. You never do. You're very good at remembering spells, and strange people out of your past, but when it comes to other things, you're impossible. You promised Ithian that a cure would be found for Berzel before the next full moon had set. And it was. So you've kept your promise," said Princess matter-of-factly.

"Is that really what I said?"

"Of course it is. I remember those things."

Kedrigern let out a whoop of joy. He took her in his arms and whirled her around, the two of them laughing uproariously. Still laughing, they left the building, hand in hand, stopping every few steps to embrace, kiss, and burst out in fresh gales of laughter.

They explained the cause of their merriment to Traffeo and invited him to join the queen, the bishop, and the other liberated prisoners of the Black Jester in a light lunch prepared by their former host's excellent cook. The company soon assembled within, and enjoyed a superb repast, during which suggestions for the Black Jester's punishment formed the chief topic of conversation.

The bishop favored burning at the stake. The queen conceded that this method was neat, and a pleasing spectacle—especially at night—but pointed out that it was relatively speedy. She spoke up for drawing and quartering. The king yawned and agreed. A florid-faced knight suggested that if they wanted something slow and nasty, exposure in an iron cage hung from the walls was just the thing. The other knight, objecting to this method as relatively painless, urged pressing to death. Additional suggestions, more complicated and poorly suited to mealtime, were made, but there was no consensus. Princess remained silent during the discussion, and after a considerable amount of loud argument, the queen bawled out, "Why don't we let Princess choose?"

Assent was hearty and unanimous. Princess looked about, blushed attractively, and said, "That's really very thoughtful of you."

"Least we can do to show our gratitude, child. Though I, for one, intend to send you a nice little remembrance from the royal treasury once we're home," said the queen, challenging the company with a ferocious look.

"May I have some time to think it over?" Princess asked.

They gladly acceded to her request. Lunch over, the group rose from the table. The king, yawning, announced his intention of taking a long nap. The queen dragooned the others into a tour of the manor grounds, a project from which only the bishop begged to be excused, pleading urgent business. Princess withdrew to a quiet corner to ponder the fate of the Black Jester.

"A good brisk walk after eating helps the liver and the lungs," the queen proclaimed.

"Your Majesty's health and vigor are striking testimony to the salubrious effects of postprandial perambulation," said the bishop with a gracious bow and a flourish. "But the stern voice of duty summons me, and I may not delay. As soon as my surviving servants have packed my gear and saddled the horses, I must proceed to the abbey on the mountain."

Kedrigern's eyebrows rose. "If I may ask, Your Excellency, what is the purpose of your visit?"

The bishop did not respond until all the others had trailed out in the wake of the queen and her loud, braying voice had faded. Then he said carefully, "Rumors have reached us of . . . dubious activities in the abbey library."

"Then there's no need for you to rush. The library's gone."

"Gone?" the bishop said in disbelief.

Kedrigern gave a brief account of the debacle at the abbey, omitting reference to the mysterious tunnel and the unhappy mission of the monks of the inner library. The bishop listened in attentive silence, his expression grave.

"A most tragic occurrence," he remarked when Kedrigern was finished. "And yet it may be the best resolution of the situation. Grim tales have been told of the contents of the great library."

"Well, library and contents are gone now. The monks are concentrating on penance and mortification."

"That, at least, is reassuring."

The bishop left to urge the pace of his servants, and Kedrigern went to the corner of the room, where Princess sat on a bench by the window, deep in thought. He settled at her side.

"I can't do it," she said, not looking at him. Her hands were tightly clenched, her jaw taut.

"What is it you can't do, my dear?"

"Have a hand in the Black Jester's execution. I may be softhearted, Keddie, but listening to all those people making cruel suggestions . . . no, I can't."

"I'm relieved to hear it," Kedrigern said, moving closer and putting his arm around her.

"What will they think of me?" she said woefully, resting her head on Kedrigern's shoulder, sighing wearily.

"Let that lot think what they want. The queen's a bully, the king's a pudding, and the rest just want revenge."

"The Black Jester did awful things, but he was in the grip of magic when he did them. He's really a sad little man. I believe he's genuinely sorry for all he's done," said Princess, her voice full of feeling.

"There's another thing to consider, my dear: I owe the Black Jester something. Thanks to him, I kept my promise to Ithian and saved my reputation. It would be most ungrateful, after that, for my wife to execute him."

Princess sat bolt upright. "That decides it. The Black Jester lives. But we can't just let him go." She looked at Kedrigern in perplexity.

"If I may make a suggestion . . ."

"Please do."

"The bishop is on his way to the abbey. The abbey is the ideal place for a penitent. The Black Jester is a penitent. *Ergo . . .*"

She took his face in both her hands and kissed him with great enthusiasm, then sprang up and tugged him to his feet. "Let's go and tell the bishop. Then we can start packing and

be on our way before the queen comes back and tries to or-
ganize games."

The bishop was pleased with Princess's decision, and the
Black Jester, hauled trembling from the dungeon, was much
relieved and effusive in his gratitude. With the bishop as witness, he bestowed his house and lands on Princess, her heirs
and assigns, in perpetuity. He departed from the manor in the
firm grip of the servants, all the while proclaiming her kindness.

"That was nice of him. I don't know what I'll do with this
place, but it's always good to have a bit of property," she said
when the bishop's party had left.

"Shall we make a quick tour of inspection before we go?"

"I've seen most of the house. Perhaps a peek at the
kitchen."

"Lead on, my dear."

As they approached the kitchen, they heard a cracked,
whining voice say, "I'll try anything, your honor, anything at
all. There's nothing for me now. I'm a fine cook, I am, but
nobody wants an ugly fat old man around the kitchen. Spoils
the appetite, they say. Now that the Black Jester's gone, I'll
never find another place. Go ahead, your honor. I'm ready."

"The cook," Princess whispered.

A droning voice followed, then a burst of girlish laughter,
and then a deep masculine shout of triumph, followed by min-
gled sounds of delight and celebration. Entering, they saw a
beautiful maiden clutching at a baggy food-stained tunic and
apron that were three times too large for her slender yet
shapely figure. She stood in cracked and battered old shoes
that swam on her little feet. She blinked at Kedrigern and
Princess as they entered, then gave a musical laugh and tossed
her rich, tumbling, honey-colored curls.

"There *is* a counterspell!" cried Traffeo from the far side of
the kitchen, waving *The Book of Five Blue Snails* over his
head. "And it works!"

Further investigation of the kitchen seemed an exercise in
anticlimax. They congratulated the transformed cook and
Traffeo, as well, and left them to their celebration. Nothing

remained now but to locate Berzel and Zorsch, pack their belongings, and slip away.

The young couple were seated under an apple tree, holding hands. They were unaware of intruders upon their solitude; indeed, they were unaware of anything but each other. Princess sighed and looked upon them fondly.

"They want to marry."

"Really?"

"Absolutely. The very minute they return to Othion."

Kedrigern was beside himself with glee. Their love was certain to infuriate Ithian; their desire to marry would send him into a rage. It was a perfect start. Kedrigern smiled thinly in anticipation. He had plans for Ithian.

···⟩ Sixteen ⟨···

twinkle, twinkle

"I'VE BEEN THINKING it over, and I've decided to give Berzel and Zorsch the Black Jester's house and lands as a wedding present," Princess abruptly announced as she and Kedrigern rode side by side at the head of the group.

"That's very generous of you."

"Well, it wouldn't be much use to us, would it? And it will soften some of Ithian's objections to the match."

"Ithian's objections don't concern me one little bit. Ithian will have other things to worry about before I'm finished with him," said Kedrigern ominously.

"Now, you mustn't be too severe. We don't want to spoil the mood of the wedding," Princess reminded him.

"Ithian treated you abominably. He must pay."

"You didn't feel that way about the Black Jester."

"In the case of the Black Jester there were mitigating circumstances; Ithian's disgraceful behavior was entirely his own idea. It cannot simply be brushed aside."

"I don't like to hear you talk that way. I'm willing to overlook his misconduct for Berzel's sake. The poor child has lost her mother—think how she'd feel if you turned her father into something awful."

"What do you suggest?"

"A profound and humble apology will satisfy me."

"You want to let him off much too easily," Kedrigern said, his face set like flint.

"It won't be easy for him at all. His daughter wants to marry a commoner. That's a very difficult thing for a king to accept."

"Nonsense. One is constantly hearing stories of kings who marry commoners, so why would they object to a daughter's doing it?"

"One *never* hears such stories," said Princess with cold dignity.

"What about the story of King Manatule and the swine-herd's beautiful daughter? There's a perfect example for you."

"I know of no such person."

"I read about him in a chronicle. It seems there was an old man in Manatule's kingdom, and he had three beautiful daughters. They lived in a—"

"His wife deserves a bit of credit, too, doesn't she? The old man didn't have three beautiful daughters all by himself, I'm sure," Princess broke in crossly.

"Of course he didn't. That goes without saying."

"It usually does, when a man's telling the story. It's always 'There was an old man' or 'There were these two men at an inn' or something like that. Why couldn't it be an old woman with three handsome sons? Would that spoil everything?"

Kedrigern thought for a moment, then said, "Yes, it would. But I can mention the mother, if it will make you feel better."

"Please do."

"All right, then. There was a man who had an incredibly beautiful, sweet, loving wife who presented him with three lovely daughters. When the wife died, the man was—"

"Oh, fine. Mention her once and then kill her off. That's a nice way to treat a woman," said Princess, glaring at him.

Kedrigern threw up his hands helplessly. In his most diplomatic manner, he said "She has to go, my dear. The daughters' problems stem from the absence of a mother's guidance."

"Oh." Princess appeared slightly mollified. "Well, go on."

"King Manatule was unmarried. He heard about the three beautiful girls and resolved to marry one of them. He rode to the cottage—"

"This is ridiculous, Keddie, absolutely ridiculous! Kings don't just dash off and marry some old peasant's daughter on a whim! There are months and months of negotiations and bargaining and conferences before a king even *meets* the woman he's to marry," said Princess.

"I'm only telling you what I read in the chronicle. Please, my dear, just accept the fact that this particular king—an eccentric, madcap young fellow—decided that he simply had to marry one of the old man's daughters."

"If that's how he managed his personal life, I hate to think of the way his kingdom must have been run. It sounds to me as though he'd been spelled," said Princess suspiciously.

"The chronicle doesn't say. Anyway, Manatule rode to the old man's cottage and declared his intention. The old man fell to his knees and said, 'If it please Your Majesty, I must reveal a sad truth about my girls: Lovely they are, and fair, but one of them always lies, one never lies, and one lies only in matters concerning the family.'

"'And which is which?' demanded the king, looking closely at all three girls, who were equally beautiful.

"'Alas, Your Majesty, my wits are failing and I can never keep track,' the old man confessed. 'Your Majesty must find that out for himself.'"

"I'd like to see some old peasant talk that way to a king," said Princess grimly. "He'd soon learn something about etiquette."

"Manatule encouraged plain speaking among his subjects. So Annie, the first daughter, said, 'I'm the one who never lies, Your Majesty.' Libbie, the second daughter, said, 'She's lying, Your Majesty—I'm the one who never lies.' The third daughter, Bella, smiled very sweetly—they all had lovely smiles—and said, 'They're both lying, Your Majesty. I'm the one who never lies.'"

Princess covered a yawn. "And . . . ?"

"Manatule was confused. He questioned them further.

Annie said, 'Those two are lying, Your Majesty,' and Bella insisted that she never lied, but Libbie said, 'Yes, you do, and so does Annie.' 'I do not,' said Annie. 'She does so,' said Bella. 'And why wouldn't she? We all do,' said Libbie. 'Except for me!' piped up Annie. Bella shook her head and said, 'You just told a whopper.' 'I did not! Ask Daddy,' said Annie. 'Daddy's the biggest liar in the family. Did you hear what he told this nice king?' Libbie said. Well, this went on until Manatule got thoroughly disgusted and had his men behead the lot of them. On his way back to the castle, he stopped at a swineherd's hovel for a drink of water and saw the swineherd's beautiful daughter. He carried her off to his castle, had her well scrubbed, and they were married that very night," Kedrigern concluded, beaming at her.

"I've never heard anything so farfetched and silly in all my life. Really, if that's the sort of thing they write about kings, it's no wonder Ithian acts like a foolish boy. He's probably been reading chronicles," she said.

"What's wrong with the story?" looking hurt.

"To begin with, no king would ever be so wasteful. The first thing Manatule would have done if he had any brains at all—which is certainly doubtful—is to figure out which sister is which. Obviously, Bella is the one who never lies."

"She is? I never worked it out."

"It's very clear. And he would have her marry the Royal Treasurer. *That* would keep accounts straight. Annie, who always lies, is the perfect wife for the Foreign Secretary. And he'd marry Libbie himself. She only lies about family matters, and with a family like that, you'd want some lying."

Kedrigern was silent for a considerable distance, then he turned to Princess and said respectfully, "You must have been a great help to your parents before Bertha's spell . . . incapacitated you."

"I can't remember. But I like to think so. I do vaguely recall a well-run kingdom," she said with a soft sigh of nostalgia.

Very soon the trail narrowed, and they rode on in single file, thus rendering conversation all but impossible. Kedrigern passed the time contemplating Ithian's punishment. Princess might be inclined to leniency; he was not. But for her sake— and because he, too, liked the young couple and did not wish to cast a pall over their nuptials—he abandoned the thought of inflicting any truly catastrophic chastisement on Ithian. A nice distinction had to be drawn between revenge and justice, and it had to be perfectly clear that Kedrigern was firmly on the side of justice. If he could work in a little revenge, that was all right, too, but it could not be obvious. Giving Ithian the fright of his life might be the best all-around solution, he concluded; and having settled that in his mind, he had only to decide on the means.

Next morning, when they had been riding scarcely more than an hour, Princess excitedly called a halt. Fluttering upward from her saddle, she flew to Kedrigern's side and announced, "This is where I met Berzel. We have a complete wardrobe nearby, protected by a spell. I think we should change, and enter Othion looking our best."

"You look splendid now, my dear. And Berzel looks very nice, too."

"Keddie, we're practically in rags. You might shake out your cloak and scrape the mud off your boots while Berzel and I are changing. You want to make an impression on Ithian."

"I don't intend to impress him with my apparel," said the wizard.

"Now, now. Remember what we agreed. Nothing too severe."

"Considering the way he behaved toward you—and toward me, in my absence—I can't imagine what would be too severe."

"I don't want you spoiling things for Berzel and Zorsch."

"I won't. I'll just give him a good scare."

"Not too much of a scare. We don't want his hair white and his wits scattered for the wedding."

"All right!" cried Kedrigern, throwing up his hands in frustration. "I'll hit him with a slight disquietude! A minor anxiety! A *frisson* of vexation!"

"Don't be difficult," said Princess, flying off.

Kedrigern wanted to be not merely difficult, but impossible. Princess simply would not understand. One did not allow insults to pass unpunished; one could not, if the wizard's profession were to be honored. Let Ithian off with an apology, and every petty pelting king in every grubby little kingdom in the land would learn about it and take it as a license to go lurching after wizards' wives as soon as the wizard was off somewhere on a difficult and perilous quest. Steps had to be taken.

And yet he did not want to upset Princess, or spoil the happiness of the young. It was a dilemma. At times like this Kedrigern almost wished he were a carpenter. A carpenter could worry about one thing at a time: Select good wood, measure it accurately, cut it carefully, join it firmly, and the job was done and on he went to the next piece. Carpentry was orderly. As a wizard, he sometimes felt like a man required to forge armor out of the webs to be spun by unborn spiders. It could be a frustrating profession.

Princess and Berzel rejoined them, resplendently gowned, cloaked, and bejeweled, and they continued to Othion. At midday they had their first sight of the walls, from a knoll at the edge of the forest.

"How shall we announce ourselves?" Traffeo asked.

"I have several suggestions," Kedrigern responded through clenched teeth. Princess gave him a hard look, but said nothing.

"Dear Princess, will you do something magical to let all Othion know of our return?" Berzel asked.

"That's not really in my line. Perhaps Kedrigern can come up with something. Something appropriate," Princess said, with emphasis on the final word.

"How about a chorus of spirit voices?" Traffeo asked the company.

"I prefer disembodied screechings," said Kedrigern, his eyes fixed on the city walls.

"You can't do that. It would terrify all of Othion," Princess quickly pointed out.

"I know," Kedrigern said coldly.

"Fairies blowing tiny silver trumpets!" Berzel exclaimed.

"Oh, that would be so dear and sweet! Do it, Master Kedrigern, please!"

"How about demons beating kettledrums made of ogres' skulls? Would that do?"

Berzel blinked and looked about in confusion. "Fairies would be ever so much cuter," she said weakly, glancing to Princess for support.

Kedrigern turned to look at her thoughtfully. He scratched his chin, and then he smiled a calm, private little smile. "Why don't we rest here for a time and think about a proper announcement?"

"But Daddy's men may have seen us from the walls. He'll be wondering who we are," Berzel said.

"So he will," Kedrigern said as he dismounted.

Scarcely had they seated themselves on blankets and taken a sip from their water bottles when a fanfare blared forth from the towers of Othion. Kedrigern rose, drew out his medallion, and peered through the Aperture of True Vision. At his back arose a flurry of voices.

"They've seen us, all right."

"How shall we respond?"

"Oh, do let's get fairies with little silver trumpets!"

"Perhaps we should wait."

"What if the royal guard come out?"

Kedrigern, silent, watched as the royal guard did in fact appear, marching from the gate and forming up on both sides. Behind them rode Ithian. He rode between their ranks and continued, alone, toward the knoll. Kedrigern tucked away his medallion and turned to the others.

"We need do nothing," he said. "Ithian is coming out to greet us in person. He's by himself."

"A touching gesture of goodwill," said Princess.

Kedrigern snorted, but said nothing. He stood apart, with folded arms, and waited. Ithian arrived on a magnificent white stallion with a scarlet caparison richly ornamented. His appearance did not suggest penitence to Kedrigern, but still he kept his peace. Ithian dismounted and walked to where Princess sat. Removing his hat, he fell to one knee before her.

"We apologize for our behavior toward you, honored lady.

We were distraught by our daughter's sufferings and poign-
antly aware of our own losses. We gave way to our feelings,"
he said for all to hear.

Just a bit too smooth, Kedrigern thought. It was glib. It
sounded like a speech that had been practiced before a mirror,
not a sincere utterance from a repentant heart. Cynical, that's
what it was. Say a few humble words, look contrite, and bide
your time until the next defenseless woman falls into your
clutches. Transparent cynicism, every word of it. Princess
would never fall for such rot, he told himself.

"It is a handsome apology, and I accept it. You are for-
given," she said, extending her hand.

"What about me?" Kedrigern cried.

"Ah, yes, Master Kedrigern," said Ithian, rising and
brushing his knee. "Have you kept your promise? Is our
daughter cured?"

Kedrigern reddened. For a moment, he was inarticulate
with rage, and then Princess was at his side, clutching his arm
firmly and whispering, "Don't spoil the wedding!"

"Daddy, it's all over! I'll never turn into a wolf again!"
Berzel exclaimed, running to her father's arms, all her past
resentment forgotten.

"We are pleased to hear it. And were you cured before the
setting of the full moon?"

"Practically at moonrise, Daddy."

"We see. Well, wizard, it appears that we owe you a fee."

"You owe me more than that," Kedrigern said in a tight,
strained voice.

"We can settle the details back at the castle," Ithian said
casually, turning his back on Kedrigern. He looked at Zorsch.
"Who is this?"

"That's Zorsch, Daddy. You remember Zorsch. We're
going to be married!" Berzel cried happily.

"We will decide when you marry, child, and to whom.
You, Zorsch—are you a prince?"

"No. No, not exactly a prince, Your Majesty."

"You must call him *Daddy*!" Berzel exclaimed.

Ithian silenced her with an imperious look. Returning his
attention to Zorsch, he examined him from head to toe. "If

you are not exactly a prince, what, exactly, are you? A duke? Earl? Baron?" he inquired, his tone becoming more scornful at each downward step in rank. "Are you a mere knight?"

"No. Not a knight. I'm . . . I serve my lady Princess and Master Kedrigern," Zorsch said uncomfortably.

"A servant!" Ithian bellowed. "Do you dare to think of marrying our Berzel? Upstart, you will pay dearly for this presumption!"

"Daddy!"

"Be silent, girl!" Ithian snapped. He turned to Kedrigern and Princess, his features contorted and empurpled with royal wrath. "And you, whom we entrusted with our daughter, have encouraged this lackey's ambitions. We see it all now, the whole fiendish plot to separate our daughter from ourselves, to inflame us with passion, to suborn our Wizard Royal. The world will learn of this! Your names will be accursed in every kingdom! Every palace! We will . . . You shall never . . ." he sputtered, shaking a beringed fist at them.

Princess's nostrils flared. Her lips set thinly. Her eyes narrowed. To Kedrigern, she said, "Go to it."

Kedrigern was prepared. He murmured a phrase and moved his hand in an intricate gesture. Ithian ceased his sputtering. His high color paled, and he looked surprised. Smiling blandly, Kedrigern said, "If Your Majesty will withdraw with us, perhaps we can talk this over."

Arm in arm, Princess and Kedrigern walked at an unhurried pace to the shelter of the trees. Ithian fidgeted for a moment, rocking from side to side, looking all about him, and then he skipped after them, flapping his arms like a toddler in abandoned play. Traffeo, Berzel, and Zorsch looked on in disbelief.

When Ithian joined them, he stared at Princess and Kedrigern in stark terror. "We went skippity-wippity-woo!" he gurgled.

"You certainly did," said Princess.

"How did you like it, Ithian?" Kedrigern asked.

The king's eyes and mouth widened into perfect little *O*'s of astonishment. "Oooh, we's the cutest little kingsy-wingsy in the whole wide world! We feels all sick in our little tummykins when we thinks how cute we is, we do!" He crinkled up his nose and blew them a kiss, but the look in his eyes was ghastly.

"Yes, I imagine you would," said Kedrigern in a detached manner. "And how do you suppose the good people of Othion will like you in your present condition? And your council? And the royal guard?"

"They won't like it one teenie-weenie bit, Mister Wizard Man, we just knows they won't! They might even rise upsy-wupsy, and throw us right off our great big throne!"

"Maybe they'll even chop off your little headsie-weadsie," said Princess with a cheerful smile.

"Oooh, they will, they *will*, those nasty mans!" Ithian squealed, stamping his feet and shaking his fists.

Coolly, clinically, Kedrigern said, "This is a cuteness spell, my dear. Not a pleasant sight. Observe how the subject is fully aware of his cuteness at all times, yet unable to avoid behaving in an adorable manner."

"Fascinating," Princess said.

"You don't see many cuteness spells nowadays. They're used chiefly to counter love charms. You get someone behaving like this for an hour or two, and no one could love him, charm or no charm."

"I can believe that."

"And this is only the first stage. He'll get cuter and cuter, day by day, until—"

"Oooh, please, Mister Wizard Man and Missus Wizard lady, please don't do this to poor little us, please! We'll never do nothing naughty or say mean things, never ever! And we'll rule our subjects just as wisely as ever we can, and we'll let our little girlykins marry her Zorschie-worschie and live in the palace, and *everything*!" Ithian said, looking at them with pleading, desperate eyes as he swung his body from side to side and dug his toe in the dirt.

"Mmm. And all those intemperate remarks? Those wild accusations?"

"And the insults?" Princess added.

"We is sorry," said Ithian, and his nether lip protruded in a pout as a tear trickled down his cheek. "If Mister Wizard Man

takes nasty old spell off us, we promises to be the goodest
little kingsie-poo you ever did see."

Kedrigern studied him critically, saying not a word. Ithian's lip quivered, and he wailed, with the first trace of an
adorable lisp, "Pwease, Mister Wizard Man, pwetty pwetty
pwease! We has an awful urge to skip and womp, and wun
awound and fall down boom on our widdle fannykins, and if
we isn't out of this weal quick—"

"Oh, all right," said Kedrigern, appalled by the spectacle.
This was getting to be too much to bear. He had cast some
harsh spells in his time, but seeing a man blasted with cuteness gave him a turn. There were some things that should not
be done, not to arrogant kings, barbarians, or even to alchemists. Better a toad than a gurgling, winsome moppet of
forty-two, he told himself as he spoke the words of disenchantment.

Ithian twitched, blinked rapidly several times, and then
spoke, very cautiously at first. "Master Kedrigern, we thank
you for releasing us."

"Don't mention it, Your Majesty."

"We have wronged you both, and we shall make amends.
We have wronged others, too, and that shall be put right
forthwith," said Ithian. His customary pomposity had modu-
lated into a becoming dignity. "Berzel shall wed the man of
her choice. The wedding will be three days hence, and all
Othion will join in the celebration. We beg you to attend as
our honored guests."

"We accept with pleasure," said Princess before Kedrigern
could plead urgent business awaiting him at home. "And as a
wedding present," she added, "we bestow on the newlyweds
the house and lands that were formerly the property of the
Black Jester."

"That monster?! Have you and our dear Berzel encountered
the Black Jester?" Ithian cried in alarm.

"He is a monster no longer, thanks to my wife," Kedrigern
assured him.

"Berzel was herself of some assistance, as was Zorsch,"
Princess said demurely.

"Perhaps we have misjudged this Zorsch. He is a comely

youth. Given the proper clothing and a title or two, he may prove suitable."

"Berzel finds him suitable just as he is," Princess pointed out.

"We were thinking of the future in Othion," said Ithian gravely. He laid a hand on Kedrigern's shoulder. "As for ourselves, we have learned an important lesson this day, thanks to you. When the festivities are over, we will leave Othion in the care of our daughter and her consort, and withdraw to some quiet retreat for pious meditation."

"I know just the place," said Kedrigern.

"We will discuss it further in Othion, at a feast to honor the happy events of this day. Let us away."

Ithian rode back to Othion with Berzel on one side and Zorsch on the other. He chatted amiably and affectionately with both of them, and did not neglect his Wizard Royal. He behaved like a changed man, and Princess regarded him with satisfaction from her place at Berzel's side. Kedrigern rode behind Princess. His expression was pensive.

"Is something wrong? I should think you'd be very happy," she said, riding to his side.

"I'm all right," he said despondently.

"You ought to feel better than that. Berzel and Zorsch are cured, Ithian's a new and much nicer man, and we're going to be honored guests at a feast and a royal wedding."

"I know," he said with a sigh.

"Well, then, cheer up."

"I don't want to be a guest at anything. I want to go home."

"We'll be home before you know it. Enjoy yourself while you can."

"I enjoy myself at home. I miss my books. And Spot's cooking. And the garden, and napping in the dooryard on sunny afternoons."

"I enjoy our home, too. But it's good to get out and see people."

"I've *seen* people. I want to be back on Silent Thunder Mountain. Vosconu's messenger will be arriving any day, and

I'd like to be there when he comes. Vosconu's an old client and a good one."

"We'll be home in plenty of time," she said, giving his hand a comforting little pat.

"Royal weddings can go on and on and on, my dear. We could be here for weeks. Months."

"Hardly that long. Ithian wants to go off and meditate, and Berzel and Zorsch will be anxious to start running Othion. We'll be home soon, and moping won't hurry things along."

"I suppose not," said Kedrigern, attempting a smile.

"There. That's better," Princess said, and giving him another fond pat on the hand, she rode off to rejoin Berzel.

She was right, he knew. Celebrations did not go on forever. People went back to their business, and honored guests were free to return to their homes. It would probably be a very pleasant few days, in fact. Superb food, comfortable accommodations, gratitude and respect and awe on every face, a generous reward from the royal coffers, cheers and congratulations at every turn. All very nice.

He raised his head and smiled more broadly. The cottage was in Spot's capable hands. It was the least unpleasant time of the year to be traveling, and they would be going in the best of all possible directions: homeward.

Until then, he would enjoy the rewards. He had done his work well, and earned them. He would smell the flowers, sip the wines, and savor the luxuries of Othion. He would pass hours in shoptalk with Traffeo, and they would work together to decipher the contents of *The Book of Five Blue Snails*. They might find all sorts of helpful things: counterspells, disenchantments, unensorcellments, perhaps even some fine points on wand use, for Princess. It would all be very relaxing and rewarding.

And a few days of it would be quite enough. Then home to Silent Thunder Mountain, and no more wandering for a long, long time.